**DO NOT REMOVE
CARDS FROM POCKET**

ALLEN COUNTY PUBLIC LIBRARY

FORT WAYNE, INDIANA 46802

You may return this book to any agency, branch,
or bookmobile of the Allen County Public Library.

DEMCO

PENGUIN BOOKS

SHANGHAI QUITTESS

Tony Kenrick was born in Australia and has lived in New York, Toronto, San Francisco, Mallorca, and currently Kent, England. He claims his hobbies are emptying his refrigerator, collapsing from the bank, and has two children: one in advertising, the other "taking a course in industrial espionage." Author of The Nighttime Guy, he is at work on his thirteenth novel.

SHANGHAI SURPRISE

TONY KENRICK

PENGUIN BOOKS

PENGUIN BOOKS
Viking Penguin Inc., 40 West 23rd Street,
New York, New York 10010, U.S.A.
Penguin Books Ltd, Harmondsworth, Middlesex, England
Penguin Books Australia Ltd, Ringwood, Victoria, Australia
Penguin Books Canada Limited, 2801 John Street,
Markham, Ontario, Canada L3R 1B4
Penguin Books (N.Z.) Ltd, 182–190 Wairau Road,
Auckland 10, New Zealand

First published in the United States of America by
Doubleday & Company, Inc., under the title *Faraday's Flowers*, 1985
Published in Penguin Books 1986

Printed in the United States of America by
Offset Paperback Mfrs., Inc., Dallas, Pennsylvania
Set in Times Roman

SHANGHAI
SURPRISE

7104021

1

With a brown cigarette dangling in his mouth at an insolent angle, the third mate, who doubled as steward for the six passengers, blew out smoke and rapped again on the open cabin door.

"Señor Wasey..."

On the bunk the rumpled bedcovers shifted a little.

"You wanna see somethin' funny? *Es muy cómico.*"

Wasey slowly rolled over, opened his eyes, and met the scolding gaze of the mustachioed Spanish grandee pictured on the label of a rum bottle standing on the side table. Had the illustration been full-figure the level of rum left in the bottle would barely have come up to the grandee's shoes.

Wasey looked away, scraped his tongue against his teeth, and made an attempt at speech.

"Wha'?"

The mate picked a piece of tobacco off his tongue and flicked it to the floor where Wasey's clothes were piled. "Out onna dock. Your ties."

Wasey blinked and frowned at the man, standing there leaning against the cabin door in filthy dungarees and the battered black derby he wore instead of a cap.

"What're you talking about?"

The mate was having a good time. "Your ties." The derby moved in a lazy sideways nod. "Outside onna dock."

"My *ties?*" Wasey, very much awake now, jumped out of the bunk, pushed by the man at the door, ran out on deck, and winced as the sunshine, bouncing off the iron roof of the oldest dock in Shanghai, smote him between the eyes. It was a perfect morning; in fact, so far the weather conditions, in the spring of 1940, had been perfect all over China—Ch'in Ming weather, as the Chinese called it, clear and bright with high blue skies. But at that par-

1

ticular moment Wasey wouldn't have cared if a hurricane had been raging.

"Hey!" he yelled. "Wait!" He sprinted along the deck, slid expertly down a companionway, using only the hand-rails, reached the gangplank and dashed down it, stubbing his toe on one of the cleats. He arrived on the dock and hopped along to where the forward derrick had just de-posited his wooden crate. Stenciled on its sides were the words *G. W. Trading Co.*

"Hey, Marcos! What the hell's going on? What're you doing with my shipment?"

Marcos, the captain of the freighter, a Filipino like the rest of the crew, wore a red and yellow butterfly shirt under his grubby white uniform, the jacket of which boasted one brass button and five wooden ones. A carelessly ashed cigar had burned a large brown hole in the left sleeve, and the braid of the gold bars on the shoulders had come unwound and stood up like frazzled pot cleaners.

He glanced up from the document he was signing for the wharf boss and boredly took in the gringo and his pajama bottoms.

"Su cheque es goma."

"My chekay es what?"

"Goma." Captain Marcos searched his memory. "Es rubber."

"Bullshit! Who the hell told you that?"

Marcos handed the clipboard to the wharf boss, a blank-faced Chinese who'd just spat noisily and was busy hawk-ing up another good one.

"Company wire. They say you get off here."

"Here?" Wasey was incredulous. "This is Shanghai. I'm not getting off in Shanghai. I paid for Los Angeles."

The captain took a cigar from behind his ear, stuck it in his mouth, and lit it. "You don' pay for no place. Company say stinkin' check no stinkin' good."

"The company's nuts. I put that money in the bank myself."

"Stinkin' bank no stinkin' good," said the captain.

That stopped Wasey cold; that was a shock, that was. A stunner. He closed his eyes. "Oh, no."

Marcos began to walk towards the gangway but Wasey jumped and grabbed his elbow. "Captain. Hold it! I'll have the money two days after we dock in L.A. I can't miss with this shipment, novelty ties. They're a knockout."

"Company say you get off here."

Wasey's voice rose a notch. "You can't leave me here. I can't sell neckties in Shanghai, for crissakes." Wasey looked about him for support but it was a slack time and there were few people around: some coolies staggering under the weight of wool bales, a peddler pushing a wine cart, and a couple of missionaries in severe black uniforms.

He appealed to the wharf boss. "Tell him you can't sell ties in Shanghai. Who am I supposed to sell 'em to? The French? The English? These are novelty ties. I got seventy gross. I can't unload seventy gross of novelty ties in Shanghai."

The wharf boss's face had opened in amazement; a Big Nose speaking, not in pidgin, or his own accursed tongue, but in perfect Shanghai dialect!

"Tell this turtle egg, will you?" Wasey pleaded.

Turtle egg! Wonder of wonders. Surely this was not a Devil, the wharf boss thought, but a tiger in disguise.

Captain Marcos, unimpressed by Wasey's fluent burst of Chinese, began to move towards his ship, but Wasey reached out and grabbed his elbow.

"C'mon, Captain. Gimme a break, huh?"

Marcos removed the cigar from his mouth and casually pressed the glowing end against the back of Wasey's hand.

Wasey snatched his hand away. "Sonofa*bitch!*"

He started for the captain but the man quickly thrust his cigar into his mouth, dived into his pocket, and produced a small revolver. Wasey stopped in his tracks.

The captain wagged the barrel at him like a warning finger, then turned and walked towards the gangway.

3

Wasey let out breath and blew on it. "Marcos!" he called.

The captain ignored him.

"There's a drawbridge in L.A. When you get there, do me a favor, okay? Rent a car, wait till it opens, and drive on through."

Marcos continued up the gangplank of his rusty ship.

"Wait a minute," Wasey yelled. "I want my stuff."

Right on cue, the fourth mate appeared and threw something over the rail. A beat-up suitcase arced through the air, landed on the dock, and burst open in an explosion of underwear and socks.

"I'll sue you for this," Wasey shouted. He picked up the suit jacket that was lying there, dug out the wallet inside and checked it. It was thin and limp. Wasey wheeled round, yelled up at the ship.

"Ten bucks! There was ten bucks in this wallet!"

The fourth mate gave a little wave. "My teep," he said.

"Tip?" Wasey was outraged. "You thieving little crook! Come down here. I'll give you a tip. I'll give you a boot in the ass!"

He continued to rail at the mate, unaware of a smaller, quieter, and much more dignified argument that was going on behind him.

"I don't agree, Mr. Burns. He's all wrong."

"I'm not so sure about that. You heard his Chinese. He seems to speak it like a native."

It was the two missionaries in the black uniforms, a man and a woman. They'd stopped a little way off and had watched the exchange between Wasey and the captain.

The woman, young and good-looking in a strict kind of way, frowned and said, "He's uncouth. A ruffian. We couldn't be associated with someone like that."

The man, twenty years older than the woman, was looking at Wasey with great interest. "If they can help us it doesn't matter who we're associated with. I'm going to speak with him."

The young woman didn't like it but she went with her

companion as he approached Wasey, who was telling the fourth mate at the top of his voice what a splendid, upright louse he was.

"Excuse me, sir."

Wasey hardly glanced at him. "What?" he said rudely.

"Can we be of some assistance?"

"Oh sure. You have a torpedo I could borrow?"

Up on the ship the captain appeared on the bridge.

Wasey cupped his hands. "UP YOURS, MARCOS, YOU HEARTLESS BASTARD."

"Mr. Burns," the woman said.

The man hushed her with a movement of his hand. "We couldn't help overhearing. You've been off-loaded, it seems."

"Goddamn right. Seventy gross of ties to get to L.A. and I'm stranded and flat broke." Wasey cupped his hands again. "FUCKING PIRATES!"

There was a sharp intake of breath. "Mr. Burns," the woman said more forcefully.

The missionary continued talking to Wasey. "We could help you get to Los Angeles."

That brought Wasey's head around and he took a real look at the man. He was mid-sized, mid-forties, with an unremarkable face whose main feature, besides plain, thin-rimmed glasses, was a beard worn full but neatly trimmed. His uniform was smartly pressed and suited his trim figure well, and with his peaked cap sitting high on his head he could have doubled for a World War I British naval officer.

Wasey grunted. "What are you going to do? Pray?"

"No. I'm going to give you a chance to earn the money."

"Thanks a lot, but I don't think I'm cut out for a soup kitchen."

"All you'd have to do is help us with some inquiries. You speak the local dialect fluently, correct?"

"For all the good it's doing me." Wasey paused. "What kind of inquiries?"

As if he hadn't heard him the other man said, "My name

is Burns. This is Miss Tatlock. And your name is . . . ?"

"Wasey. What kind of inquiries?"

"We're trying to locate something. If you help us find it I'll pay your fare to Los Angeles. Including your shipment."

"What exactly are you looking for?"

"Why don't we let Miss Tatlock find you a hotel where you can freshen up." He glanced pointedly at the woman, who only half muted an objection. "Then she can bring you to my office and we can discuss this further in some measure of comfort and privacy."

Wasey looked back at the freighter. The gangplank was being rolled away and a couple of wharf coolies were standing by the mooring ropes ready to cast off. He made a disgusted sound in his teeth, raised his arms and let them fall to his sides. "Well," he said, "I sure haven't had any other offers." He pointed to his crate. "My shipment will have to be stored. That's a dollar a day right there."

"Go ahead and arrange it," Burns said. He turned to the woman. "I'll be in my office, Miss Tatlock."

"Mr. Burns," she said, tight-lipped, "may I see you for a moment?"

"Later," he said firmly, nodded at Wasey, and walked off towards the gates.

"Looks like you've been overruled, Miss Tatlock," Wasey said. He gathered up his clothes from the dock, shoved them into his ruined suitcase, and slung his topcoat over his shoulder. "All ready. Shall we go?"

Wasey, with a two-day stubble, one eye slightly bloodshot from last night's drinking, his hair all mussed, wearing pajama bottoms and carrying a busted suitcase trailing a shirt sleeve, was clearly not Miss Tatlock's idea of an ideal traveling companion.

"You could at least put on your topcoat. And some shoes," she said coldly.

Wasey, his earlier anger burned off, resigned himself to

being bullied. He put the suitcase down, opened it, and eased his sockless feet into a pair of brown and white two-toned brogues. He slipped on his rumpled topcoat, went over to talk to the wharf boss about his crate, then rejoined the woman and set out with her for the gates.

She walked briskly, almost striding, and Wasey had to hurry to keep up.

"You're not crazy about me, are you, Miss Tatlock?"

The only answer was the prim click of her low-heeled shoes on the cobblestone wharf.

"Well, maybe once you get to know me a little better—"

She spoke on top of him. "I think there's very little chance of that, Mr. Wasey. I'm sure our association will be an extremely brief one. There's no doubt in my mind that you'll prove to be totally unsuitable for this job."

"For what job? What am I supposed to find?"

"Mr. Burns will explain everything. You're his choice, not mine."

Wasey was about to come back at her on that when he spotted something that brought forth a grateful sigh. "Oh, thank God."

The wine peddler was coming towards them, the bottles in his wooden cart clinking musically together.

"Hey, Miss Tatlock, advance me ten cents, would you? I'm dry as a bone."

"I will do no such thing."

"Come on, Miss Tatlock, I need a shot after my recent ordeal."

"No."

"Why the hell not?"

"I'm against strong drink."

"Well, I'm all for it."

She raked him with a withering glance. "That, Mr. Wasey, is quite obvious."

The wine peddler passed them, and Wasey turned and

walked backwards a few steps as he wistfully watched his chance go by. He swung back and said moodily, "You're no fun at all, Miss Tatlock."

"There are more important things in life than fun, Mr. Wasey."

"Like what, for instance?"

"Like helping your fellow man."

Wasey pointed back at the wine peddler. "You just had a golden opportunity to help your fellow man."

"I'm talking about alleviating pain and suffering."

Wasey swallowed on a parched throat. "So am I."

They reached the gate and the cab rank. Most of the taxis had been taken by the passengers from a cruise ship that had docked earlier on, but there were still a couple hanging round for stragglers. They chose one that was in pretty good condition for a Shanghai taxi: an old Essex with broken springs, bald tires, and two smashed headlights.

"Which hotel?" Wasey asked. "I usually stay at the Condor. It's about a three-cab ride from here."

"A three-cab ride? What's that?"

"How long have you been in Shanghai, Miss Tatlock?"

"Not long."

"Yeah, well, you see, the taxis they have here tend to be a little ancient. You usually get about a mile or two before they quit on you and you have to get out and get another one."

"I'm sure this taxi will be fine. Now, about this hotel, the Condor. What's it like?"

"Great. The restaurant has Swatow cooking, and the room service is terrific."

Miss Tatlock did not approve. "This isn't a vacation you're on, Mr. Wasey. Something plain but adequate is all that's required."

Wasey said facetiously, "Well, there's always the Hotel Penang. No bar, no restaurant, and they change the towels regularly every New Year's Eve."

"Fine," Miss Tatlock said. "Hotel Penang," she told the driver.

"Hey, wait a second. I wasn't being serious."

"I doubt you know the meaning of the word, Mr. Wasey."

Wasey slouched in the seat as the cab moved off. He brooded and watched his companion, who was pointedly ignoring him. He was idly wondering what she really looked like. With not a trace of makeup, and her hair pulled back in a tight bun, she'd gone out of her way to make herself look unexceptional. But she'd been unable to disguise the prettiness of her features: the perky nose, the large hazel eyes, the full line of her lips. The uniform did nothing for her either: the mannish jacket and the overlong skirt, the crisp white blouse caught high up at the neck by some kind of badge, the black stockings and the sensible shoes . . . if this woman had a voluptuous figure her outfit was designed to keep it a secret.

"I bet that's your philosophy, Miss Tatlock. Plain but adequate in all things. The clothes you wear, the food you eat, and so on."

There was no comment from the other side of the seat.

"Do you have boyfriend, Miss Tatlock?"

"Mr. Wasey. My personal life is no concern of yours."

"Do you?"

With icy exasperation Miss Tatlock said, "If you must know, I am engaged to be married."

"Ah-hah! And tell me, your fiancé, is he also plain but adequate?"

"Mr. Wasey! There is no need for this conversation. There is no need for any conversation." Miss Tatlock swiveled her head and gazed determinedly at the city outside. She'd chosen a good time; the cab had just swung out of a side street and joined the clamor of the Bund. Automobiles, tramcars, trucks, rickshaws, pedicabs, yellow double-decker buses, and wave after wave of bicycles swept down the wide curve of the avenue. On the left was a solid phalanx of Victorian

9

office blocks, domed and spired and clock-towered. On the right was the quay and the river, which carried even more traffic than the avenue. Thousands of mat-covered boats, lighters that serviced the freighters anchored out in the river, formed a wide, almost solid extension of the boulevard. Beyond the freighters, flying the flags of half the world, was a parade of tugs and sampans, and working junks with sails like weathered tents open to the wind and eyes painted on their split bows. Low-riding river steamers with fat barges lashed to their sides plodded along farther out, hooting loudly at the black-funneled ferries heading downriver towards Woosung. On the opposite bank, over in Pootung, two sad-looking Chinese destroyers had had their guns removed and were now no more of a threat than the ancient dredger moored next to them.

At the north end of the river, towards the Yangtze, a Japanese heavy cruiser lay stolidly in the water, its guns trained on the town. It was the only immediate sign that the city, like most of the country, was suffering under a cruel occupation.

In spite of Wasey's prediction the cab made it all the way to the Penang Hotel, which turned out to be neat and clean, if a little spartan, which was quite all right with Miss Tatlock. There was no trouble with the desk clerk; he didn't seem fazed by a guest checking in wearing a topcoat, striped pajama bottoms and two-toned shoes. Miss Tatlock paid for Wasey's room in advance and sat down in the little lobby to wait for him. Twenty minutes later, when he rejoined her there, she got a surprise.

"God bless hot water," Wasey said. "I feel like a new man."

He looked like a new man; he was wearing a shirt and tie and a gray seersucker suit that, while it could have used a press, still draped nicely on his bony shoulders. He had sandy-colored hair, too fluffy to hold a part, and a face, now that it was freshly shaved and clear-eyed, that had a fresh, open look to it with good firm lines in the nose and jaw. Even with the loud two-toned shoes he looked quite presentable.

Miss Tatlock masked her reaction. She rose and said, "Shall we go?"

"Lead on," Wasey said.

Miss Tatlock stopped. "What's that on your tie?"

Wasey looked delighted. "You noticed it, huh?" He unbuttoned his jacket and displayed the tie in all its glory.

Miss Tatlock stared at the heavy white illustrations painted on the tie's blue background. Just under the knot was a cocktail glass with bubbles rising from it. Then, in descending order, came the head of a racehorse wearing the winner's garland of flowers, a pair of dice, a five-card poker hand, a chorus girl's high-kicking legs, a speeding sports car, a running greyhound, another cocktail glass, a roulette wheel, and a bottle of champagne. The last inch of the tie was taken up by the legend, written in script, *The Road to Ruin*.

"Isn't it a honey?" Wasey said. "It'll go like hotcakes."

Miss Tatlock suddenly understood. "That's what you're taking to Los Angeles? A crate full of those?"

"Right. Terrific, huh? And get this. The illustrations glow in the dark." Wasey looked round. "I'll show you." He quickly crossed the lobby and opened the door of a broom closet. "Come into the closet."

"No, thank you," Miss Tatlock said.

"They won't glow in the light. Come into the closet."

"I don't wish to see them," Miss Tatlock said firmly.

Wasey shrugged and closed the door. "Okay, but you're missing the best part."

They left the hotel and got a taxi, a Packard Clipper with no fenders and no front seat—the driver had sold it for use as a bed and drove the car perched on a fruit box. It made a mile and a half before it quit.

Their next cab, a Reo Speedwagon with a backfiring engine and a steering problem, was nearly at the Garden Bridge when it veered slowly left and fetched up against a building.

They walked across the bridge, which spanned the Soo-chow Creek, showed their passports to the Japanese Blue-jacket at the checkpoint, and picked up a third cab, which deposited them without mishap at the beginning of the Hongkew district.

Miss Tatlock led the way through a series of tight, nar-row alleys to a building that was very much a reflection of the district: it was old and worn out, with most of the windows cardboarded over. Wasey followed his guide up a flight of unwashed stairs to the second-floor landing. On the door ahead of them, poorly painted in Chinese, with its English equivalent underneath it, were the words *Help-ing Hand Society.* There was also a logo, a drawing of an outstretched palm holding a cross.

Miss Tatlock fished a key from her handbag and let them in. The office, only one room, was almost a blank: a couple of wooden chairs, a cheap desk with papers in orderly piles, an old filing cabinet in the corner.

"This is where you work?" Wasey asked.

"This is Mr. Burns's office."

"I guess yours isn't so lavish."

Miss Tatlock chose to educate rather than reprimand. "We have no money for frivolities, Mr. Wasey. We have a very small budget which is stretched extremely thin. All we need is a base of operations and a place to keep records, and as such this office suffices."

Wasey took a look at the only piece of decoration on the walls, a printed sheet in a thin frame. He read it out loud: "'The people are as hard as steel. They are eaten up, both soul and body, by the world. They don't seem to feel that there can be reality in anything beyond the senses. To them our doctrine is foolishness, our preaching contemptible, our talk jargon, our thoughts insanity, and our hopes and fears mere brain phantoms. . . . Think of the conversion of four hundred millions of the most proud, superstitious, and god-less people of the human race. Sometimes I am ready to give up in despair and think that China is doomed to destruction, that to raise it out of its state of moral and spiritual degradation is a matter of impossibility.'"

"A famous missionary wrote that fifty years ago, Mr. Wasey, and it's still true."

Wasey turned. Burns had come up the stairs without him hearing.

"I read it once a week. Helps keep me going."

"Inspiring stuff," Wasey said.

Burns closed the door, invited them to sit down, went behind the desk, and took his cap off. He had thin hair with a little bald patch on top. He looked at Wasey and nodded. "Much better. Miss Tatlock has obviously been looking after you."

"She's been a peach. Although she wouldn't come into the closet with me."

Miss Tatlock colored. She said quickly, "He wanted to show me his tie, Mr. Burns."

"His tie?"

"He claims it glows in the dark."

"It does glow in the dark." Wasey opened his jacket. "All of them do. They're all glowing away right now in that packing crate."

Mr. Burns caught on. "Oh, I see. Your shipment." He craned forward for a better look. "The Road to Ruin," he read out. "Oh yes, most amusing. They like novelty clothing in Los Angeles. I think you're on to something there, Mr. Wasey."

Wasey beamed. "Mr. Burns, I can see you've got a good head for business. Now, um, what do you want me to find?"

"Speaking of business," Burns said, "I assume you're in import-export?"

"That's right. Chief operating officer and majority stockholder of the G. W. Far East Trading Company. G. W. Glendon Wasey." He looked over at Miss Tatlock. "Glen."

Miss Tatlock wasn't interested.

Burns pressed on. "I would assume your business brings

13

you to Shanghai quite a bit."

"Off and on."

"So you know the town well."

"Certain parts of it, sure."

Miss Tatlock sniffed; she knew which parts *they* were.

"How old are you, Mr. Wasey?"

"I'll be thirty-four on August twenty-ninth." Again he looked at Miss Tatlock. "Virgo."

Miss Tatlock quickly looked away.

"So, Mr. Burns," Wasey went on, "now that you know all about me, what do you want me to find?"

Burns took a folded white handkerchief from his pocket, removed his glasses, and began to polish the lenses. "First let me tell you something about us. I'm with the Helping Hand Society. Miss Tatlock is with the Door of Hope. Both groups are similar with parallel objectives. And both groups are underfunded and woefully understaffed. In fact, Miss Tatlock and I are the sole representatives of our respective organizations in Shanghai. So we've joined forces."

"Makes sense," Wasey allowed. "You can save twice as many souls."

Burns gave him a tiny smile. "You might say that we're, er, not in that end of the business. While both our organizations are founded on firm Christian principles, our primary aim is to render aid and assistance for this life, rather than the next."

"I'm all for that," Wasey said. "Nobody knows if there's going to be a next."

Burns coughed and let the remark pass. "As I was explaining, Mr. Wasey, we've been looking for someone to help us. We haven't been able to find anybody here, so we've been covering the docks each day to check on the new arrivals." He paused for a second. "When was the last time you were in Shanghai?"

"About three months back. January, I think."

"Then I can tell you that the political situation has worsened considerably. The Japanese have put a stranglehold on the city. They don't dare come into the International Settlement, but they're everywhere else."

"Yeah, I saw the marines at the Garden Bridge. They're getting pretty bold."

"As for the war itself," Burns went on, "it's going terribly. The government is conducting the war with an atrocious disregard for human life, and the casualties are appalling. Right at this moment there are literally hundreds of thousands of Chinese soldiers lying in filthy field hospitals, and nothing's been done for them. One doctor for every five thousand men if they're lucky."

"I've heard the United States might come into the war," Wasey said. "That should help."

Miss Tatlock spoke up. "Who will it help, Mr. Wasey? All those soldiers in agony?"

Wasey shuffled his feet. "Well, what about American aid? Doesn't Washington send medical supplies over here?"

"Oh yes," Miss Tatlock said bitterly. "They send medical supplies. And maybe five percent of the shipment gets through."

"The Japanese get it, huh?"

"No. The Chinese generals do. They sell it to the heroin dealers. Go down to the French Concession any day of the week and you'll see the army wives buying out the stores."

"The corruption is colossal," Burns said. "It's absolutely scandalous."

Wasey shrugged his hands. "That's the way China works. They don't see it as corruption, to them it's just business as usual. There's nothing you can do about it."

Miss Tatlock bristled. "That's where you're wrong, Mr. Wasey. There's a lot we can do about it. We have a chance to get medical supplies to those poor wounded soldiers without the authorities knowing anything about it."

Burns made a restraining gesture. "Let me take it from here, Miss Tatlock." He stroked a finger down the side of his beard and considered his approach. "I'm not sure if you know it, Mr. Wasey, but when a field hospital makes up a list of urgently needed supplies, there's one item that's always on the top, and that's morphine. And as we've just told you, it's not getting through."

Wasey moved his head. "Uh-huh."

"Do you know what morphine's derived from?" Burns asked.

"No."

"Opium."

Burns let that sink in, then said, "We have a chance to get our hands on half a ton of it. And have it processed into morphine."

Wasey's eyebrows went up. "You have a government official on the payroll?"

"Nothing like that."

"Then how—"

"The Chinese government doesn't know about this opium."

"You're not trying to tell me this opium is illegal, are you?"

Burns nodded.

Wasey looked at Burns, looked at Miss Tatlock, then slowly pointed a finger at them both. *"You* two? You're going to fool around with the opium racket?"

"We're not fooling, and we're not fools, Mr. Wasey." Miss Tatlock's voice had iron in it.

"I'm not so sure about that, Miss Tatlock. Don't you know who runs the opium racket? The gangs. You can't get involved with people like that. They'll sprinkle you into their rice and eat you for lunch."

"We know about the gangs, the secret societies," Burns said. "We're well aware of what kind of business they're in, drugs, prostitution, extortion, and so on. But they're not one hundred percent evil. They also act as a kind of national benevolent association. For instance, they're always the biggest contributors to flood and famine relief."

"Hearts of gold and knives of steel, Mr. Burns. You'd be crazy to mess with them."

"We don't intend to mess with them. This half a ton of opium I mentioned . . . it doesn't belong to them."

"Who does it belong to?"

Burns got up from his desk and went over to the grimy window. The sound of cartwheels on cobblestones drifted up through it, and the cry of a duck peddler echoing off the narrow walls of the alley. In the building opposite, almost within reach, a woman put a yellow fish in a glass bowl on a window ledge so it could swim in a patch of sun. Burns turned back to Wasey. "Have you ever heard of a man in Shanghai named Faraday? Walter Faraday?"

"Doesn't ring a bell."

"Apparently he was quite an operator. Bit of a legend round here. A scoundrel, of course. A thief, and worse."

"It's his opium? This Faraday guy?"

"It was. He's dead now. He got into trouble with one of the gangs."

"I told you," Wasey said.

"Not because of the opium. They say he acquired that legitimately, brought in a shipment from India with the gangs' permission. No, the story is he cheated a stranger at cards, somebody who turned out to be a visiting relation of one of the head gangsters. It was taken as an extreme insult and Faraday was killed."

"What happened to the opium?"

"He apparently had some warning, and hid it somewhere." Burns slowed his words. "It's never been found."

Wasey slowly rocked in his chair. He tipped his head back and closed his eyes. "Oh God," he said. "The man wants me to find a cache of opium." He massaged his face and barked out a laugh. "I thought you wanted me to look for the mission dog. Or a parishioner who'd wandered off somewhere. Something nice and safe like that."

"I wouldn't ask you if I thought it was going to be

dangerous, Mr. Wasey. I'm convinced the gangs will stay out of it because the opium isn't theirs and they're not greedy."

"Then if it's such a piece of cake, why don't you look for it?"

Burns seemed a little embarrassed. "Because I'm afraid I'm just not learning the language fast enough. This is a new posting for me. I've only been in China for three months, and Miss Tatlock's only been here for four weeks. And what this job needs is somebody who can speak and understand the local dialect perfectly."

"Mr. Burns, do you honestly think that that's all it's going to take? That you can just walk up to people and ask them if they've seen half a ton of opium floating around anywhere?"

"I think if you ask enough people, then eventually you'll get an answer that might lead somewhere."

"Like the river," Wasey said.

Tightly, Miss Tatlock said, "We're wasting time, Mr. Burns. We not only need someone who speaks the language but someone with a bit of gumption too."

"You're right, Miss Tatlock, I don't have much gumption. But I do have a certain amount of common sense. And I can tell you right now that two missionaries and a man trying to sell seventy gross of glow-in-the-dark ties is not what you use to find a fortune in hidden opium."

Nobody spoke for a moment, then Burns broke the silence. "What about those ties, Mr. Wasey? You still have to get them to Los Angeles, and you have no money."

Wasey couldn't argue with that, and Burns followed up quickly.

"Why not give this a try? Just ask four or five people. If you come away with only a lead, however slight, I'll go through with my end of the agreement."

Wasey was tempted. "Just a lead? I don't actually have to find the stuff?"

"That's correct."

"Who would I ask?"

"There's a man named Tuttle who I want you to meet. Unfortunately he's away for a few days. But knowing Shanghai as you do, I'm sure you could think of a few people who might have their ears to the ground."

"Yeah, I guess I could," Wasey admitted.

"You have to agree it's a good deal we're offering you, Mr. Wasey. A steamer ticket in return for what amounts to a couple of days' legwork."

Wasey thought about his shipment; if somebody beat him to L.A. with the same kind of ties, which was a definite possibility, he'd be in a hell of a hole. He said, "I'd have to throw a little money around..."

"Miss Tatlock will supply it."

"She's coming with me?"

"I think it would be a good idea," Burns said. "There are a few more details you should know about, and Miss Tatlock can fill you in as you go."

Wasey winked at her. "Well, Miss Tatlock, together again."

She broadsided him with a look, then rose smartly. "I suggest we get started."

Wasey got up too, and Burns crossed to the door, opened it, and held out his hand. He said, "Good luck, Mr. Wasey. I must confess that I don't share your pessimism." He allowed himself a smile. "I think two missionaries and a tie salesman could well turn out to be a winning combination."

Faced with such confidence, all Wasey could do was smile right back. "You might be right, Mr. Burns, but it'll take a miracle."

Burns pointed to the logo on the door, the hand holding a cross. "You're forgetting my calling, Mr. Wasey," he said. "I believe in miracles."

2

Wasey's foot had hardly touched the alley before Miss Tatlock demanded to know whom he thought they should ask first. Wasey told her he'd have to think about it, looked around trying to orient himself, then started in the direction of the Kiangsi Road. They went through a series of side streets into an area that was just as poor as the one they'd come from but made a lot more lively by a number of open-air stalls.

A dentist wearing a filthy blue apron offered to check Wasey's teeth. A wooden table set up on the sidewalk carried his stock in trade: two jars of purple ointment, some bent metal picks, a few sets of dentures in a cracked glass case, and a high mound of decayed yellow teeth, evidence of his professional skill with the pair of rusty forceps he held in his fingernail-bitten hand.

Also available in the medical department, a little farther along, were the services of a doctor and his assistant. On their table was a collection of whistles, bells, gongs, and wooden rattles which, in the hands of the healer who knew what he was doing, could be blown, rung, struck, and shaken in such a manner as to drive out the evil spirits that had caused a patient's malady. There was also a chart set up illustrating all five organs: the eyes, the eyebrows, the nose, the mouth, and the ears.

Not far from the doctor a beautician kept up a steady stream of chatter. For clear facial skin she recommended a mask of egg white, hens' blood, and peach blossoms be applied before retiring, a jelly of wood shavings for glossy black hair, and for colored fingernails balsam flowers mixed with fine yellow tobacco, crushed in a mortar with burnt alum, then wrapped and rewrapped seven times in a mulberry leaf.

Wasey inquired but Miss Tatlock wasn't interested in getting her advice.

The stall next to it wasn't as specialized and sold new hinges, old doorknobs, chopped firewood, blackbirds, carpet snakes, goldfish, baby sloths, and hot water for tea.

The neighboring stall confined its offerings to wine and rice beer, but Miss Tatlock refused to let Wasey sample the wares.

Wasey pressed on for a way, then stopped outside of a restaurant. It was open to the street, with a chef standing behind a long wooden counter and ducks hanging from bamboo frames, delicious-looking birds bloated and glazed with a varnish of melted rock sugar and red bean paste. There were various pots bubbling over a wood-fired stove, most of the food prepared and ready.

Miss Tatlock frowned. "Why are we stop— Oh, I see. Yes, I suppose the proprietor of a restaurant would be a good person to ask."

Instead of answering Wasey stepped back and allowed Miss Tatlock to precede him.

There was no one in the restaurant except an old woman picking tiny feathers out of a swift's nest for the house specialty. Wasey went over to the counter, checked the fare, then ordered from the chef. Once again Miss Tatlock was ahead of him and allowed that it made sense to give the place some custom if they wanted information. They took a table and were immediately brought a bowl of sugared lotus leaves, a teapot and two cups. Miss Tatlock poured a cup for herself but Wasey covered his with his hand. "I've ordered a different kind," he said.

Miss Tatlock got right down to business. "As Mr. Burns told you, there are a few more things you need to know. According to his information, Faraday never had time to refine the opium. It's still in its original form. . . . Poppies."

"Half a ton of poppies? What, in bales?"

"I believe so."

She stopped speaking as the chef put down a teapot in front of Wasey, who quickly poured a cup, drained it, poured a second cup, drained that, then sighed with satisfaction. "Sorry," he said. "Go ahead."

"I also believe," Miss Tatlock went on, "that the Chinese slang for opium poppies is 'flowers.' That's right, isn't it?"

"Correct," Wasey said, pouring from his teapot again. "That's what they call opium addicts here, slaves of the flower."

"So what we're looking for, Mr. Wasey, is Faraday's flowers. Mr. Burns understands that that's what they're known as."

Wasey raised his cup and proposed a toast. *"Kan-pei,"* he said, and drank.

Miss Tatlock stiffened. "Mr. Wasey. Are you listening to me?"

"Absolutely. What we're looking for is Faraday's flowers."

The chef interrupted them, bustling over and laying down a number of covered bowls, steam rising from them.

"You've been in China a month, that right, Miss Tatlock?"

"Yes."

"What do you think of Chinese food?"

"My interest in food, Mr. Wasey, is confined to finding ways of supplying it to those in need. Not in consuming it myself."

Wasey dished fish fillets in tart sauce into his bowl, a hot rice cake and a tea-dyed pear. "If you want to learn about China, Miss Tatlock, you'll have to learn about its cooking. It's a big part of the culture. And you'll also improve your Chinese."

Grudgingly she conceded that he might have a point, and turned her attention to the bowls. "What are these called?" she asked, lifting a lid.

"Ch'in-niu. Dragon claws."

"They look like pickled chickens' feet."

"That's what they are," Wasey replied, helping himself to more fish fillets.

Miss Tatlock picked up a claw, tentatively nibbled at it, then put it straight down again.

"They're an acquired taste," Wasey told her.

"Why aren't you eating them?"

Wasey waved his chopsticks innocently. "I never acquired the taste."

Miss Tatlock glared at him and might have said something if the chef hadn't arrived with two more bowls.

"Ah!" Wasey said, lifting a lid. "Now this is Chinese cooking at its most inventive. It's called 'improved egg.' They take an egg, push a pin through the top, and drain it. Then they beat the yolk, blend it with chicken stock and crushed mushrooms, and pour the mixture back into the shell. They seal the hole with a piece of paper, then bury the egg in a mound of rice and steam it till it's cooked."

"How do you eat it?"

"Take the paper off and suck."

"No, thanks," said Miss Tatlock.

Wasey drank from his cup, then lifted another lid, brought the bowl up to his nose, and inhaled deeply. "Mmmm! If there's one thing I love it's the smell of puffed fish maw in cream stock."

He pushed some of the dish into Miss Tatlock's bowl.

A little awkwardly she got some onto her chopsticks and tried it. She made a face and swallowed quickly. "I don't care for it," she said, passing the bowl to Wasey.

"No, thanks," Wasey said, "I only like the smell."

Miss Tatlock smoldered at him but Wasey didn't seem to notice. He poured from the teapot again and raised the cup. *"Kan-pei."*

Miss Tatlock, suspicious, said, "What kind of tea is that?"

"It's, um, Moo Goo Gai Pan. Very bitter. You wouldn't like it."

She pounced on his reply. "If you know I wouldn't like it, then why haven't you insisted I try it?" She reached for the pot, brought it to her nose, and sniffed it. "Why, this is alcohol!"

"Alcohol?" Wasey blinked and looked at his cup. "I thought it tasted funny."

Miss Tatlock banged the pot down onto the table. "Mr. Wasey. You know very well how I feel about strong drink. And while I'm paying the bills you will please abstain."

Wasey gave a little sign of surrender. "You drive a hard bargain, Miss Tatlock."

"I suggest you talk to the proprietor now."

"I can't send the chickens' feet back, you already ate some."

"I am not talking about the chickens' feet." Miss Tatlock took a breath and collected herself. "I suggest you ask him about the flowers."

Wasey looked puzzled. "What would he know about the flowers? He runs a small restaurant."

"But that's why we came in here. You said so."

"You said so. I came in here because I haven't had a thing to eat or drink all morning."

Miss Tatlock opened her mouth, then snapped it closed. She dug into her handbag and thrust money at Wasey. "I shall wait for you outside. Please bring me a receipt and the change."

She got up and marched away, almost colliding with the chef, who was on the point of delivering yet another steaming bowl.

"Alas," Wasey said. "We must go. The young mistress has an appointment."

The chef held out the bowl in dismay. "But I have prepared pig's tripe soup."

Wasey sighed deeply. "She will indeed be heartbroken."

* * *

Miss Tatlock took twenty angry paces before she stopped and wheeled on him. "I have something to say to you, Mr. Wasey. I do not intend to be teased anymore. I do not intend to be made a fool of. You are flippant, facetious, and, I suspect, sorely lacking in moral fiber. However, I am duty bound to Mr. Burns to work with you, and I shall try. We have made a bargain, you and I and he, and I expect you to live up to it. I expect you to give it your best. Do I make myself clear?"

Wasey was suitably contrite. "Yes, ma'am."

"Very well. Now. Apart from city and government officials, whom we cannot approach, what kind of person would be well informed about what goes on in Shanghai?"

Wasey considered it. "My first guess would be the rickshaw king."

"Who is that?"

"I don't know his name but he's the guy who runs all the rickshaws. Every city in China has a rickshaw king. They usually know what's going on because the pullers hear things."

"How do we locate him?"

"Simple. Take a rickshaw."

With a stern look on her pretty face Miss Tatlock said, "We'll take a taxi. I do not believe in using my fellow man as a beast of burden."

"You'd take a taxi to see the taxi king," Wasey explained patiently. "But there isn't any taxi king, because nobody in his right mind would own more than one Shanghai taxi. If we want to see the rickshaw king, we have to take a rickshaw."

Miss Tatlock hesitated for only a moment. "Very well. Just this once."

A few blocks' walk brought them into the bustle of the Kiangsi Road not far from one of the big hotels. There was a group of rickshaw men standing outside the doors waiting for customers.

"Block your ears, Miss Tatlock. The pullers all get on

okay until one of them gets a fare, then all the others hate him and call him names."

"Thank you for the warning, Mr. Wasey, but it's imperative that I learn Chinese, and I'd be grateful if you'd translate at every opportunity. Especially the language of the poor, the people I'll be working with."

The rickshaw pullers spotted them and leaped at them like a pack of starving dogs. They shouted prices, each one undercutting another without even knowing the destination. Wasey chose a big rickshaw which had a pusher behind as well as a puller in front, and helped Miss Tatlock up onto the padded seat.

Immediately the two lucky coolies were bombarded with insults.

"Translate please, Mr. Wasey."

"Dog butcher," Wasey said.

"And that?"

"Cat eater."

Miss Tatlock was leaning forward, concentrating on the shouted words.

"And that?"

"Your father fucks chickens."

Miss Tatlock cut the lesson short.

It was a long ride and a noisy one, partly because of the traffic din but mainly because the two coolies grunted, hawked, and spat every step of the way, and yelled frightful imprecations at careless pedestrians. The puller trotted between the traces in the alarming Shanghai fashion, head down, contemptuous of all motorized vehicles, while the pusher never looked up once. Yet, as Wasey told Miss Tatlock, the rickshaw was by far the safest means of transportation and accidents were rare.

Wasey knew they'd arrived when he saw the pile of broken rickshaws, too dilapidated even for the Chinese district over in Chapei. The street, a lane of broken cobblestones, was a jumble of reed and bamboo houses propped up at impossible angles by long curving poles. The only large building in sight, which might once have been a market, was open to the weather now, the precious iron sections of its corrugated roof long since acquired by the locals. The big red Chinese characters which had been painted along the side were peeled into meaningless curls and slashes, the doors had been stolen, and every pane of glass removed.

The rickshaw stopped near a group of pullers who were standing in an impatient circle, slapping down coins and grunting encouragement to two crickets which were teased with straws into a fighting rage.

Wasey went over to make inquiries. "I'm looking for the king," he announced. "Who can help me?"

Eyebrows lifted. A Devil speaking like any normal person! One of the men, the bookie for the group, gave Wasey some directions. Wasey thanked him, then lingered a moment.

"Two cash on the brown one," he said.

"Done!" said the bookie.

It was a short fight. The combatants clashed, jaws snapped, and one of the insects limped away with a broken leg. Its owner, adding insult to injury, called it a gutless pig and stepped on it. Wasey murmured something to the bookie, then went over to where Miss Tatlock was waiting.

"Did you find out?" she asked.

"Down the alley and all the way to the back." He stopped her as she began to move off. "Er, Miss Tatlock, I, um, owe a man some money."

Miss Tatlock bridled. "You didn't bet on that barbarous spectacle, did you?"

Wasey looked disgusted. "I would've won if it hadn't been fixed. My cricket took a dive."

"How much do you owe?"

"A nickel Shanghai."

"Very well," Miss Tatlock said. She opened her purse and handed over a coin, the equivalent of half an American

27

cent. "But understand this, Mr. Wasey. I do not intend to settle any more of your gambling debts."

Wasey went over, paid the bookie, came back, and led the way down a narrow lane. The aroma was the standard one for the coolie section: bean curd sizzling in peanut oil, fish heads, the pickled odor of *yi-ts'eh*—the salted mustard greens that were the staple diet—and the raw yellow-soap smell of thrown-out laundry water soaking into the dirt of the alley. When they reached the last house Wasey pushed aside a rice-sack curtain, and they entered.

The room was dark, and made darker still by a hardened-earth floor. In the center charcoal burned in an old kerosene can: heat, light, and cooking stove all in one. There was a rough table, a few unmatched chairs, and a cot made of boards nailed to one wall. The rickshaw king certainly didn't live like royalty.

They moved through a smelly hall and out into an open backyard area where several rickshaws were being repaired. They were old ones bought cheap from the big companies whose names they still bore: Everlasting Remembrance, Steadfast Righteousness, Able to Fly Company. Two men were hammering at a wheel closely watched by a third, who was wrapped in a torn padded quilt, an older man with a plump tummy and a star burst of lines around his eyes. He turned at their approach. He was used to visits from Big Nose—usually inspectors from the Municipal Council come to complain about an unsafe vehicle. But no inspector ever wore cream-on-shit shoes and a painted scroll around his neck. Nor had one ever been accompanied by a young and handsome Jesus lady with her hair lashed to a rock at the back of her head.

"Honored sir," Wasey began. "You are the rickshaw king?"

Local dialect instead of pidgin! It could not possibly be an inspector. The king indicated his humble surroundings. "Alas, royalty in name only."

"We are welcome?" Wasey asked.

"As the Blue Heaven is my witness."

Wasey nodded at Miss Tatlock, said to the other man, "My *mei mei* does not speak the Divine Tongue and begs to be excused on the grounds of extreme stupidity."

The rickshaw man gracefully excused her. He peered at the rolling dice and the cocktail glass on Wasey's tie. "My compliments on your attire, sir."

Wasey pointed to the Road to Ruin legend and translated, taking into account the different values of a different culture. "It says, the Path to Paradise. It lights up at night without the aid of matches."

The king caught his breath. "A quality beyond price."

Wasey began to undo the tie. "My heart would fly if you would accept it."

"Your loss would be too great."

"I have others."

The rickshaw king was surprised. "You have more than one?"

"I have ten thousand."

The king was astonished. "An extensive wardrobe, to be sure."

There was no need to give him the tie, the offer alone sufficing to show goodwill.

"Honored sir," Wasey began again. "I understand that you know this peerless city as well as anyone."

"Perhaps better."

"I'm told you know who lives here and what they hold most dear."

The man waved an arm at the two coolies at work on the rickshaw. "I have many birds. They bring back numerous seeds of information."

Wasey thought the analogy an apt one; most pullers did look like birds, skin and bones, the rags they wore like thin trailing feathers.

"We are seeking to recover something of some worth that has been mislaid. We are willing to pay handsomely for any hint as to its whereabouts."

The rickshaw king waited.

"You have perhaps heard the name Faraday?" Wasey asked.

The king confirmed it.

Behind him Wasey had felt Miss Tatlock tense when he mentioned the name.

"We are looking for his flowers."

"Ah," the king said. "Faraday's flowers." He began to nod his head.

"Would you know, honored sir, where we might begin our search?"

The king kept nodding for a moment, then stopped and began to shake his head the other way.

"Or who to ask?"

The king just kept on shaking his head.

"Perhaps one of your pullers might know."

"Everything is possible."

Recognizing a blank wall, Wasey turned, took Miss Tatlock's elbow, and led her out of the room.

Walking along the lane, she said, "Do you think he knows?"

"If he does he isn't saying."

"Perhaps we should have paid him some money."

"He would have asked for it if he'd had information to sell. I told you we weren't going to get anywhere."

"It's only our first try, Mr. Wasey. You can't judge from that."

"Believe me, Miss Tatlock, that's the kind of treatment we're going to get whoever we ask. A polite smile, if we're lucky, and zero help."

"I think you're wrong. Please suggest somebody else we can see."

Wasey, knowing it was useless to argue, was forced to consider her directive. "Well, we've done rickshaws, so we've covered the land. Maybe we should try the sea."

* * *

Although officially called the Whangpoo, Shanghai's river had several local names depending on the particular stretch. At the northern end, opposite the citadels of business, it was known as the River of Serenity. At the opposite end, where a thousand houseboats floated on a sluggish tide, it was called the River of Robust Scent.

Getting out of a cab opposite that section, Wasey said, "Smells healthy, doesn't it?"

Miss Tatlock walked with him to the low stone balustrade of the quay, and looked out over the great sweep of water that blinked and bounced in the sunlight. An armored launch cruised slowly down a lane of houseboats, a machine gun mounted on deck, a dozen soldiers with rifles ringing the cabin. The big flag it flew, the red and white blaze of the rising sun, made a cruel snapping sound in the breeze. Miss Tatlock watched it in cold silence, then her eye was drawn to something else, something in the river that looked like a logjam. There was a barge near it, and men pushing at the logs with boat hooks.

Wasey saw what she was looking at. "They're corpses," he said. "They sew them into sacks."

"Who does?"

Wasey pointed south. "The authorities in Nantao. They're opium victims who've starved to death. The relatives are supposed to bury them, but that costs money, so they're often left on the street to be picked up, like garbage. They're dumped into the river on the outgoing tide with the hope that they'll make it all the way to the Yangtze."

Miss Tatlock watched the river, then set her jaw. "We've got to find those poppies, Mr. Wasey. Not just for the morphine we'll get but to stop it reaching the streets as opium."

"Well, we're trying. That's why we came down here to talk to the lighter boss. In a port city like this he rates pretty high."

They began to walk towards a sign that advertised a

water taxi service. They went down steps to a dock and hopped on board a sampan which had a burbling outboard motor rigged up on a long boom astern.

Wasey had a word with the boatman, then sat down next to Miss Tatlock. "One thing," he said. "The lighter boss is usually a pretty tough cookie. They're not famous for being exquisite in manner or speech. I'll probably have to show him some money."

"How much will you need?"

"A U.S. dollar should do the trick."

Miss Tatlock handed him a bill, then held on tight as the boatman took the craft away fast. He steered it down a line of lighters and expertly brought the boat alongside a freight junk parked at the end of the row. Its sailing days were long gone; it had no mast, and it listed heavily to one side. Washing was threaded on bamboo poles, and blankets had been spread over the mat roof of the cabin to catch the afternoon sun. They climbed aboard and moved along the incline of the deck, past a woman who was hauling up clothes she'd washed in the muddy yellow river. The small child at her side wore a lifeline, a cloth cord tethered to a fat sack of flour.

Wasey led the way into the living quarters, a tunnel-shaped affair that was kitchen, dining room, and bedroom all in one, a wild jumble of rope, cats, chickens, barrels, floats, and people. A group of rowdy children were playing a game of *cha-tzu,* shouting each time one of them rolled the seven tiny stones. An aged grandparent sat watching them, while in another corner two teenage girls cut rags to resole slippers.

Wasey had no trouble spotting the man he was after; he was sitting at a makeshift table shoveling noodles into his mouth as if he were stopping up a hole in a wall. He was a hard, heavy man with a rough face, and the black shorts and gray sleeveless undershirt he wore showed off a lot of bunchy muscle.

Nobody had so much as glanced at Wasey or Miss Tatlock, apparently used to strangers coming and going. And when Wasey spoke the man at the table didn't even look at him, his eyes staying greedily on a charcoal brazier where a woman stirred a sizzling pan.

"I'm told that Shanghai lives because of its port and that nothing moves in or out of the port that the lighter boss doesn't know about."

The lighter boss acknowledged nothing, so Wasey piled on the flattery.

"I'm told that the lighter boss is, therefore, the most powerful man in the city, perhaps in the entire province of Kiangsu. That nothing of any importance happens without his knowledge."

Wasey's only answer was a snap-snap-snap as the man worked his chopsticks in a quick burst of movement, the noodle bowl jammed to his mouth.

"I am looking for something, and information as to its whereabouts would be of major interest and would not go lightly rewarded."

"How much?" the man grunted through a gob-stopper of pasta.

Wasey produced the dollar bill, and with a fast movement the other man reached out, snatched it between his chopsticks, dropped it onto the table, then paused as something caught his attention. Once again the chopsticks darted out, but this time they seized Wasey's tie. The man lifted it to peer at the drawing of the chorus girl's legs, snorted, and dropped it. He rapped impatiently on the table, and the woman at the brazier sped to him with a steaming pan: fish liver and intestines mixed with eggs and ginger. The man scooped it into his bowl, took a swig from a bottle of vinegar, sprayed it onto his food, dumped sugar onto it, and hungrily attacked it.

"I am looking for flowers," Wasey said. "Faraday's flowers."

The words had no effect on the lighter boss.

"Can you give me a name? Someone I can ask?"

Still eating, the man shook his head.

"You are sure?"

The lighter boss didn't like having his word questioned. He glowered at Wasey, glanced at Miss Tatlock for the first time, then rumbled something menacing.

Wasey turned around. "No dice. Let's go."

Miss Tatlock was indignant. "He owes me a dollar. He took that money and gave nothing in return. Ask for it back."

"He'll probably say no."

"Ask him!" she demanded.

Wasey turned back to the man, who was just taking another swig from the vinegar bottle, and passed on Miss Tatlock's request. For an answer the lighter boss leaned forward and spat the vinegar over Wasey's two-tone shoes.

Wasey faced Miss Tatlock again. "I think that's a no."

Furious at the man's unfairness, Miss Tatlock took a fast step forward and reached for the dollar on the table.

The boss moved fast; his chopsticks pinned Miss Tatlock's wrist to the table.

"Mr. Wasey," she cried. "Help me!"

"I don't have any chopsticks," Wasey said.

The boss reached over with his left hand, took the dollar bill, and stuffed it down his undershirt. Then he released Miss Tatlock.

"You bully!" she said to him, then swung round and marched away.

When Wasey joined her out on the deck she rounded on him. "Why didn't you come to my defense?"

Wasey shrugged. "It wasn't my fight."

"And just why not, I'd like to know!"

"It wasn't my money."

Miss Tatlock simmered all the way back in the water taxi and didn't speak till they were standing on the quay. She said sharply, "Next!"

Wasey breathed out deeply. "Why bother, Miss Tatlock, it's hopeless."

"Next!"

There were battle flags in her eyes, so Wasey quickly came up with somebody.

He told her that an important man in Chinese society, and one who was often party to quite a few secrets, was the owner of any old and established insurance company. Not one of the big English or American firms, he pointed out, but a local one that specialized in the Chinese type of insurance.

"Where are these businesses located?" Miss Tatlock asked.

"Most of them are in the lower Nanking Road."

"Very well, that's where we'll go," Miss Tatlock declared.

There was no trouble with the cab they got until it had made a hundred yards and the two front tires blew out. Wasey bemoaned the fact that Miss Tatlock refused to take rickshaws and, sitting in the rear seat of a second taxi, holding on tight, he enlarged on the danger they were in. "They're deathtraps, these things. Four out of five traffic fatalities in this town are caused by taxis and their crazy drivers."

"Can't they bring in a new traffic law?" Miss Tatlock asked.

"They did. But it's a very Chinese one. As of this year, if a person driving a car kills somebody, a wax effigy of the victim is set up in a room and the driver has to look at it for an hour or two. They figure the driver will feel sorry and mend his reckless ways."

"I don't think that's strong enough."

"You're right. There was one cabdriver who felt sorry three times in two months."

"That's scandalous," Miss Tatlock said. "Did he go to jail?"

"Oh no. Matter of fact, he had another accident. They made him take the three effigies home and put them in his dining room. Nearly drove his wife crazy. They were a family of four, but every night there were seven at the table."

Wasey's pessimism wasn't borne out on that particular trip, the cab delivering them promptly and safely at the lower part of the Nanking River. It was a staid, respectable area given over to the careful management of finance and the polite pursuit of commerce. Here shiny new Fords and Studebakers were parked on clean-swept streets, and men wore snap-brim felt hats and tartan woolen scarfs with their long quilted gowns and real leather shoes.

The insurance shops were grouped together, their black banner signs hanging down in long flapping verticals, the gold lettering in Chinese and English. The shops themselves ran all the way from large glossy affairs to simple counters, just a clerk in a teller's cage and a list of that day's special offerings.

Wasey checked with several passersby, financial-looking types, and the consensus seemed to be that the oldest and most venerable insurance office was the Ho Chong Insurance and Exchange Company Limited, Inc., and that Ho Chong himself had as good a grasp on community goings-on as anybody in the district.

They found the place easily enough, a fine, solid-looking establishment with dark camphorwood wall panels and an enormous teak table that stretched clear across the floor. In the back several clerks were busy with brush and ink stone and abacus, the Reckoning Tray, as it was called.

As Wasey and Miss Tatlock entered the door the owner, fat and jolly, broke into a blubbery smile and waddled up to the teak table. He bowed and said, in English, "Good afternoon, lady and gentleman. My calling name is Ho Chong. The welcome is extending deeply."

Wasey thanked him.

"You have desires to insure your parts?" He pointed to some large display cards propped up on the table. Each one illustrated a different part of the body with a price beneath it. Unlike the policies of Western companies, most of the insurance written by Chinese firms was not for life insurance—that is, the whole body—but for those selected areas held most precious by the customer.

"If the rate is fair," Wasey answered.

"Eminently fair. Regard this." Ho Chong held up an illustrated card. "The neck, the left elbow, and both knees for just four Shanghai dollars a month."

When Wasey said it was a little pricey Ho Chong held up another card. "Then how about the armpits, the genitals, and both ankles for just three Shanghai dollars a month?"

Wasey looked doubtful. "I don't know if I need the ankles."

The fat man picked up a third card. "Then I suggest the armpits, the genitals, and the big toe of your choice for just two Shanghai dollars a month."

Wasey wasn't crazy about the offer and made a counterproposal. "How about the armpits, the genitals, and both big toes for two dollars a month?"

Ho Chong recognized a sharp trader but still wanted a deal he could live with. "I could do the armpits, both toes, and the epiglottis for two dollars a month."

"No, for that price I'd need the genitals, too. How about the epiglottis, the genitals, the—"

"*Mr. Wasey!*" It was Miss Tatlock. "Could you please conclude this."

Wasey gave Ho Chong an apologetic shrug. "I'll just take a straight kneecap and ankles."

The fat man asked Wasey to fill out a form, then directed his attention to Miss Tatlock. "And you, reverend lady, you would also secure coverage for a treasured part?"

"No, thank you."

Ho Chong never gave up easily. "The lips and ears perhaps?"

"Thank you, no."

"The thighs and buttocks?"

"Definitely not."

"Then surely your breasts and vagina?"

"*No!*" said Miss Tatlock. With her face a fine shade of red she stared fixedly at the camphorwood paneling.

Wasey explained to the disappointed proprietor. "I don't think they're in much danger."

"Mis-ter *Wasey!* Could we please conclude our business here."

Wasey meekly asked her for two dollars, gave the money and the signed form to Ho Chong, then waved his hand around him. "Your shop looks most prosperous, sir. You must have insured many parts of many people."

Ho Chong smiled and boasted, "Indeed. Half the parts of half the people in Shanghai."

"May I ask if you ever did business with a man named Faraday?"

"No. And a thousand thanks to Father Heaven. A bad risk indeed, and so he proved."

Wasey said, "He is reputed to have had some flowers."

"Ah yes." Ho Chong's fat face broadened. "Faraday's flowers. Well known in the city."

Miss Tatlock sounded pressing and urgent. "We want to talk to someone who might know where they are. We'll pay them well for information."

Ho Chong half closed his heavy eyelids and pondered. "I do not know their location. But there is one who might."

"Who?" Wasey and Miss Tatlock said it together.

Ho Chong was still considering it. "But he's a hard man and rough. If annoyed he would spit on your head."

"Who? Who?"

"The lighter boss."

Miss Tatlock's shoulders sank.

Wasey sighed and looked down at his stained two-tone shoes. He said thoughtfully, "He must've been working his way up."

Miss Tatlock's disappointment lasted for about fifty feet along the Nanking Road, then her head lifted, her step quickened, and her words had snap to them. "Where to now, Mr. Wasey?"

"Anywhere we can buy a towel."

"A towel? Whatever for?"

"So we can throw it in. We're not getting anywhere, Miss Tatlock. It's obvious."

"Sometimes the obvious can be very deceiving, Mr. Wasey."

"Come on, Miss Tatlock, the shot's not on the table. Let's forget it."

"There's an old saying, Mr. Wasey, corny perhaps, but good advice. If at first you don't succeed, try, try again."

"Well, we didn't succeed at first. And we have tried, tried again. And all I've got to show for it is a bleached pair of Florsheims and an insurance policy for my ankles."

She said fiercely, "You're a quitter, Mr. Wasey. I knew you were."

"We're chasing a rainbow, Miss Tatlock."

"No, we are not. A rainbow is an optical illusion. Half a ton of opium poppies is a physical fact."

"Then how come nobody seems to know where they are?"

"Because we haven't yet found the right person to ask."

"I don't know who else to ask, Miss Tatlock. I'm fresh out of ideas."

Miss Tatlock locked eyes with him for a moment, then checked her watch. "Very well, we'll stop for today. I suggest you sleep on it tonight and we'll meet with Mr. Burns in the morning."

"What good's that going to do? That's where we started."

Miss Tatlock didn't appear to have heard him. She opened her handbag and held out a bill. "You'll need money for dinner."

"That wouldn't even buy me breakfast."

"If I give you more you'll only use it for drink."

"All right, give me some more and I promise to use it for food." He took the bill. "I'll use this for drink."

39

Miss Tatlock's handbag closed with a frugal click. "I expect to see you in Mr. Burns's office tomorrow morning. Nine o'clock sharp."

Wasey waited. He threw her a tired salute. "Whatever you say, sergeant."

3

When he got back to his hotel Wasey got a pleasant surprise. Raking around in his suitcase, he found five Hong Kong dollars in the pocket of an unwashed shirt, which meant his evening wasn't going to be an entire loss like his day.

What a ball of wax it had been. He lay down on the bed and tried to focus on the sudden change in his fortunes; instead of being on the high seas, bound for a commercial bonanza in Los Angeles, he was stuck in Shanghai, embroiled in a madcap scheme with a couple of wide-eyed missionaries. It was crazy, but there it was. He tried to think whom he could wire for money, somebody he didn't already owe money to. It was difficult, and he fell asleep with the effort.

It was getting dark when he woke up. He took a fast shower, then went downstairs to do something about a drink. He had a beer in the bar next door, which bucked him up a bit, then another, which aroused his appetite. He went into the first restaurant he came to. It had six wooden benches set over a shallow pond with eels swimming beneath the diners' feet. There was a set menu, three dishes only; a cold plate as a starter; beef gristle stewed into submission and served in bean paste, then eel split down the center, chopped up, and sautéed in peanut oil. With it came a side dish of ducks' feet boiled in pork broth, the delicate webbing being regarded as a taste thrill. Wasey enjoyed it all, drank a large pot of Sau Mei tea, then left the place feeling happier about things.

The area he was in was far from being the naughtiest district in the city, but seeing as how the entire International Settlement seemed to be devoted to evening entertainment of a particular kind, every area had its share of nightclub touts, all of whom wore dark blue suits, rubbed their hands a lot, and spoke a smattering of several languages. In a fifty-yard walk from the restaurant Wasey was offered a chance to witness floor shows which featured, in order of soliciting, twenty-seven different ways, thirty-eight different ways, and forty-four different ways. In the next fifty yards he was offered spectacles of a different kind.

"Sir! A girl and a donkey."

"Sir! Two girls and a donkey."

"Sir! Two girls and two donkeys."

And there was one offer that stopped him. "Sir! Two donkeys."

"How many girls?" Wasey asked.

"No girls, just donkeys."

He was also offered a chance to see Shanghai's famous sex circus, a show in an actual big top in which all the performers—jugglers, clowns, acrobats, aerialists, wire walkers—not only performed entirely nude but did so while having "united happiness." The tout for that particular extravaganza carried a stack of advertising fliers. He took one look at Wasey's two-tone shoes and hand-painted tie and gave him a flier printed in English. Scanning it, Wasey was charmed by the blurb pertaining to the trapeze artists. "See Ch'ien and Ting Ling attempt the dangerous double flying fuck without a net."

Wasey resisted all the touts' blandishments and chose to have a drink in a bar. But he was still treated to a floor show of a peculiar kind. In fact, he was part of it.

After he'd had a few drinks he was invited into a back room to play chess with a young lady. The chessboard was five feet square and mounted on a low table. The chessmen were oversized, too. The young woman, who was naked, stood on the table and moved the pieces with a part of her anatomy not normally associated with such an intellectual game. She was a smart player and Wasey had to resign after less than a dozen moves, although he claimed that she'd disturbed his concentration.

It was while he was strolling back to the hotel that he

got, if not an answer to the question he'd been asking that day, certainly an acknowledgment that he'd been inquiring.

A rickshaw puller trotted up alongside him. "Flowers," the man said.

Wasey stopped. The puller was thin and frail, and the rags he wore made him look like someone who'd been hastily bandaged.

"What?"

"Man know where flowers. You come." The coolie, from some other province, spoke Shanghai as if the words hurt his mouth.

"Who sent you? Did the king send you?"

"You come. Man know where flowers."

Wasey had no thought of caution. The reverse was true. He climbed up into the rickshaw convinced he was about to earn his fare to Los Angeles. The puller started off, made an immediate turn, and darted into a series of side streets. Wasey was soon lost; it was hard to get his bearings without being able to recognize something, and all he was seeing, as the rickshaw rocked and jounced over the cobblestones, was what looked like the same lane: identical two-story stucco apartment blocks on each side connected by narrow passageways, each with a single dim yellow streetlight fighting a losing battle against yards and yards of thick darkness. But he knew that it was hard to go very far in any one direction in the city without coming to water—the entire place had been built on a swamp. If you went east you came to the Whangpoo, Soochow Creek if you went north, the lakes if you went far enough west, Siccawei Creek if you went south, and south was where they seemed to be heading.

He was sure of it a little while later when they came out into a side street and he saw the godowns bulking ahead of him. They were shaped like airplane hangars, vast wooden warehouses that had been built as part of the city's river transportation system.

He got a solid reminder of that as a reeking cart rumbled past them heading for the creek. Only half of Shanghai had sewers; the rest of the city had to be content with outhouses, the tin receptacles from which were collected each week and dumped in the honey cart. This strange cargo was then taken to a barge, towed down the Whangpoo, and thrown into the Yangtze fourteen miles away.

Wasey had never figured out why it was called the honey cart. He pinched his nose until the vehicle had mercifully outdistanced them, then turned his attention to the godown they appeared to be heading for. It was larger than the others, older and more lopsided, the sign above the big double delivery doors too faded to read.

The rickshaw coolie slowed to a walk, stopped, dropped the traces, and stood there with his pigeon chest heaving, sweat soaking through the rag around his forehead and trickling down over his sucked-in face. "Inside," he panted. "Flower man inside."

Wasey got down and went forward. A small entry door squealed back when he pushed it, and the stink hit him immediately, unmistakably the same one as the honey cart, only much more virulent.

He wondered why anyone would choose this god-awful place for a rendezvous until he realized that a warehouse was exactly the kind of place where you'd store half a ton of opium poppies.

With both hands covering his face, and trying hard not to gag, he crossed to a second door and opened it. Inside, at one end of a long featureless room, a man was sitting on a chair. He seemed oblivious to the appalling stench and sat there placidly, perfectly at ease, as if he couldn't imagine more congenial surroundings.

He stood up, the smile on his face deepening, and beckoned to Wasey with a gesture that seemed to promise untold delights. Wasey went towards him, starting to speak.

He didn't get a chance.

Halfway across the room, the dark creaking floorboards

44

turned into painted newspapers, impossible to spot in the dim light. And as his foot tore through them, his body followed, pitching forward and tearing through the fake floor.

He fell with a cry, tumbled several feet through the air, and landed with a thick heavy splash in a huge vat that was positioned below. It was the source of the venomous stench in the room above and, as Wasey plunged headfirst into it, he still couldn't figure out why they called it honey.

4

Wasey didn't arrive in Burns's office the next morning until nine-forty, which didn't surprise Miss Tatlock at all. What did surprise her was the way he looked. He was wearing a Chinese gown that hung on him in folds, his face was a glowing pink, and his hair was mussed and damp, as if he'd just recently stepped out of a shower.

"Good morning, Mr. Wasey," Burns said. Then, unable to keep from commenting, "You've gone native, I see."

"Would you care to hear why?" Wasey sounded angry and unhappy. "A funny thing happened to me on my way home last night." He slumped into a chair and told them about it.

Miss Tatlock squinched up her face. "Why, that's awful!"

Wasey shot her a hard look. "I thought so, too."

Burns ran a hand over his beard and looked uncomfortable and itchy. "That's a terrible thing, Mr. Wasey. It seems you've been the victim of a dreadful practical joke."

"Mr. Burns . . ." Wasey rolled his eyes. "How can you be so naïve? That wasn't a prank, that was a warning for me not to be so nosy."

"From whom?" Miss Tatlock asked.

"From the goddamn Red Society, that's whom. Where do you think I've been all night? Getting clean in the Honan Road Steam Baths, that's where. Lying in a steaming-hot tub of water with just my eyes showing. Believe me, I had plenty of time to talk to the locals, and there is no question about it. Dropping people into the honey pot is a little trick the Red Society is famous for. They do it to discourage people. Well, I'm discouraged, Miss Tatlock, I'm through. The next time there could be crocodiles swimming around in there."

"Mr. Wasey," Burns began. "I hope you know I sympathize deeply with what has—"

"Good, I need sympathy. And I also need twenty American dollars to replace the clothes I had to throw away." He held out a handful of gown. "I had to borrow this tent from one of the bath attendants."

"I'll be happy to reimburse you," Burns said.

Wasey looked resentfully at Miss Tatlock. "My best pair of Florsheims."

"I'm sorry about the shoes," Miss Tatlock said.

"And that was my only spare Road to Ruin tie."

"I'm not sorry about the tie," Miss Tatlock said.

Burns chimed in quickly before Wasey could respond. "As I was about to say, Mr. Wasey, I sympathize with what happened to you. However, you have no proof that one of the gangs was responsible."

"Of course they were responsible. I covered half of Shanghai yesterday blabbing about opium."

"It probably had nothing to do with the opium," Miss Tatlock said. "What were you doing last night? Before it happened?"

"I was having a quiet game of chess, as a matter of fact."

"Speaking of yesterday," Burns said, "Miss Tatlock has given me a full report on your inquiries. I'm very impressed with you, Mr. Wasey. And so is Miss Tatlock."

"Impressed?" Wasey checked with Miss Tatlock. She looked at the floor. "I sure didn't get that impression."

With grudging fairness Miss Tatlock said, "While there were certain aspects of your behavior yesterday that I found reprehensible, I'd be less than honest if I didn't say that you surprised me with your ability to think of people to ask. And your ability to ask them."

"That's why it's important you stay with us," Burns said. "We've been going down to the docks every morning for a long time, and we never found anyone else we thought could do the job."

"You thought I could do it, Mr. Burns. Your offsider didn't."

With some effort Miss Tatlock said, "I admit I was wrong."

Burns leaned forward, intense. "Give it one more try. Please. That opium could help stop the suffering of thousands."

Wasey lifted his hands and let them fall to his lap. "Hell, I can't think of anyone else to ask anyway."

Burns brightened. "I might be able to help you there. I mentioned a man named Tuttle yesterday. Knows the city very well. He'll be back in town tomorrow, and I'm sure he'll have some ideas."

"I'd like to help you. But I've already stuck my neck out once."

Miss Tatlock spoke. "Mr. Wasey, what happened to you was disgusting. But you weren't actually harmed. As Mr. Burns said, somebody may just have been playing a practical joke on a Westerner. You know we aren't popular here. Somebody told me that there are still some Chinese who think we come from a spirit world. They think we're so different that, underneath our clothes, our bones are outside our bodies."

"Yeah, I know that, Miss Tatlock. It's called *nahkuning*. So what?"

"Just that what happened to you could have happened to any foreigner. I'm sure you've just had bad luck."

"It's going to get worse if I keep asking questions."

"Why don't we do this . . ." Burns was taking some bills from his wallet. "Take this money and buy some new clothes. See what you can find out today, and tomorrow talk to Tuttle. Remember, Mr. Wasey, I'm still willing to buy you and your shipment a ticket to the States. All I want is a lead."

The combination of a promised ticket later and actual money now was a hard one to resist, and Wasey gave in.

"Okay. I'll talk to this guy Tuttle. But I'm not promising anything."

He held out his hand for the money, but Burns smiled and passed it the other way. "Miss Tatlock is the banker," he said.

They went to a department store on the Rue Amiral Bayle that Wasey had heard about during his all-night bath. It was called Little Sing Sing. While it was smaller than the city's major department store, which was known as Big Sing Sing, the prices were somewhat lower because all the merchandise was stolen. But far from being tucked away in a back alley, as might be expected, the store was located quite openly in the middle of a large shopping district. Coming into the street floor, which was stacked to the roof with merchandise, Wasey wondered idly how much squeeze would have to be paid for such an arrangement.

A middle-aged Chinese, a happy bubbling type, dressed in a suit and tie, came hurrying towards them with a bright urgency as if he had exciting news to impart. He said in English, running the words together in a high piping voice, "Hello yes please got very many plenty things you bet."

"A fine selection indeed," Wasey answered in Shanghai.

The man's eyes lit up and he switched languages immediately. "A scholar! Your pardon, sir. I should have guessed from your fine gown and elegant bearing."

"A mistake of minuscule importance. And may I compliment you on your command of English?"

"Thank you, but I fear I made a grammatical error, did I not?"

"If you did it was one so small as to escape my notice," Wasey answered.

The man beamed. "I am Hsiao Sing Sing, and you and your *mei mei* are welcome in my humble emporium." He led the way onto the floor. "What may I show you?" Sing

Sing asked, touching items as he walked by them. "Italian marble, Spanish leather, Swiss watches?"

"Menswear," Wasey said.

"Right this way." Sing Sing turned them over to a subordinate, and twenty minutes later Wasey was wearing a double-breasted silk suit stolen off a ship from Singapore, a pair of white moccasins, part of a missing Australian shipment, and a shirt and tie both of which had had the labels removed.

Miss Tatlock, examining a tag, said, "These prices seem exceptionally low. What kind of a store is this?"

"It's a discount house," Wasey answered.

She went off to explore on her own as Sing Sing arrived back.

"What else may I show you? German cameras, French perfumes, Chinese brocade?" He paused beside an oak refectory table that could have seated twenty people. "Or perhaps something on a larger scale. I have immediately available a 1940 De Soto opera coupé in maroon and tan, a '39 Delage D Eight Sport with pontoon fenders and mahogany interior, and a boat-tailed Auburn Speedster with wire wheels and chromed supercharger pipes."

When Wasey failed to respond immediately the sales pitch was instantly changed. "Or if the lady enjoys an early-morning canter in Jessfield Park, I have a fine thoroughbred on order, this year's winner of the Hong Kong Gold Cup, re-marked, of course. Or perhaps a day on the water is her pleasure. I can supply you with anything from a sporty Italian speedboat to a fully equipped oceangoing junk armed with six Browning machine guns."

"Tempting indeed," Wasey admitted. "But what I am really looking for is flowers."

Sing Sing made a self-effacing gesture. "A man of discernment. Forgive me. If you would follow me to my office . . ."

He led the way across the floor, took a left at an immense

stone temple lion, and continued on to a glassed-in room tucked away in a corner. One wall was lined with oversized books—photo albums, as it turned out. Sing Sing selected one, laid it down on a genuine Hepplewhite desk, and opened it to the first page. Several teenage girls looked back at Wasey, blank-faced and a little stunned. As Sing Sing turned the pages they got younger and younger.

"Perfect young flowers," Sing Sing said. "Bright bouquets to perfume the dark of long winter nights."

"Not those kind of flowers. I'm looking for some that belonged to a man named Faraday."

"Ah," Sing Sing said. "Faraday's flowers. Very valuable. However, I do not deal in jewelry, opium, currency, gold bullion, or fine art. But I would be happy to pass you on to an acquaintance or two who do make a market in such commodities, and may well be induced to be of service."

He wrote down two names for Wasey, told him a little about each person, then asked if there was anything else he might be interested in.

Wasey took a fast look to make sure Miss Tatlock was still out of earshot. "Yes. A gun."

The store owner wasn't at all perturbed; he simply reached for another book and opened it. "A German twenty-millimeter aircraft cannon suitable for mounting on a wheeled carriage."

"A mite too large, I fear."

"Then perhaps this would suit. An Italian six-point-five Scotti Brescia carbine with fixed bayonet."

"A fine weapon, but surely a trifle bulky on one's person."

"A pistol! Why not a pistol?"

When Wasey allowed that he might look tolerantly upon such an item, Sing Sing got down another album.

"A forty-five-caliber Military Pattern Mauser. Or a Tokarev automatic, the Russian version of the famous Colt.

51

It lacks perhaps the balance and the pointing qualities of the American original, but is, nevertheless, most versatile."

Wasey stabbed with his finger. "What's this one?"

"But of course. A most compact piece. A Japanese Baby Nambu. Seven millimeter, semiautomatic, seven-round inline detachable box magazine. Barleycorn sights at the front, vee notch at the rear."

"How much?"

"Would eight American dollars be acceptable?"

"Not as acceptable as four American dollars."

Sing Sing looked troubled. "Normally I would be honored to accommodate you, sir, but this is the year of the snake, and being born in the year of the ram as I was, any double multiple of two does not augur well for me."

"The snake and the ram," Wasey said in mock alarm. "A calamitous conjunction, to be sure. But one, I believe, in harmony with any double multiple of three. So six dollars would prove fortuitous for you."

Sing Sing, who'd been going to ask seven, was a trifle put out to be bested at his own game, but was gracious in defeat. He excused himself, disappeared downstairs somewhere, and returned with a small black box, inside of which was a small black automatic.

"I thought you might also like this," Sing Sing said. He held out something that Wasey at first thought was a cigarette lighter.

"I don't smoke."

Sing Sing grinned. "It is an antipersonnel grenade. Also Japanese. Small, as you can see, but powerful, nonetheless." He pointed to a little notched wheel on top. "The first notch sets the fuse for five seconds. The second notch sets it for twenty minutes, so it can also be used as a miniature time bomb."

"How much?"

"Two dollars."

"I'll take it." What the hell, Wasey thought, if he was

in trouble with a gang a grenade was just the kind of weapon he might need.

He slipped the box, and the tiny grenade, into his jacket, arranged to buy them on credit, shook hands with Sing Sing, and rejoined Miss Tatlock.

"What was all that about?" she asked.

"I thought I'd try him. He gave me a couple of names to check out."

"That's excellent, Mr. Wasey." Walking out of the store, she said. "What's in the box?"

"What box?"

"The one he gave you?"

"Oh, that. Just a little gift for shopping there. They do that sometimes in China."

"What is it?"

"I don't know. I didn't look."

"But I saw you look."

"Miss Tatlock. It's just a small gift from one man to another."

Miss Tatlock suspected booze. "Let me see it."

"Okay. But I don't think you'll like it." Her suspicions stronger than ever, Miss Tatlock watched Wasey take the box from his pocket. "They're rubbers," Wasey said.

"A man doesn't give another man pencil eras—" Miss Tatlock stopped. "Oh," she said, and waved the box away as if it were on fire.

5

Tracking down the first man Sing Sing had suggested didn't turn out to be so easy. Sing Sing hadn't known his address, only that he could be found in one of several of the city's teahouses, and a tour of these proved to be an education for Miss Tatlock, who'd never been to one before. They came in all shapes and sizes, everything from the first-class ones on Yates Road, where plump matrons in Paris originals sat in carved blackwood chairs nibbling glazed pastry fishes, to the filthy hovels up near Paoshan where wretched beggars crept in after hours and slept on the tables. The teahouse Wasey found his man in was somewhere in between the two, a large busy establishment on the Foochow Road, a narrow street of evil reputation in the heart of what was known as the Blue Chamber District. It was on the second floor of a low building, up a wide staircase crowded with peddlers selling scrolls, pottery, sheepskin coats, toys, and switches of long black hair. An open balcony ran round the exterior where people could sit and watch the action in the street below, but inside the place was jammed, too. In spite of the late-morning sunshine the naked bulbs which hung from the ceiling burned brightly, laying a hot white glare over the packed tables. Waitresses hurried around—serving more wine than tea—children cried, dice cups thumped down, and a line of painted young girls in long satin dresses and heavy makeup were being loudly paraded around by a clutching woman who'd rented them for the day.

Wasey managed to find a table, and ordered a pot of T'it Kwoon Yam, knowing Miss Tatlock would object to anything stronger.

"Do you see the man?" she asked, looking around.

"We'll give him a while," Wasey said. He sat back and regarded her. They hadn't said too much in the other tea-

54

houses; she hadn't quite forgiven him for the mortifications of the previous day, but all the same, Wasey thought he detected a certain softening on her part, which he assumed was due to her revised opinion of his suitability for the job. It crossed his mind that it might also have something to do with his new clothes, and the fact that she probably thought he looked more presentable now that he no longer wore two-tone shoes or what she had referred to as "that dreadful tie." Maybe she even suspected that he wasn't a total ogre now that she was getting a little more used to him. He was about to broach the subject, but Miss Tatlock, working at improving her Chinese, spoke first.

"Mr. Wasey, when you ordered the tea, did the waitress call me your *mei mei?*"

"Yes, ma'am."

"I've noticed other people have, too. What does it mean?"

"Mei Mei? Sweetheart. Girlfriend."

Miss Tatlock reacted with sharp surprise, and more than a touch of indignation. "Why on earth would anyone think that?"

"Why shouldn't they? Missionaries have boyfriends. You have one yourself, if I remember rightly."

"He is *not* my boyfriend. He is my fiancé."

"It's the same thing. It just makes anything that happens on the front-porch swing a bit more legal. Anyway, what's so ridiculous about you being my girlfriend?"

"Don't be absurd."

"Come on, tell me. What?"

"For one thing, we have absolutely nothing in common."

"How do you know that? We hardly know anything about each other." His eyes roamed her face for a moment. "Tell me. Do you always wear your hair in a bun?"

He thought he was going to be reprimanded, but instead she said simply, "Always."

"Why?"

"It's neat, unfussy, and approved by the Society."

"Ah, yes, the Society. What's its name again?"

"The Door of Hope."

"Where is it headquartered?"

"Baltimore."

"But you're from Boston, right?"

"Why do you say that?"

"Because you're so prim and proper."

"Proper I may be, Mr. Wasey, but I do not regard myself as prim."

"My dear Miss Tatlock. Any girl as pretty as you who wears long skirts and always has her hair in a bun is prim."

Miss Tatlock, a little flustered, welcomed the arrival of their tea. Wasey poured for them both, then said, "So where are you from?"

"Rhode Island. Providence."

"No kidding? I know Providence. I used to date a girl from Brown."

"Really." Miss Tatlock didn't sound interested.

"Where's your fiancé from?"

Again she looked as if she might reprimand him, but again she held back. "Vershire, Vermont."

"What does he do?"

"He teaches divinity at Dartmouth."

"Now there's a coincidence. This girl I used to date from Brown, I took her to a football game once, and they were playing Dartmouth. Boy, did Brown kill 'em." Wasey took a sip of tea. "Really waxed 'em." Took another sip of tea. "Wiped the field with 'em."

"Mr. Wasey. I am not interested in athletics. Neither is my fiancé."

"Reads a lot, huh?"

Miss Tatlock switched the subject. She surprised Wasey by asking a personal question, mild as it was. "How did you learn to speak Chinese so well?"

"I was born here. Lived here till I was twelve, then went back to the States to go to school."

"Was your father working here?"

"Yup. Hydraulic engineer. Worked with John Ripley Freeman on the Yellow River Project. And later with O. J. Todd."

Miss Tatlock appeared almost animated. "I know about that project. The Door of Hope started its operations here right after the Yellow River floods."

"So there you are," Wasey said. "The Yellow River floods. And you didn't think we had anything in common."

His attention was distracted by a new arrival in the room, a bony and wizened old man who carried a case in one hand and a long stick wrapped in a yellow cover in the other. "This could be our boy," Wasey said.

The man went from table to table but got no takers till Wasey hailed him.

"Master," Wasey said, in deference to the man's advanced age, "I'm told your performance is a thing of wonder, and well worth two cash."

"Three cash," the old man replied, and Wasey nodded, the bargain struck.

The man began to unpack his apparatus, took the yellow cover off the stick to reveal something that looked like an umbrella without the cloth. And it opened like one. It was made of wood with five spokes, and dangling from four of them were miniature models of a pagoda, a chair, a ladder, and a water cask attached to a tiny trapeze. Glued to the trapeze was a piece of red celluloid cut to resemble flames. The fifth spoke supported a wire wheel, a broad one with an axle through its center.

The man opened his case and brought out three things: a model of a water seller, whose twin flagons he filled with water from a flask; a prettily engraved brass bell; and a white mouse, which he placed on the stick. When the mouse scampered to the top of the stick, its owner went into his act.

"Fire! Fire!" he cried in a cracked voice. "Run, little

rat! Save your house!" He tinkled the bell and the mouse scurried down the first spoke, entered the wheel, and ran as the wheel revolved.

"Run, little rat, the flames are brighter." The man tinkled the bell a second time, and the mouse left the wheel, went up the spoke, down the next one, and entered the little pagoda.

"Buddha cannot help you. You must put the fire out yourself."

The bell sounded; the mouse fled the pagoda, zipped to the next spoke, ran down it, and perched on the tiny chair at its end.

"Hurry, little rat, hurry," its owner urged. "This is no time to rest. Run down the ladder to the water seller."

He rang the bell again. The mouse flew to the next spoke, climbed down the rungs of the ladder, climbed up them again, shot to the top of the stick, and perched there nervously.

"Calamity!" The old man sounded genuinely worried. "All hope had fled. The flames win."

Wasey was caught up in the drama. "Why?"

His shoulders slumped, the man pointed sadly at the three coins Wasey had placed on the table. "The water seller wants four." Wasey groaned. "A bandit without a heart." He put down another coin, and the trainer picked up the water seller, poured water into the cask on the little trapeze, and with increased urgency shook his bell.

The mouse immediately dashed down the last spoke to the trapeze, hauled up the string attached to the cask, clutched it in its tiny paws, and, responding to another ring of the bell, hopped towards the celluloid flames and poured water on them.

The trainer sighed his relief. "Just in time."

"A near thing," Wasey agreed.

As the man retrieved his mouse and began packing up, Wasey placed another coin on the table. The trainer watched and shrewdly waited to see how he was expected to earn it.

Wasey said, "A rodent of such prowess must surely have performed before many people in Shanghai."

"Before governors, thieves, and madmen," the trainer replied.

"Thieves?" Wasey asked, watching the man. "Has it ever performed for one named Faraday?"

"Alas, there is much rust in my memory." Wasey offered the coin as a lubricant. "Faraday. Ah, yes, I remember."

"He had some flowers, Master."

The old man showed the stumps of his yellowed teeth. "Faraday's flowers. Reputed to be worth a fortune."

"I was told you might know their location."

The old man looked wistfully at the coins Wasey was jingling in his hand but pleaded ignorance. He apologized, finished packing, and left the teahouse in a hurry.

Tiredly, Wasey dropped the coins back into his pocket. "Everybody knows Faraday. Everybody's heard about his flowers. But nobody knows where they are."

Rising from her chair, Miss Tatlock said, with great purpose, "We'll find somebody. This is only our second day."

"Funny," Wasey said, swirling the cold tea in his cup, "it seems a whole lot longer."

Luck Su was the name of the second man Sing Sing had written down: he was the owner of a dance hall on the Avenue Pétain not far from the Polish Legation. It was called the Hollywood, and while it wasn't as big as its competitors, Ciro's and the Frisco, it was still a very popular venue for the taxi dance. On the way there Wasey explained that the taxi dance was a unique institution in Shanghai. With a straight face he said, "They're not the kind of dance halls you're used to, Miss Tatlock."

"I am not used to any dance halls, Mr. Wasey."

"Okay, but if you were used to them, you wouldn't be used to this kind. They cut right across Shanghai society. You'll never see an upper-class Chinese girl at the movies or the theater here, but you'll see them at the taxi dance. The parents don't mind. Even though there are a lot of hard-drinking sailors at these places, not to mention ladies of easy virtue." Wasey thought about it. "And ladies of even easier virtue."

Miss Tatlock burned him with a look but, a second later, hesitated over a question. "Mr. Wasey . . . what exactly is a taxi dance?"

"A guy buys a ticket to dance with a hostess. The better-looking the hostess, the more tickets she costs. Don't you ever read the gossip column in the local English paper?"

"Of course not."

"They get a lot of publicity in that. You see things like: Last night Miss Brilliant Jade, glamorous fifty-ticket girl at Ciro's, broke a heel doing a sultry tango with an ardent admirer."

"I see," said Miss Tatlock.

"At the other end of the scale you can buy a flat-chested rhumba, or a bad-breath fox-trot, for four or five tickets."

"That's unfair. Penalizing a woman because of her physical qualities."

"You're right," Wasey said, trying to look concerned. "I'm against that kind of thing myself."

When they arrived at the dance hall they found that, even though it was only an afternoon session, it was very well attended. The lobby was jammed with people lining up to buy tickets, then having a fast drink at the enormous bar before going inside. Wasey would have liked to do the same himself but, with Miss Tatlock beside him, he had to settle for tickets.

The ballroom itself, warm, crowded, and brilliantly lit, had a tuxedoed orchestra on a raised stage and dancers gliding in formal locks and twists on a huge expanse of polished floor. There was a plush reserved section populated, for the most part, by elegant young men and women with servants in attendance, and with its sofas, banquettes, and crisp white tables it looked a lot like a high-priced restaurant. The taxi girls, sitting cross-legged on bamboo chairs, were ringed around the inner edge of the dance floor looking as if being asked to dance was the last thing on their minds. Most were Chinese, but there were also Koreans, Japanese, Russians, Portuguese, as well as one or two English girls.

Wasey steered Miss Tatlock into the hall, stopped a waiter, and dropped some coins onto his tray. "Where do I find Luck Su?"

The waiter regarded the money as if it were something messy he'd have to clean up. "Never heard of him."

"You should have. He's your boss."

The waiter gave him the money back. "He's not here now."

Wasey got the message: the boss didn't like to be disturbed by strangers. He put the money back on the tray. "Who's the number one girl here?"

This time the money was accepted. "Miss Precious Pearl," the waiter said, nodding to his right.

"And who is the least favored?"

The waiter nodded to his left. "Miss Perfect Carp."

Wasey said to Miss Tatlock, "Wait here, okay?"

"What are you going to do?"

"Trip the light fantastic." He began to move away, then stopped and turned. Amongst all the flouncy tulle dresses and satin and silk cheongsams, her strict black uniform looked wildly out of place. "And listen," Wasey added, "don't dance with anyone for less than five tickets."

He made his way round the circle of chairs and had no trouble identifying the number one girl. She'd just accepted two entire rolls of red tickets from an American marine and, with queenly detachment, was getting up to dance. She had a spectacular figure which pushed at fabulous angles at the red silk dress she wore. It was a long dress, almost ankle length, but sleeveless and split high, so there was a great deal of voluptuous skin on display.

Wasey had no trouble identifying the other girl either. Miss Perfect Carp was a dumpy, morose-looking girl with one eye decidedly out of alignment. She looked up in surprise when the nice-looking yellow-haired foreigner stopped in front of her, a surprise that deepened when he spoke in her own language. Previously the only things the foreigners had ever said to her were variations of "I give you one more tickee. You me nookie nookie."

"I'd like to dance," Wasey said. "How many tickets are you?"

Seeing it was a foreigner, who were all rich, the girl immediately doubled her price. "Two."

"I'll give you a hundred," Wasey said, and slowly and in plain sight handed all the tickets he'd bought to the speechless girl.

Everybody saw it. Everybody had watched in amazement as the well-dressed American had stopped in front of Perfect Carp, who usually only ever got drunken nearsighted English sailors on a budget, but now she was breaking Precious Pearl's record.

Wasey took the stunned girl in his arms and moved her onto the dance floor. The orchestra, Filipinos like most of the musicians in Shanghai, had taken a break, leaving only five of their number on the stand. They were now playing Hawaiian music.

"May I ask you a question?"

"Anything," the girl breathed.

"Luck Su. Where's his office?"

The girl knew she shouldn't tell; it was one of the rules. But a hundred tickets! "The door at the side of the stage. Go through there and down the corridor."

Wasey thanked her, waited till the music finished, delivered the new queen of the Hollywood Dance Hall back to her throne, then rejoined Miss Tatlock. "Right. This way," he said, and followed the directions to the owner's office.

The man was annoyed when they arrived unannounced. He was seated behind a desk going over a ledger, which he quickly slammed shut. There were two other men in the room, thick-shouldered hoods in George Raft suits and bright yellow ties. Whatever Luck Su was, he wasn't just the owner of a taxi dance hall.

He said loudly, in Shanghai street slang, "Who the fuck are you?"

"A man with a couple of questions," Wasey answered. His heart was hammering; he hadn't expected anything like this. Beside him Miss Tatlock seemed perfectly cool. One of the hoods started towards them but froze when Wasey took out the box Sing Sing had sold him and quickly opened it. "The first question is this," Wasey said into the tense silence. "I bought this gun from Sing Sing. Do you suppose it'll work?" It was a nice way of threatening them without pulling the gun.

Luck Su, a pockmarked cadaver of a man, was clearly the kind who'd consider it an affront to have a pistol pointed at him. He gave a brief nod and said, "He sells good stuff. Now who are you?"

"A man with a couple of questions."

"Who told you where to find me?"

"One of the girls."

The man's fingers pressed hard into his desk. "Which one?"

"Miss Lucky Star. She left last week."

The dance hall owner frowned, shot a glance at one of his bodyguards, who shrugged. Wasey had correctly guessed that, with sixty or seventy girls, they'd only know the names of the big earners.

"Bitch," Luck Su said. "What do you want?"

"Did you ever meet a guy named Faraday?"

"Maybe."

"Did you hear of his flowers?"

"I don't know. I'd have to think about it."

"I have fifty American dollars in the safe at my hotel," Wasey lied. "It's yours if you help me."

For the smallest part of a moment Wasey thought he saw temptation bite at the man, but then he went cold again.

"Can't help you."

"A hundred dollars."

"Still can't help you. Now would you mind getting the hell out of here?"

Wasey didn't wait to be asked twice; he guided Miss Tatlock outside, where she flared at him.

"What is the meaning of that gun?"

"Protection, Miss Tatlock."

"I'm dead against guns. Guns are evil things."

"I'm not crazy about them myself. I've never had one before and I'm not even sure I can use this one."

"Nevertheless, I strongly object to you carrying one."

"I'll tell you something, Miss Tatlock. If I hadn't been carrying one in there, those boys would have rumpled the lapels of both our jackets."

Through a defiant mouth Miss Tatlock said, "I'm not afraid of them."

"Well, I am. I'm five ten, one sixty, and no good at fisticuffs. I'm crazy to go along with you on this wild idea but, seeing as I am, I need a safeguard. I'm not about to get roughed up or have any more cute practical jokes played on me. So that's the price of admission, Miss Tatlock. If you want me along, the gun goes with me."

Faced with an ultimatum, Miss Tatlock tried to back down gracefully. "Do you promise to leave it in its box?"

"I'll have it gift-wrapped if you like. Just as long as I get to keep it handy."

6

They spent the rest of the afternoon in the Central Records room of the Honan Road police station, but ran into a blank wall there, too. Wasey had thought they might get a name or two from Faraday's file, but it took a sighing clerk over an hour to find it, and it turned out to be worthless.

"Look at this," Wasey said, disgusted. "Walter Faraday. No address, no description, no photograph, no prints. One arrest for public nuisance." He handed the sheet to Miss Tatlock, who couldn't read it anyway.

"Nothing about accomplices?"

"You don't need an accomplice to make a nuisance of yourself."

"I don't understand. He was a major criminal."

"That's only down there so the cops can say he had a record. He paid them off, Miss Tatlock. He had to have a file because the cops would've been embarrassed to admit they didn't have one on such a big-time crook. So they gave him one that means nothing."

"That's scandalous."

"That's China."

Wasey turned to the waiting clerk and spoke to him in dialect. "What's your name?"

"Ch'en She, sir."

"We're looking for something that belonged to this man, Ch'en She. If there are any other files you could check, anybody you could ask, I'd be happy to pay for your extra time."

It was a surprise for the clerk; nobody had even offered him squeeze before. That was always reserved for the uniformed police officers, and none of it found its way to the back rooms. He nervously adjusted the half glasses on his flat face, unsure of how to proceed but unwilling to let the offer go. "It might be possible," he said. He brushed a hand over his thin hair, a short, middle-aged man with a round little body.

It meant another long wait while the clerk hunted through another hopelessly inefficient filing system in a back office. It was getting dark outside when he returned and announced that he'd set up a meeting with someone who might be able to help them. He gave Wasey an address and told him to meet him there in an hour, and they killed the time by walking to the place. It was in a street that the guidebooks usually describe as "colorful," which in this case was a euphemism for a roaring, garishly lit alley full of knock-down-and-drag-out honky-tonk bars. Miss Tatlock had never seen so many so close together—there was nothing *but* bars, one after the other, lining the street in a double row. The buildings that housed them were all two stories high, all made of brick, and all had splashy signs coming right down to the sidewalk, flooding the jammed pavement with a Technicolor sea. The crowds that waded through it were brilliant cerise one moment, bright bottle green the next, blazing white the next, although they were pretty colorful in themselves.

Wasey hadn't got three feet into the maze of people before a woman, easily seven months pregnant, offered herself to him for the equivalent of ten cents American. She was brushed aside by a man wearing a dress and a satin jacket lined with goatskin, his mouth heavily rouged, who offered his attractions for half that sum.

Another man hailed him from the entrance to a passageway. "No waiting!" he cried. "Sir, no waiting over here."

Behind him Wasey glimpsed the service for which there was no holdup: a half-dressed woman was bent over, the plump cheeks of her naked bottom wiggling invitingly. Standing near her, barely able to function in the confines of the tiny lane, a Dutch sailor was taking advantage of the curbside service with another woman.

Walking on Miss Tatlock's left, Wasey had obstructed

her view of the alley, and she'd thought that somebody had been calling out for help.

"What was going on down there?" she asked, concerned.

"Just business as usual."

She insisted on knowing. "What was happening?"

"It was just a man enjoying a Shanghai knee trembler."

"What's that?"

"It's, er, the smart new cocktail everybody's drinking this year."

"Oh," said Miss Tatlock.

Wasey fought off a dozen other offers of various kinds and led Miss Tatlock through the mad throng, trying to identify the bar he was after, the Seven Seas. He found it halfway up the street, and arrived outside limping slightly after an overzealous prostitute had cried "Tonight!" in his face and grabbed at his crotch.

Ch'en She, the file clerk, was waiting there, extremely uneasy in the surroundings.

Instead of greeting him Wasey said, "What do they call this street again?"

"Rue Chu Pao San," the clerk replied. "It's known locally as Blood Alley."

"A reasonable assessment," Wasey said. He looked at the bar, which appeared to be identical with the rest. "Is he in here? The man we're supposed to see?"

The file clerk nodded. "I checked the records. This man has been arrested repeatedly but has never spent even a night in jail. He must be high in the underworld, and therefore might know something about this Faraday person."

"What does he do?"

"He is a caffeine dealer. He owns some tea-drying ovens in the Kinchow ghetto. According to his file, this is where he does his retail business."

"Let's go and meet him," Wasey said.

It was dark inside, almost as dark as the exterior was

bright. The brick floor was littered with matches and cigarette ends, there were tripod stools drawn up to low wooden tables, and a stand-up bar ran the length of one wall with a tarnished brass foot rail fronting it. The big mirror behind the bottles was cracked and pitted in several places, and large pieces of it sagged dangerously. A blade of the electric fan in the ceiling had been broken off, and somebody had stomped in the bulbous jukebox in the corner.

The customers looked to be a cross section of the mob outside on the street, although there were few Chinese present, and most of those seemed to be pimps either taking a breather or trying to drum up trade among sailors of several nations. Practically all of the sailors were drinking with one hand and playing Double Six with the other, and making loud, drunken remarks in a variety of languages.

Wasey checked to see Miss Tatlock's reaction, but she seemed as unaffected by the tough bar as she had been by the sinful street outside. The file clerk pushed at his half glasses, looked timidly around him. "A rough place, indeed."

His observation was borne out almost immediately when one of the sailors, a beefy type, jumped to his feet, upsetting a table and a dice board, and threw himself at an equally large opponent. At the same time the bartender snatched up a whistle and blew it long and hard.

"Stop it this instant!" Miss Tatlock cried to the two battling men. She spun round on Wasey. "Make them stop! They'll hurt each other."

"Hey, fellas," Wasey mumbled. 'Cut it out."

Ten seconds later, in answer to the bartender's signal, two black-clad thugs poured in through the door brandishing heavy wooden clubs. They poleaxed the two sailors—each with a single crunching blow—left them where they fell, went to the bar, swept up the money the barman slapped down, then ran out to sell their services somewhere else.

"Those awful brutes," Miss Tatlock said, and sped to

the two supine men to administer first aid.

The place went back to normal: games were resumed, glasses were picked up, and nobody took any notice of the Jesus lady and the two unconscious forms.

In a small, gulping voice Ch'en She, the file clerk, said, "I suggest we conclude our business and leave."

Wasey didn't argue. "Where's our man?" he asked, spotting him as he said it. It had to be him. Only a Chinese drug dealer would dress like that: he looked as if he might have stepped in for a cooling drink during the summer of 1910. He wore white shoes, a white shirt with a pale striped tie, white pants with a red cummerbund at the waist, a dark blue blazer, a straw skimmer on his head with a red hatband that matched his cummerbund, and he had hooked a light whangee cane to his arm. He'd even made an attempt at a handlebar mustache that curled thinly under his nose and faded out into waxed ends. He was definitely the most dapper Chinese Wasey had ever run into, the very model of the jaunty Edwardian.

When they went up to him, the man said, "How many?" and opened the Gladstone bag at his feet. Inside, wrapped in rice paper, were a dozen one-pound bricks of crystallized caffeine. The man's beautifully pressed clothes stank of chloroform, the chemical used to extract the drug from tea, and in spite of the Florida water he'd doused himself with, he still smelled like an operating room.

The file clerk explained that they weren't there to buy, telling him the reason why they'd come.

"So," Ch'en She concluded, "I naturally assumed that you, sir, might have known this man Faraday, and might know where certain items that once belonged to him could be found."

The caffeine dealer mulled it over, his eyes flicking between Wasey and the clerk. He said, "I take it that payment is to be expected for such information..."

"A substantial one," Wasey assured him.

"Well, then. Although I was not personally acquainted

with the gentleman in question, I have many associates who might have been." The dealer thought about it some more, then said, "Let me make a few phone calls. There is a man named Chunshou, who knows many people in Shanghai. If you, sir," he said to Wasey, "were to wait somewhere for thirty or forty minutes, perhaps I could persuade him to see you. Where are you staying?"

"The Penang Hotel."

"Too far," the dealer said. He considered it for a moment. "Have you dined yet?"

"No."

"Ah. Then I suggest the Hopei. It's nearby, the food is acceptable, and if you mention my name you will be well looked after. You could wait for Chunshou there."

"Fine," Wasey said. "We'll do that."

"I think it best," the dealer said, "if this gentleman remains with me. We have, er, business to discuss."

It was an obvious allusion to the divvying up of the reward, so Wasey left them to it. He got directions to the restaurant, then he and Miss Tatlock took their leave, pausing only to make way for a couple of red-turbaned Sikh policemen who arrived to pick up the two sailors.

Outside, Wasey said, "Don't hold your breath, but I think we might be getting somewhere. A guy's going to meet us in a restaurant."

"Who is he?"

"I don't know him, but the man who's sending him, who I just met, is a genuine, card-carrying member of the underworld. So it looks promising."

The news cheered Miss Tatlock immensely, and they arrived at the restaurant on fairly good terms.

It was a big open place with a floral-pattern tiled floor, dark bentwood chairs drawn up to stiff white tablecloths, a huge Welsh dresser at one end, and canvas-sheet fans on pulleys above the diners' heads. When the headwaiter showed them to a table and began to recite the menu, Wasey told him that he'd been sent by "the gentleman in white at the Seven Seas." Instantly they were moved to a larger table and fawned on. A waiter rushed in with chilled glasses of Shantung beer, and Miss Tatlock, instead of protesting vigorously, merely pushed hers towards Wasey, who mimed a heart attack. Then the food started to arrive, special dishes reserved for special guests: sweet fried noodles sprinkled with pepper oil and hot sauce, thin wheat cakes wrapped around poached eggs and spring onions, a dish of crunchy silver tree fungus in light syrup, duck buns, and baked carp in lamb broth.

They didn't say much while they were eating, they'd had a long day. But by the time they'd got to the dessert, which was Shanghai Dust—host chestnut puree laced with leatherflower honey—they were feeling a lot better and more relaxed.

Wasey said, "Thanks for letting me have the beer. Can I order a real drink now?"

Miss Tatlock opened her mouth on a word that had no chance of becoming a yes, so Wasey leaped to his own defense.

"Look, I could've ordered booze soup and I didn't."

Miss Tatlock still didn't approve but she was sporting about it. "Very well, if you must."

"Good girl." Wasey signaled a waiter and put an imaginary cup to his mouth. Then he watched Miss Tatlock, letting his eyes wander over her hair and craning his head to one side to peek at her bun.

"It's still there, Mr. Wasey."

"Just checking." There was a pause. "I used to date a girl whose mother wanted her to be a missionary, like you. But she wasn't that crazy about the idea and decided to be what she'd always wanted to be."

"I agree with being independent and making your own decisions. What did she want to be?"

"A waitress in a lumberjack camp."

Miss Tatlock looked at him.

Wasey said, "What made you decide to be a missionary

anyway? I think I know why you're not a waitress in a lumberjack camp."

Miss Tatlock didn't snap at him as she might have done the day before; she appeared to have come to terms with his flip manner and accept it as an unchangeable part of his makeup. "When I finished college I worked as a secretary for a firm that was rich and successful. They manufactured an expensive gadget designed to help the American housewife cook food faster so that she didn't have to rush home from the beauty parlor. It occurred to me one day that a lot of people in the world didn't have any food to cook faster. No food, no home, no prospects. All they had that they could count on was suffering. So I thought it might be a better idea if I stopped working for people who were very rich and started working for people who were very poor."

"But why a missionary in China? There are poor people in Providence."

"I checked the various societies. Most of them have strings attached. They'll help people but in turn they try to sway them towards religion. The Door of Hope is a Christian body but it exists solely to help people, and expects nothing in return."

Wasey tapped the table lightly. "I like that. Pure giving. The other way it's more like a swap."

"That's exactly what it is, Mr. Wasey. That's very well put."

"So how did you end up here?"

"I went where the Society sent me. With a barbarous war raging in China, the need was most urgent here."

"So we both ended up in Shanghai unexpectedly," Wasey said. He reached for the cup of pomegranate brandy that a waiter delivered. *"Kan-pei."*

Watching him drink, Miss Tatlock said, "What will you do after Los Angeles?"

"Assuming I ever get there, I'll flog the ties and look for another deal someplace else."

"Is that how it works, import-export?"

"Yep. After I sell the ties I check with my contacts in L.A. They tell me that a couple of tons of, let's say roofing nails, could make money for anybody who can get them to Java maybe. So I hear of a guy in Burma, or wherever, who has roofing nails he wants to sell. I hop a freighter to Burma, buy the nails, sail 'em to Java, and unload them at a profit. Then I take the money I made on that deal, ask around again, and hear that Singapore is desperately short of canned asparagus. So I make inquiries and come up with a guy in Brisbane who's sitting on a load of canned asparagus. I hop down there, buy the asparagus, sail it to Singapore, and sell it. And so on."

"And can you always count on a profit?"

"No, ma'am. Somebody may have heard the same thing and beaten you to Singapore."

"What do you do then?"

"You get tired of eating asparagus."

"It sounds like you spend an awful lot of time away from home."

"All of it. I don't have a home."

"Just freighter cabins and hotel rooms?"

"That's right. The decor's not much and it can get a little cramped, but there's no mortgage, no crabgrass, and you never get a bill from the phone company." Wasey glanced at a clock on the wall. "I don't know what's happened to our rendezvous. He should've been here by now."

Miss Tatlock's face fell. "You didn't tell me that. How late is he?"

"He's certainly overdue. Let's give him another half hour."

They gave him three more half hours, then they left.

They returned to the Seven Seas, but there was no sign of the dealer or Ch'en She.

"I told him where I was staying," Wasey said. "Maybe there's a message for me back at the hotel."

They walked a few blocks looking for a cab, Miss Tatlock's disappointment showing in her silence. Wasey asked her where she lived. "Not far from you." Her voice was leaden.

"Which hotel?"

"It's not a hotel. I board with two other missionaries."

Earlier in the evening Wasey would have got off a comment on that but he said nothing now; she was really down.

They got a cab and Wasey dropped her off at her address, telling her they'd meet in the morning, then continued on to his hotel.

He was right about a message being left for him; the desk man handed it over. It said, "Ch'en She is waiting for you upstairs."

Wasey rode up in the elevator glad he'd have something to tell Miss Tatlock.

He heard the sound the moment he let himself into his room. It was a soft dripping that he assumed was a bathroom tap, but he was wrong about that, as he saw when he switched on the light.

There was something in his bed, covered by the spread. And the dripping noise was being made by the blood that was leaking from it.

With sharp slivers of ice darting through him, Wasey spent a long time staring at the bed. Then he inched towards it, took a breath, and pulled back the spread.

He should have vomited, should have thrown up the meal he'd just eaten, but the horrific sight paralyzed his physical reflexes.

A single word shot into his brain: *nahkuning*, the word that he'd told Miss Tatlock was Shanghai slang for "foreigner." Bones on the outside, it meant, and that was exactly what was lying in Wasey's bed.

Ch'en She, the half glasses still on his face, had been neatly and expertly boned, and his skeleton had been taped to the outside of his plump shapeless body.

7

"It's open," Wasey called at the door of his new room at nine the next morning.

Miss Tatlock, coming in, stopped when she saw Wasey lying bare-chested in bed. "Excuse me. I'll wait for you outside."

"I won't be going outside."

"What do you mean?" She saw something dark in Wasey's face. "What happened last night? Why have you changed rooms?"

"Because they're still scrubbing down my old one." He told her what he'd found in his bed when he'd got back.

Miss Tatlock went white. "Good Lord! How ghastly!" She turned her head away and shuddered. "That poor man. What kind of person could do such a monstrous thing?"

"A butcher. A real one. The gangs hire them. The cops came last night after the hotel called them. They took one look at what was left of Ch'en She and snapped their notebooks shut. They recognized a gang killing and they don't interfere with respectable people like that."

"They were certain it was the work of a gang?"

"They even knew which one. The Green Society. Apparently boning people is a habit of theirs."

"That poor man must have known something. Or found out something."

"I don't think so. They just used him as a messenger boy. And the message is: 'Don't let this happen to you.'"

"It may be out of place to say so, Mr. Wasey, but it does prove we're making progress. We must be getting close or they wouldn't have done such a barbaric thing."

Wasey shifted in his bed, put his hands behind his head. "Close or far away, it no longer concerns me. I'm out of it."

"But you can't quit now. Not when we're getting some-where."

With weary patience, Wasey said, "My dear Miss Tat-lock. I have already got as far as I'm getting. I've upset the Red Society, and now I've upset the Green Society. If I keep on I'm only going to upset a society of another color. Not to mention the original two societies, who will no doubt be affronted by my rudeness in ignoring them and will send round men in aprons."

"But you're only guessing that might happen. You're thinking the worst. Nobody's contacted you. Nobody's actually threatened your life. Maybe they were just trying to scare you off."

"Well, if they were, it worked."

"Mr. Wasey," Miss Tatlock said. "I really feel confident about this. I really feel we're making headway. But if you quit now Mr. Burns and I will be back where we started. We'll have lost all our momentum."

"If I stay with you I may lose a lot more than my momentum."

Miss Tatlock spoke right on top of him. "You're doing such a good job, I've already told you that. And it's be-ginning to show results. What happened to that man was hideous but it proves we're getting closer to the opium and that's the important thing. I'm convinced that if you give it one more try we'll get a real lead and you can book your ticket for Los Angeles."

"No, thanks. I'm out."

"Don't you want to get to Los Angeles?"

"Sure. But I don't want to float there in a canvas sack."

Miss Tatlock, desperately casting around, suddenly re-membered something: "Tuttle. The man at the Shanghai *Post*. He's back in town today, and Mr. Burns is positive he'll be able to help us."

"I'm out of it. *Finito*. The end."

"Two more days. Fifty dollars on top of your fare if you'll just give it two more days."

Wasey crossed his arms, shook his head. "Not interested."

"A hundred dollars, then. You tell me. What do you want?"

"Death from natural causes. I have a sister and three nieces, Miss Tatlock, and I do not want a coroner sending them a certificate that says 'manner of death: filleted.'"

She argued with him for another five minutes, promising, cajoling, flattering, but Wasey stubbornly kept his arms folded and his head shaking a negative. Finally Miss Tatlock seemed to run out of ammunition and became very quiet. A curious look appeared on her face, a kind of reluctant resolve, and she watched Wasey for a few moments before speaking again.

"Very well. Then there is only one thing left for me to do."

"What's that?" Wasey asked, not terribly interested.

Miss Tatlock walked to the door and slowly closed it. "Put you under an obligation."

"I already told you. I don't want your money. I'll raise the price of a ticket some other way. Something nice and safe."

Miss Tatlock wasn't listening. She went over to a small chest of drawers, put down her handbag, reached up, and began to pull a long hairpin from the bun behind her head.

"If you try to stick me with that I'll—" Wasey broke off. Miss Tatlock had put the hairpin down and was taking out some small bobby pins. A possible explanation suggested itself but Wasey rejected it as absurd. "Hey, Miss Tatlock." His voice sounded funny. "What kind of an obligation are you talking about?"

Miss Tatlock's hair tumbled down like a silky brown waterfall.

Wasey knew he had to be wrong; it couldn't be *that*. "Hey, er, you're not thinking . . . that is, you're not, er . . ."

With her back to him Miss Tatlock began to unbutton her uniform jacket.

Wasey sat up, then flopped back against his pillow. "Oh my God!" he said. "Miss Tatlock, is it really you over there?"

Miss Tatlock took off her jacket and folded it carefully. She spoke to the wall. "Finding that opium, Mr. Wasey, may well be the most important thing I'll ever do. And I can't find it without your help."

She reached for the badge that closed her blouse at the neck. Wasey was flabbergasted. And a little outraged. "But that's blackmail. You can't do that."

Miss Tatlock took off her blouse and revealed a plain white bra that stretched across the creamy skin of her back. "I don't regard it as blackmail. I'm merely putting you under an obligation so you'll have to help me."

"Well, that's blackmail. And I strongly . . . object."

Miss Tatlock climbed out of her long black skirt. As she bent forward the line of her bottom pressed against her cotton slip.

Wasey swallowed. "Cut it out, Miss Tatlock, you're going too far."

Miss Tatlock wriggled out of her slip, which did wonderful things for the briefs she wore.

"You don't fool me, Miss Tatlock. You're bluffing. You're not going to take off anything else."

She reached behind her and undid her bra.

"Okay, keep going. Go all the way. It won't do you an ounce of good."

Miss Tatlock put two fingers inside the elastic of her pants, slid them down, and stepped out of them. She tossed them on top of the rest of her clothes, and turned round.

Wasey stared, then blinked rapidly; he couldn't get over the sight. "Miss Tat-lock," he breathed. "You have a major body."

She walked briskly to the bed, threw back the sheet, got in next to him, and fixed her eyes on the ceiling.

Wasey was still ogling her figure. "Wow-wee!"

"Mr. Wasey, we have a long day ahead of us. Would you please get on with it."

"Keep talking like that and you'll enflame me."

"I'm waiting, Mr. Wasey."

"You can go ahead and wait. I don't mind enjoying the view but I refuse to do anything that'll put me under obligation."

With an action that a postal clerk might have used to stamp a letter, Miss Tatlock took his hand and placed it on her left breast.

"That doesn't obligate me one tiny bit," Wasey said.

Miss Tatlock breathed in deeply and her breast stirred under his palm.

"You're a very firm girl. Soft, too," Wasey said, shaping an outline. An erect nipple rose beneath his fingers and he bent his head and tongued it. "Nice," said Wasey, "but still not obligated."

Miss Tatlock took his hand and dumped it down on her hip. Wasey sucked in his breath. "Mmmm, I love jutting hips." He slid his hand around its curve, over the soft swell of her tummy, and down over her legs. "Oh, yes," Wasey murmured. He dropped his face into the crook of her neck, smelled her freshly washed hair, moved his hand over thighs that were slowly opening, touched the tips of his fingers against a warm moistness. "Gorgeous," he said. "Beautiful. But it doesn't obligate me."

Miss Tatlock reached down, brushing her hand against his pajama bottoms and one or two other things.

Wasey groaned.

She eased the pajama pants undone.

"Go ahead," Wasey said. There was very little left of his voice. "You're doing it, so it doesn't count."

She turned slightly towards him, raised her inside knee, and Wasey entered her before he knew what had happened. Not by much, but a definite joining. He froze. "Okay. But I'm not moving."

"Excuse me," Miss Tatlock said crisply, "I'm falling off the bed." She moved to correct the situation, shifting the top of her body, then the lower half, thrusting up with her hips and absorbing Wasey in the process.

With a short cry Wasey wrapped his arms around her and pumped away in an ecstasy of delight.

"Miss Tatlock," he moaned. "I've got . . . oooh . . . I've got something . . . ahhhh . . . to say to you."

"What?"

"I'M COMING!"

He spent himself in a shuddering paroxysm, lay atop her for a moment, then rolled off exhausted. He slowly got his breath back, then said, "That was fantastic. You were marvelous. Shit, I'm obligated."

Wasey called Tuttle, the man Burns and Miss Tatlock had told him about, at his newspaper, the Shanghai *Post*. Tuttle said he'd be happy to see him but wouldn't be free till much later in the day. Miss Tatlock, having no fear that Wasey wouldn't keep the appointment, being under obligation as he was, let him go by himself, as she had a mountain of paperwork to catch up on for the Door of Hope. So Wasey arrived alone at a teahouse around seven that evening.

He spotted Tuttle right away. He looked like a journalist, like a man with a deadline to meet and no time to get a haircut or get his suit pressed. He was fortyish, slightly stooped, and looked as though he could have used some sunshine and some good home cooking.

Wasey thought him a curious mixture: his clothes said "I don't care," yet his eyes were bright and intelligent, and he enunciated his words with careful consideration.

"John Tuttle, Mr. Wasey. Welcome to Shanghai."

Wasey shook his hand. "Thanks, but it's hardly my first trip."

He sat down at the man's table. The teahouse was several cuts above the last one he'd been in, the clientele mainly Chinese but with a sprinkling of Westerners.

Tuttle pushed a cup towards him and poured from a pot. "Have you tried *siu hing?* It looks like tea but thank God it doesn't taste like it."

Wasey reached for the rice wine. "We're old friends."

"So," Tuttle said. "You picked a fine time to visit Shanghai, Mr. Wasey."

"Glen. My name is Glen."

"You picked a fine time, Glen. Put one foot outside the Settlement or the Concession and there's a Jap soldier wanting to know where you're going. Have you seen the cruiser parked in front of the customs house? Its guns are pointing this way. It's not polite."

"I agree. However, it's not the Japanese who've been giving me trouble. It's the Chinese. It appears that I've annoyed a couple of the local secret societies."

"Which ones?"

"The Red and the Green."

"The Red *and* the Green? That's pretty good going. Did they threaten you?"

When he told Tuttle what had happened the journalist winced. "Gawd!"

"That's why I'm carrying this." Wasey patted the box that was peeking out of his jacket pocket.

Tuttle looked puzzled. "What is it, chocolates?"

"It's a gun."

"What's it doing in a box?"

"Guns make me nervous," Wasey said. It was true; before leaving the hotel he'd taken the Baby Nambu out of the box and stuck it into his belt, but he'd hated the feel of it, so he'd put it back in the box and put the whole thing back into his pocket.

Tuttle said, "Well, I just hope you don't have to use it in a hurry."

"Me, too. I wouldn't exactly be as fast as Buck Jones."

"At the risk of being impertinent," Tuttle said, "what have the gangs got against you?"

"I assume you've heard of a guy named Faraday?"

"The great Walter Faraday. Oh, yes. He was something of a legend around this town."

"A crook of the first water, so I've been told."

"True," Tuttle answered. "But he wasn't just a thug with a gun in his hand. He had class, our Mr. Faraday. He was a top drug dealer, a master thief, and a pretty good con man, too. He was a hell of an actor. He disguised himself once, makeup and the whole works. Posed as a bank examiner and walked out the back door with a couple of teller's trays full of money."

Wasey inhaled the wine in his cup, then drank it down. "I'm looking for something that belonged to him."

Tuttle smiled. "Poppies?"

"You know about them, huh?"

"Oh, sure. Everybody knows about Faraday's flowers. The Lost Dutchman gold mine of Shanghai. They're supposed to be there, they more than likely are, but nobody seems to know where."

"So I've found. I promised some people I'd check into it. I believe you know Mr. Burns."

"I've met him, yes."

"Have you met his offsider, Miss Tatlock?"

Tuttle said no.

"You should." Wasey wagged his head. "She's full of surprises, that one. Anyway, do you know anybody who could maybe give me a lead?"

Tuttle frowned over the edge of his cup. "Not offhand, but I should be able to dig up somebody." He drank and said, "I don't know about you, but I'm starving. Do you like crab?"

They left the teahouse and walked through an inner part of the city that was solid with people. The area had been swelled three years previously when the Japanese had driven thousands of people from the Hongkew district into the International Settlement, and bodies thronged through the streets, packed in like a crowd at a carnival.

Few of them were going anywhere, most were just walking around waiting for the sidewalks and the doorways and the apartment halls to clear so they could find a place to lie down. Voices called, arguments started, raucous laughter and shrill obscenities shared equal time. Running children bumped against the crush, one little boy succeeding somehow in towing behind him a lantern on wheels, a paper rabbit with a lighted candle in its tummy miraculously unscorched and untrammeled. Two young girls, fresh flowers in their hair, danced in perfect harmony, beating long bamboo jingle sticks against their bodies in time to the song they sang. But the precious few coins they were receiving dried up immediately when their thunder was stolen by a black bear wearing a long yellow dress and carrying an oiled-paper umbrella opened over its shoulder. The people howled and congratulated its trainer, and those who could spared a coin.

"The bear's supposed to be a satire of somebody," Tuttle said. "But just who, I've never found out."

"A Yangchow *ma-tzu*, a maidservant," Wasey told him. "For some reason they all have large feet and they waddle when they walk, just like that bear."

Tuttle laughed. "I'd better let you be the guide."

The parade continued, a lot of peddlers now with their wares strung across their shoulders on bamboo canes: a man selling firewood chopped into brick-size blocks; another selling fat yellow *tung-kua* melons; an old woman with a basket full of *chun-ya,* preserved leaves to flavor tea; a man bowed down by the weight of two casks of mountain water fresh from an icy stream. And there was one peddler whom Wasey wanted to stop—he carried an entire restaurant on his back: two tall bamboo stands containing everything he needed, a metal pan and a ladle hooked to the side of a glowing clay stove with bowls warming in racks underneath and, in the other stand, red bean sauce, soy oil, scallions, and mounds of fresh noodles.

83

"You want noodles, we'll have noodles," Tuttle promised. "But not here."

He led Wasey through the crowds to an area where they thinned a bit, and the air was pungent with the smell of woodsmoke and cooking charcoal. Tuttle stopped in front of a wineshop, and not, as Wasey supposed, just to get a drink. He pointed to the sign painted in white paste on the window, and Wasey read it out. "'Drunk by moonlight, with goblets flying.' Pretty, but what does it mean?"

Tuttle propelled him into the shop. "It means at least you've come to Shanghai at a good time to eat."

They had to stoop to pass under bottles in bright paper wrappers, hundreds of them, dangling on colored cords from the roof beams. They edged their way around huge bamboo-covered wine crocks and out into a roofless courtyard where space had been cleared for chairs and wooden benches.

"In the spring the wineshops are the best places to eat in the city," Tuttle said, taking a seat. "Maybe the entire country."

A woman slapped bowls down onto their table, dished something out, and flew away.

"Sea blubber, slivered turnips, and peanuts," Tuttle announced. "Eat up. It's terrific."

Wasey dipped chopsticks into the sweet-salty jellyfish and cleared his bowl. The woman was back, as he finished, with more dishes: grilled perch with crab roe and noodles, ducks' tongues, cold smoked chicken.

"Leave room for the main course," Tuttle said as a small boy trotted in out of breath from his run from a nearby shop. He wore thick cloth covers on his hands to protect them from the red-hot handles of the covered pan he carried. He dropped it with a thud onto the table and whipped off the lid, releasing a fragrant cloud of steam that rose from a tumbled heap of red-peppered crabs. The woman arrived with vinegar, chopped ginger, and soy sauce, then hurried unbidden to a large beehive copper kettle where wine bottles warmed over hot water. She selected one, opened it, plonked it on the table, and left the two foreigners tearing off shells, sucking at crab claws, and dousing the fiery taste with cup after cup of hot kaoliang wine.

"Now do you understand that sign?" Tuttle asked. He pointed above him at the night sky and picked up the bottle. "Drunk by moonlight, with goblets flying." He poured from the bottle and they both picked up cups. *"Kan-pei,"* they said.

They ate in silence for a while, then slowed down and just sat sipping the wine.

"This thing with the poppies," Tuttle said. "That's why the gangs are mad at you, I take it."

"I sure can't think of anything else."

"Well, you're encroaching on their territory and they wouldn't like that. Still, I think you'll be okay. They may slap your wrist but I'd doubt they'd do anything more."

"That's comforting, but what makes you think so?"

"Because you're a foreigner," Tuttle said. "And whenever a foreigner's killed in the Settlement or the Concession, the Council complains to the bankers and threatens to withdraw the city's money."

Wasey didn't get it. "The bankers? How does that affect the gangs?"

"They run the gangs," Tuttle said blandly. "Most of the big ones, anyway."

"I didn't know that. My God, what a town."

"The Athens of the East, they call it."

Wasey said, "I assume that if it's a Chinese that's killed nobody complains."

"Of course not. There's a sign that pretty well sums it up in the Koukaza, the French Park. It says 'No dogs or Chinese allowed.'"

"Yeah, I've seen it."

Tuttle thought some more. "Another thing in your favor is that Chiang Kai-shek has put the word out to take it easy on Americans. He's counting on us for help against the Japanese one of these days."

"Will the gangs listen to him?"

"Sure. He's an old and valued customer. A dozen years back they lent him fifteen million bucks for smashing the Commie pickets. Somehow the loan was never repaid."

"Must've slipped his mind," Wasey said. "Christ, is there anyone who's not on the take in this country?"

"Not that I know of," Tuttle answered. "There's an entire war raging, right? But there's still trade going on between Chungking and the Japs here in Shanghai. Chungking sends them tungsten and foodstuffs—war materials, for heaven's sake—and the Japs send back, you won't believe this, silk stockings and fountain pens. Somebody broke the story in the States, and do you know how Chiang explained it? He said it was all part of his plan to undermine the Japanese economy." The journalist took a long swallow from his cup and dabbed at his mouth with a knuckle. "Okay, that's enough politics for one night." He pushed his chair back. "Let's go. I've got an idea."

Tuttle paid for the meal, led Wasey out into the street, through some alleys, and into one of the big boulevards, where they found a cab in reasonable condition.

Wasey asked where they were going.

"You ever heard of Beulah's?"

"Sure. But I never got around to visiting."

"Some people say it's the best house in the country, some say it's the worst. But Beulah's been in business for years and knows half of Shanghai. She might be able to help you."

Tuttle stopped talking then and settled back in the seat and closed his eyes, apparently beginning to feel the effects of the wine he'd drunk. Wasey watched the traffic thinning out ahead, the driver no longer sounding the horn at every corner. The crowded rush of the downtown section had given way to sidewalks and small residences, and the further west they drove, the larger the houses became.

Finally, when they turned into Bubbling Well Road, the

houses disappeared and only long high brick walls showed, the street well lit and swept clean, no rickshaws, no coolies, no sign of people at all except for late-model cars parked here and there.

A minute later the taxi slowed, passed through high iron gates, and scrunched the gravel of a long curving drive. The house it stopped in front of was enormous: a white monstrosity with a portico supported by Corinthian pillars, and a double set of steps looping up to the front door.

"Who lives here?" Wasey asked. "Margaret Mitchell?"

Tuttle paid the cabdriver. "Early Chinese Antebellum they call it. Very popular in the Settlement. In the Concession they go in more for small French châteaus."

They started up the steps, which were lit by the flames of burning pitch staves stuck into wrought-iron brackets.

"Beulah used to have about fifty of these on each side of the drive," Tuttle told Wasey. "She had fifty Chinese footmen all dressed like Monsieur Beaucaire holding the things until a drunken chauffeur drove too close one night and burnt up the top of his boss's Duesenberg."

"Sounds like a colorful lady. Is she French?"

"Russian. Her real name's Natasha Kurznetsov. She came here in 1917 with all the other White Russians and made her money peddling her hips on Soochow Street. Then a textile magnate bankrolled her and she bought this spread."

When Tuttle rang the bell the door was opened instantly by a short slight man looking ridiculous in tails. Tuttle said, in Chinese, "How are you, Yeng?"

The other man bowed. "You are fatter, sir," he said, which, in China, was a compliment between two men.

As they went by him Tuttle murmured to Wasey, "Yeng's the bouncer. A Tai Chi master. All he has to do is put one finger on you and it's all over."

They moved into a classic foyer: black and white marble floor, ornate pilasters rising to a molded ceiling, wall niches, and a great staircase that swept up to a second-floor landing.

"We wait here for Beulah's entrance," Tuttle whispered. "And here she comes."

A woman came down the staircase rounding its perfect curve, one hand smoothing the polished banister, the other fluttering a silk fan. She wore a full-length, off-the-shoulder gown of pink and white chiffon, and she came floating down to them like a Southern beauty descending to flirt with a group of dashing admirers.

"Johnny," she cooed—she pronounced it "Shonney"—"such a long time. Where have you been, you naughty boy?" Her accent was as thick as her makeup, which was caked over the wrinkles under her jaw, a two-hour-old mask on a fifty-five-year-old face. Her wig was a miracle of curls and tresses, straw yellow and shiny bright, and the dress would have been perfect had it not had to stretch over a huge bosom and battleship hips.

"Miss Beulah," Tuttle said, taking her bejeweled hand and leaning over it. "It's been too long." He turned to his right. "May I present Mr. Wasey. Beulah Belle Lovelace."

The woman simpered. "But how handsome. The girls will be delighted."

A servant appeared and had a word in her ear, and the madam excused herself. "You know where the bar is, Johnny. Get Mr. Wasey a drink and bring him back for the show. It's just about to start."

She moved away in a billowing waddle and Tuttle led his guest further into the house to a large room where tasseled lanterns gave a sheen to blue rugs and rosewood furniture and high floor vases. There was a bar in a corner; Tuttle ordered a tumbler of vodka for each of them.

Wasey said, "What kind of a show is it? As if I didn't know."

"Better than most. It stars Lothar and Sheena."

"Who's Lothar and Sheena?"

"Don't you read the funnies? Lothar is Mandrake the Magician's giant Nubian slave. And Sheena's queen of the jungle. Beulah chose the names, not me."

Wasey followed Tuttle down a tapestry-hung corridor to a room that had been converted into a small theater. About a dozen men sat on folding chairs, some with drinks in their hands, some chatting, some just waiting for the red velvet curtains to open on the little raised stage up front. The men were of various ages and nationalities; Wasey heard English, French, Italian, as well as Japanese, this last spoken by two intense-looking Orientals who were sitting in the first row. The only words he caught sounded like "Lowtarr chi Sheenarr," which led him to believe they'd been to Beulah's before.

A murmur went up as a man entered the room and made his way to the front of the stage, where he sat down behind a conga drum. The drum almost hid him; he couldn't have been more than five feet and was thin as a rail. He had a dark Latin face and a hairline mustache, and wore white pants, rope-soled deck shoes, and a Hawaiian shirt that swamped his narrow frame.

"That's José," Tuttle told Wasey. "During the day he's a cook at the Cuban Embassy."

José began to beat the drum softly at a mid tempo with the accent on the first beat—*one*-two-three-four, *one*-two-three-four—then the curtains jerked apart in three separate movements. A jungle scene was revealed: in the foreground, layers of lumpy green cotton fabric signifying grass, and in the background stylized trees fabricated from bamboo and crepe paper. The backdrop had received the most attention: elephants, lions, and tigers had been painted on it—by a Chinese artist, from the look of the tigers, which had scales, two rows of sharp teeth, and long red tongues. From backstage came the amplified scratch of a record player followed by the sounds of lions roaring, elephants trumpeting, monkeys chattering, and a kookaburra, transplanted somehow to the wrong continent, pealing with laughter. The stage remained empty for a few moments, then a blond young woman stepped out from behind the curtains.

The group of men buzzed at her appearance, and Wasey distinctly heard a voice say, "Sheenarr."

The woman was wearing a short leather skirt and a halter top, a costume that her chorus-girl figure swelled to exciting dimensions. She carried a market basket and seemed to be pantomiming picking fruit from the crepe-paper trees, a simple maid in a sylvan setting. It was a radical departure from the Sheena that Wasey knew, who, if he remembered correctly, was usually depicted swinging through the trees with a knife between her teeth.

"Her name's Ingrid," Tuttle confided. "She's an exchange student from Stockholm."

The girl went on with her gathering for a moment or two, then the drumbeats began to increase in intensity, a worried, urgent sound that threw a shadow over the idyllic setting. Then the audience sucked in their breath as, from stage left, a huge black man appeared, his mouth hanging open and his eyes dancing with lust. He wore, in close approximation of Mandrake's assistant, a one-shouldered leopard-skin loincloth and a fez perched on his shaved head.

"Lowtarr," a voice down front said.

Again Tuttle kept Wasey abreast of the players. "Moses Jones. Used to play right tackle for the Chicago Bears."

There was only one person in the entire room who hadn't noticed the intruder, and that was the Swedish exchange student, who went on smiling at the crepe trees and filling her basket with handfuls of air. But the situation changed drastically when Lothar, advancing stealthily across the cotton grass, trod on a painted cardboard twig. Five seconds later somebody broke a stick offstage, and the girl spun round with time only for a short high scream before the big man was upon her.

The drumming increased to a furious tempo, underscoring the struggle, as Sheena, fighting desperately for her virtue, bit, kicked, and struck at the giant while the audience kidded themselves that they were on her side and muttered soft encouragements. But the giant just laughed, reached out a huge hand, and, as the audience gasped, ripped away the jungle queen's halter, releasing two of the whitest, plumpest breasts anyone had ever seen. Lothar groped at them greedily, too preoccupied with their pneumatic fullness to notice the rubber knife Sheena had succeeded in freeing from her skirt. She slashed at his heart, but the giant jumped aside and the knife traveled harmlessly down his side, harmlessly except for the fact that it ripped his leopard skin from top to bottom, the girl having made sure that the knife caught the big ring of the costume's zipper.

She gasped when she saw the size of her destiny, and there were a few gasps from the audience, too. The knife dropped from her nerveless hand, and it was a simple matter for Lothar to rip away the jungle queen's skirt, which brought forth further gasps. Sheena's bottom, satin smooth and perfectly unblemished, looked as if it had never done a hard day's work in its life, and it dimpled like angel food cake as Lothar's thick fingers dug into it, pulling her to him.

He brought the swooning girl down onto the cotton grass, and entered her with a single triumphant shove, her pose the traditional one of bewildered submission: head turned, one arm flung across her face, spread legs like dead things. The conga drum changed its beat, subsiding to a monotonous throb as Lothar moved on the girl in time with its rhythm. The drummer gradually increased the tempo and, like a racing crew responding to the coxswain, Lothar picked up the stroke.

A few moments later the audience started to buzz. Something was happening to Sheena . . . low moans were coming from her mouth, and she began to writhe slowly, hands clutching at the green cotton grass.

The drummer's fingers moved faster—Lothar's backside moved faster—as Sheena, with a shrill cry, her inner passions tapped, locked her arms and legs around her jungle lover. Together they hammered into each other, their explosive energy raising a small cloud of dust from the African veldt. The drumming rose to an insane frenzy and, as the pair onstage reached a yelping climax, sustained its thunder for several long, pulse-pounding moments, then, with perfect timing, stopped instantly as Lothar and Sheena collapsed in an exhausted heap.

The curtains jerked closed, and the dry-throated audience applauded till the curtains opened again, revealing Lothar and Sheena upright now and holding hands, breathing deeply. Lothar grinned and bowed, and Sheena dropped a shaky-kneed curtsy, then both pointed to the drummer. The Cuban cook generously directed the applause back to the two thespians.

"Author! Author!" Wasey called.

The curtains jerked closed and the zoo noises shrieked into silence as someone scratched the record taking it off.

The group of men had risen from their seats and were circulating now, and one of the Japanese came up to Wasey and began speaking to him in English.

"Ah, velly good fucking, eh?"

"Mighty velly good," Wasey answered.

"Ah, would like to be fucking Sheenarr."

"But what about Lothar?"

"Not possible. Have already inquired."

A servant arrived with the news that Beulah was ready for them, so Tuttle and Wasey excused themselves and followed the servant out of the room.

"What did you think of the show?" Tuttle asked, walking down the hall.

"I think it could use an out-of-town tryout," Wasey told him.

Tuttle said, "It got a new wrinkle a few weeks back. Moses ran into a couple of football fans and didn't turn up, so José had to go on in his place. He wore the leopard skin, which must have looked like a dressing gown on him. Anyway, when it came time for him to lose it Ingrid

92

played it straight, looked down, and fainted at the sight of a dick the size of a cigarette."

The servant took them to a room where they found the formidable figure of Miss Beulah waiting for them. The room was unfurnished save for carpets on the floor and a few chairs placed in front of a wooden runway that curved from one door to another. In a corner three Filipinos in white tuxedos were holding instruments: a violin, a piano accordion, and a bass. Beulah greeted them, and Wasey complimented her on the show they'd just seen.

"Thank you, dear boy, I have always adored the theater. But now it is time to choose your companion for tonight. Sit down, please."

She moved away to have a word with the musicians, which gave Wasey a chance to whisper to Tuttle, "Listen, I don't have any money. And I'm already into you for dinner and drinks."

"You'll get back at me," Tuttle said. "And Beulah will give you credit. If you expect her to help you, you'll have to be a customer."

"That's fine with me," Wasey replied, although he didn't think Miss Tatlock would approve.

Beulah took up a position at the side of the runway and nodded to the musicians, who began to play a fair rendition of "A Pretty Girl Is Like a Melody."

Wasey guessed what was coming, and later found out why it was coming: Tuttle told him that the Wing On department store had once held an American Week complete with an MC'd fashion show. Entranced by it, Beulah had incorporated the idea into her own presentation, so that now choosing a girl at her house was like being able to buy the models at Lord and Taylor's.

"The lovely Autumn Moon," Beulah intoned in her throaty Russian accent. And down the runway, moving to the rhythm of the music, came a pretty Chinese girl in silk pants and long jacket. She did a graceful pirouette as her mistress said, "Notice the beautiful curve of the hips, and the softness of the features. Truly a beauty. Autumn Moon."

"She's terrific," Wasey said. "I'll take her."

Tuttle nudged him. "You're not supposed to choose the first one."

"I always do," Wasey said.

As the girl exited up the runway another appeared at the other side. "And this little number," Beulah said, "is Shining Beetle." The girl was a carbon copy of the previous one and moved with the same liquid grace in time to the music of the trio. "Shining Beetle comes to us from Kansu. Notice the fine line of the bust. Thank you, Shining Beetle."

"What a honey! That's it right there."

"Don't be so hasty," Tuttle said. "It's rude."

The musicians played the girl off and greeted the next arrival, as did Beulah. "And from Hong Kong, fresh from a starring role in the cinema, comes lovely October Flower." The trio switched to "You Ought to Be in Pictures."

"Will you look at that! Okay, sold!"

But Beulah, proud of her girls and her presentation, was intent on showing her wares and ignored Wasey's impetuousness.

A dozen more girls came down the runway. They could be hired simultaneously and had names like the Two Springtimes, the Three Qualities, and the Four Seasons. For these the trio played "Tea for Two," "Three Little Words," whatever was numerically appropriate. The show culminated with the promise of a fabulous orgy, for which group the band swung into a peppy rendition of "Six Lessons from Madam Lazonga."

"So, Mr. Wasey," Beulah asked as the last of the girls made her exit. "Which do you choose?"

"The Six Virtues."

Miss Beulah eyed his five-ten, one-sixty frame. She was basically a motherly type and she sometimes had to stop some of her clients from having too much of a helping.

"I'm not sure you'd be happy."

"The Five Planets, then. I'll take the Five Planets."

Miss Beulah went on critically assessing him.

"The Four Seasons?" Wasey asked hopefully.

Tuttle snapped his fingers "Hold it!" He grinned at the madam. "One guess who I'm thinking of..."

Beulah looked at Wasey, reappraising him. "Possibly," she said.

"Is she free at the moment?" Tuttle asked.

"As a matter of fact, yes."

Wasey didn't like the private conversation. "Is who free?"

"Your concubine," Tuttle replied, and he and Beulah laughed.

There was a little more discussion, but the upshot of it was that ten minutes later Wasey and Tuttle were in a cab heading back the way they'd come.

"You had to choose somebody," Tuttle said. "So you may as well choose the best."

"Where are we going? Doesn't this girl work for Beulah?"

"Sure she does. But she's special. She works off the premises. She prefers to work at home, so to speak."

"Where's home?"

"The Great World Amusement Park."

"The *where?*"

"Glen, there's something you ought to know about this woman. She's different. She doesn't think of herself as a whore. She thinks of herself as a concubine. I know I was chortling about it back there with Beulah, but that was just for show. Beulah laughs at her, but I don't, and you shouldn't either."

"I don't get it. What do you mean, a concubine?"

"This girl sees herself as an imperial consort, and the man she looks after is her emperor."

"She sounds like a nut."

"She's not a nut. She was born a hundred years too late, that's all. She won't go with anyone she doesn't like, and never for just one night. If you want her, you have to make a commitment for several days."

"That's crazy. I'll be on my way to L.A. in several days."

"Better not tell Beulah that," Tuttle advised him.

The area they arrived at a little while later was much like the one they'd had dinner in: lanes and alleys practically roofed over by limp skeins of twisted wiring strung from rickety telegraph poles. Passing within inches of second-story balconies, the wires doubled as clotheslines, and sheets, towels, and all kinds of clothing hung like limp flags and dripped water onto the pavement below.

"This is where she lives?" Wasey asked. "You said something about a park."

"This is where we're going to buy her a present. It's called Pig Alley. You've never been here?"

He stopped Wasey in front of a shop which was still open in spite of the late hour. They went inside, into a dusty, dimly lit room crowded to the ceiling with bronze and brass and stone. There was an old man behind the counter peering through wire-rim spectacles at a book as fat as a shoe box, the forty-watt bulb above his head, like the man underneath it, nearing the end of its life. It buzzed and flickered and sent black shadows fluttering into the back of the shop, where ornate folding screens and chipped stone Buddhas stood beneath shelves of rolled silk scrolls, temple ornaments, cork pictures, tomb rubbings, and framed drawings of Khitan princes astride red pomponned ponies.

The old man looked up myopically, taking a moment to refocus his eyes. "Young sirs," he said in a crackly voice and unaccented English, "before I ask how I may assist you, perhaps you could assist me." He pointed to the open pages of his book. "Do you read Chinese? These characters here . . . the printing is as bad as my eyes."

Wasey crossed to the counter and turned the book towards him. *"T'ao-t'ieh,"* he said. "Monster mask."

"Then the *chueh* is indeed genuine," the old man said,

half to himself, bringing up from under the counter a bronze wine pitcher on which a twin-bodied dragon twisted and turned, its snarling head bug-eyed and fiercely fanged. "Late Chou," he said, excitedly tapping the book. "Look here in the *po ku t'u,* a picture of one just like it."

Tuttle wagged his finger in the air. "Feng, the only thing that's genuine on the counter is your encyclopedia. That jug isn't late Chou, it's early Chiang Kai-shek."

The dealer adjusted his glasses and took another look at Tuttle. "You've been here before?" he asked.

"The last time it was a jade Tsung column you'd found from the period of the Warring States."

The black mandarin cap the dealer wore bobbed as he ducked his head in embarrassment; his stringy white mustache drooped down to join the wisp of beard hanging from his chin.

"I am ashamed. What I took in my senile stupidity to be two eager tourists turn out to be scholars of refinement and good taste."

"And limited means," Tuttle added.

The old man's head came up, the sparkle back in his eyes. "There is something I could show you?"

"Your superb collection of dolls, Master."

"Ah. Of course." A trace of a smile appeared around the dealer's mouth. "Perhaps now I recognize you, young sir. Mr. Tuttle, is it not?" He glanced at Wasey, looking ready to giggle, then turned and shuffled towards the back of his shop.

"That's the present we're buying?" Wasey asked. "A doll?"

"A china doll. She likes to collect them. That's where she gets her name from, China Doll."

Wasey shrugged. "I guess it's better than Shining Beetle."

"Old Feng has a terrific collection. Victorian stuff."

"Why take a gift anyway? Doesn't she get paid?"

"Bet your life she gets paid. Beulah will be sending you a pretty hefty bill."

"Tell her to make it out to Tatlock, Door of Hope," Wasey said.

The dealer called to them and they moved past piles of items and through a curtain that shielded a small storeroom. There was only one thing in the room that commanded attention: a lacquered rosewood cabinet in which twenty to twenty-five dolls were displayed. The cabinet was beautifully made and expertly polished but it was the dolls that took the breath away. They stood on the cabinet shelves in three glowing lines, pressed and pleated, ruffled and laced, with not a single loose stitch or an unstuck hem. The dealer reached for one, a female doll of crisp perfection, her milky shoulders sloping into a starched blue dress of white-dotted voile, her waist impossibly narrow. She wore a blue lace bonnet on a wig of real hair that capped a puff-cheeked face of immaculate features: tiny red butterfly mouth, tiny smooth dollop of a nose, long dark eyebrows arching over bright blue paperweight eyes. But it was her glazed porcelain skin that fascinated—flawless, glossy, almost liquid in its purity.

"A *poupée modèle,*" the dealer said. "Made by Huret in France in 1844." He handed it to Tuttle, then reached for another one, a fat-faced boy with molded blond hair dressed in black velvet and ruffles. "German. Tinted bisque. About 1860. You'll notice that most of the dolls have blue eyes. That's because Queen Victoria liked blue eyes." He gave that one to Wasey to examine, but Wasey was looking at something else, and the dealer saw it.

"Ah," he said, smiling, "the gentleman is a connoisseur." He reached for a doll that was larger than the rest and in a different compartment, the dolls in this section all figures of the Chinese court. He handled it carefully, the gem of his collection, and when he described it his voice crooned with pride. "The Emperor Huang Ti. He's called the Yellow Emperor because the color signifies earth and he was born on earth-element day. He invented money, building blocks, and the compass, and organized the calendar into its present sixty-year cycle. When he died a phoenix and a unicorn appeared at his bed as testament to his benign rule."

The doll was about twenty-four inches high with a broad, deep body clothed in a gown of yellow silk, the storks embroidered on the chest prancing in a green grove of bamboo. Its ample waist was cinched by a pink leather belt decorated with carnelian brooches, the same stone being used in the round coin earrings. The long pointed beard and wriggling snake mustache were made of jet-black hair and were in sharp contrast to the whiteness of the plump porcelain face.

The dealer indicated the cloak and the headdress, which were strangely plain. "I have not finished restoring him, so he is not quite complete."

"How much?" Wasey asked. He surprised himself. He didn't see the point of taking a present, wasn't interested in Victorian dolls, but this doll was striking—the kind of thing that turns a browser into a buyer.

"Twenty-five dollars American."

"*How* much?"

"The original would be worth ten thousand times that. But this is the finest copy in the country. Made in Peking in the late eighties." The dealer looked sly. "China Doll would love it."

Tuttle laughed. "How did you know we were shopping for her?"

The old man's smile was just one more line in his face. "Two young men looking at dolls late at night . . . Besides, I remember you now, sir. You bought the Hsiang Fei doll some time ago, did you not?"

Tuttle didn't comment on that; he seemed a little embarrassed.

"Twenty-five's too rich for my blood," Wasey said, pointing. "How much is that one there?"

It was a lady of the court, smaller and less colorful than most of the other dolls, although it was interesting with its strange feathered cap.

The old man found his choice amusing. "Yu Hsuan-chi. An excellent choice for China Doll. She will be well pleased. Fifteen dollars."

Wasey haggled him down to half that, arranged for credit, and had the dealer wrap the doll. Five minutes later they were in a cab and continuing their journey.

Wasey tapped the present on his lap. "What the hell did we buy this for?"

"To influence China Doll. I told you, she has to accept you."

"I've been with a lot of hookers, and I never had to qualify before."

"She's not a hooker," Tuttle said quietly. "Not like you're talking about."

Wasey didn't pursue it any further; he remained silent, watching the traffic as they headed north, then west. He recognized the grandstands of the racecourse as the cab followed its perimeter to an area where the houses gave way to vacant allotments. The street ended in a cyclone fence, a dark, open space beyond. Wasey peered at it through his window.

"What is this place? It looks like the middle of nowhere."

"You're close. It's what's left of the Great World Amusement Park. It's where she lives, remember?"

"What's the gag, Tuttle? Nobody lives in an amusement park."

"China Doll does. I told you she was different." Tuttle got out of the cab, Wasey following, uncertain of what was going on. The reporter brought a key from his pocket, squinted at it, then handed it over. "Present from Miss Beulah. Through the gate and follow the lights."

"Follow the lights to where?"

Tuttle cocked his head to one side. "You don't want me

to spoil the surprise, do you?" He got back into the cab. "I'll call Beulah tonight. Talk to you later." The cab wheeled away, leaving Wasey with no idea of where he was, and very little idea of what he was supposed to do.

A dim bulb burned above the gate, and beyond that he could see a few tiny lights, but the rest was darkness.

Standing there with the key in one hand and the present in the other, he wondered if he wasn't in the middle of an elaborate joke — newspapermen were famous for pulling gags.

Then another thought struck him, a far more worrying one: what if it wasn't a joke, what if it was all a setup? A deserted carnival late at night, no houses anywhere, no people... He hesitated, wondering if Tuttle could be on the gangs' payroll. But would the gangs go to such lengths to set a trap, buying the doll and everything? It didn't make sense. But then nothing made much sense in this crazy city.

He looked at the gate and listened to the night. There was an eerie sound coming from beyond the fence, a soft banging as if a door was blowing back and forth in the wind. That was probably what it was, Wasey told himself, because there actually was a wind, a mild one, wafting a chill against his face and sending leaves scuttering over his shoes. He fingered the key in his hand, looked at the gate, and knew he didn't want to go in. But there was a chance of getting a lead if he did. Tuttle was high on Miss Beulah as a source of information, and that could mean a ticket to Los Angeles.

He walked forward, fitted the key into a rusty padlock, snapped it open, and went through the gate. He crossed a flat stretch of pitted asphalt to the first of the lights he'd seen from outside, a naked bulb dangling from an overhead wire. They dotted the dark ahead of him, strung about a hundred feet apart, and as he moved towards them he came upon a little ticket booth with a swaying wooden sign slapping against its frame. A short way beyond that something dark bulked against the night, a lacy black network of twisted spars. He made out the looping crisscross of a roller coaster, but as he got closer he saw that it was mangled around itself. A carousel was next, tipped on its side, the horses limbless and charred, their brass poles warped into flabby curves. Wasey began to see that the whole place was a burnt-out wreck. Dreadful flames had swept through it, quick and efficient, and the carnival had twisted and turned like meat on a spit.

The lights continued, jerry-rigged things, and Wasey followed them past more ruins: stalls, slides, a smashed Ferris wheel like a *Titanic* heeling under the stars. Then a path opened up, a stretch of ground that appeared to have acted as a firebreak, the ride on the other side seeming in better condition.

The light bulbs crossed the path and ended abruptly against a wooden structure that was only faintly scorched. Most of the paintwork had bubbled, and there were strips of canvas hanging loose, but the building itself had been saved and it stood out like the only thing left in the wake of a tornado. The sign it carried was written in English and Chinese. It said "The River Caves."

Wasey stopped, put the wrapped doll under his arm, reached into his pocket, and took the automatic out of its box. He felt comforted knowing that he had the miniature grenade, too; he was pretty sure he could use that if he had to, but the gun still spooked him.

He moved to the entrance, a wedge of darkness that would have been totally black had it not been for a faint glow coming from somewhere inside.

A soft chunking noise came to him, followed by a liquid slap and splash, and a metallic squeal. A few feet further on he saw its origin: a large waterwheel slowly churning an artificial stream. It squeaked around its ungreased axle, its buckets thumping and dipping into the water. Wasey stood very still, listening, but there were no other sounds, nothing moving except the big wooden wheel, and the water spilling out of it.

He crossed some planks and went closer to the stream that vanished into a void on both sides.

When the noise sounded it scared the hell out of him, a sudden loud bump on his right.

Something moved on the stream—a little wooden boat coming towards him like a ghost ship. He stopped it, stepped into it, and sat down on its narrow seat. It seemed a strange thing to do, getting into a ride in a ruined carnival, but nothing else presented itself.

The stream drifted the boat away, bumping it gently against the wooden banks that were no more than six feet apart. Wasey was carried towards swinging doors—he could just make them out—positioned across the stream, and the little boat nosed them open and slipped through. When they swung closed again he found himself in a blackness that was utter and complete. It was the worst moment of his life. The fear he'd been fighting off broke through and stormed all over him. He sat frozen, waiting upon his fate, allowing himself to be slowly drawn into the black nothingness, the quiet gurgle of water a ghastly sound, the gentle bumping of the boat a sickening feeling.

The splash of light shocked him with its suddenness.

It burst the dark apart on his right, and for a chilling instant he wasn't sure what he was seeing. He'd expected something horrible, menacing, but instead the scene was gentle and bucolic: a Chinese town of long ago—pavilions, a park, a placid green lake studded with islands, elegant villas and gardens with fruit trees in flower, temples and courtyards, a river with willows and fishermen, a seven-tiered pagoda, a flooded rice field, women picking mulberry leaves. The model was beautifully done and absolutely correct, each of the thousand roof tiles carved by hand, the figures dressed in the fashion of the Sung period, perfectly in scale.

The light winked out and the dark returned.

The boat drifted on.

This time he felt the slight knock when, twenty seconds later, the boat tripped a relay and another scene came to life. It was far simpler, far less busy than the previous one, but it had the same quiet serenity and feeling of peace. It was a three-dimensional reproduction of a famous Ma Yuan painting, a mountain scene in the southern countryside, sharp crags half lost in a mist, a tall scraggy plum tree in the foreground and, in the middle ground, a man in the robes of a medieval scholar contemplating a round yellow moon. Wasey was charmed by it, as he had been by the first scene, and much of his anxiety had fled, the gun limp in his hand, almost forgotten.

He was ready for the light switching off this time, but now, instead of pitch-blackness, the dark was punctuated by fantasy figures lit from behind and mounted on the black walls. Devils, ghosts and goblins, monkey gods and fox spirits glowed pink and red and green, but the figures were playful rather than fearsome, friendly and mischievous, and perfectly in keeping with the mood of the caves.

A little further on light burst in again, showing a boat race on a glassy lake. Each boat was painted red and gold and was long and narrow with a bearded dragon's head carved at the bow and a high thrashing tail at the stern. An acrobat turned somersaults on the dragon's head, and children swung in a swing beneath the tail. Eight straining oarsmen were ranged on both sides of a double cabin topped by a pagoda roof, two men in the lower section keeping time for the rowers with gong and drum, while in the upper section a man waved blue flags and another unfurled a long silk banner that billowed in an imaginary breeze. The person of rank who sat in the stern wore the crimson cap, the red and blue striped robe, and the imperial blue jacket of the eighteenth-century Ch'ings. The light winked out, and Wasey floated on, his eyes blind again, his ears hearing nothing except the trickle of water and the occasional thump of the boat brushing the bank.

The fourth scene showed the figure of a cowherd looking up with anguished longing at a woman seated at a loom. They were perhaps six feet apart and separated by a great swatch of twinkling white stars that glittered and rippled in a silver river. Across this glistening space a flock of wag-tailed birds was stretched wing to wing.

The tableau went black and the new darkness clung close for a while, then began to fade slightly, disturbed by a thin wavering light that came from up ahead. The stream curved round a corner and he saw that the flickering glow came from a candle held by a young woman waiting at a landing. She held herself like a servant with her short plump body bent fractionally forward, her eyes lowered. She leaned over to stop the boat and steadied it, and motioned for him to get out. When he'd stepped onto the landing she released the little boat and it glided to complete its journey back to the entrance. The girl bowed to him, turned, and led him down a corridor, the candle flames dancing creepy shadows around them.

So far as he could see in the fluttering light the walls were of the same rough wood as the planking underfoot, as were the walls in the room they came to. There was machinery of some kind in a corner and benches set up, one with a model of an ancient city half completed. It was apparent to Wasey that he was in the river ride's maintenance area, although the room the servant led him to next had undergone a striking change. The wooden walls had been papered from floor to ceiling in a gilded medallion pattern in which silver birds swooped on a pond full of lotus leaves. Against this dazzling background were framed pictures of ceremonial robes of the Wang Mang, the Tsin, and the Yüan dynasties. And a fine collection of Sung cartoons: a gathering of ball players and spectators—their costumes strictly regulated by occupation—two actresses in coral and white robes exchanging clasped hand greetings, and a fat actor in the part of an eye doctor, his gown covered with paper fans that had bulging eyes drawn on them.

There were classic bird and blossom woodcuts by the Master of the Ten Bamboo Studio, and a collection of New Year door gods, red-gloved, impossible figures dressed in swirling colors and stomping along in bearded, pop-eyed masks.

On another wall, underneath a row of oil lamps that lit the room, the Emperor Wen marched in regal procession towards his son and successor, the Emperor Wu, both men splendid in red and and gold and black, and wearing the high slat mortarboards that veiled their heads front and rear. The floor was covered, almost in its entirety, by a Ninghsian rug, a marvelous thing with scarlet fish swimming through a swirl of orange reeds, and with mountain and valley borders. Blue and pink were the colors of the wisps rising from the peaks, Mongol souls ascending directly to heaven. It was like a sun on the floor, that rug, warming the chill air just by its presence.

The furniture was sparse, a few chairs and tables, all of them in blond *luan* wood, beautifully carved. The cabinet against the end wall, yellow bamboo and fluted camphorwood, had been fitted and joined by a master, but its intricacies were overshadowed by what it contained.

Wasey went to it and gazed through the glass panels. It was an even better collection than the one the dealer owned on Pig Alley, although there were none of the French and German dolls, the collection being devoted entirely to figures of the Chinese court. Most of them made the doll he'd brought look second-rate, and there was one that even eclipsed the Yellow Emperor, the one the dealer had wanted twenty-five dollars for. Wasey was certain she was an empress, the costume was fabulous: a yellow satin gown embroidered with peonies, roses, and winter plum blossoms in shiny metallic thread. A shoulder cape made of dozens of pieces of red and green glass representing rubies and emeralds. Her shoes, painted porcelain, were supposed to be jade, as were her long pendant earrings and the clasps on her gown. In her left hand she carried a demon-quelling wand, wood painted to look like gold. And the headdress, which, on the original, would have brought a fortune by itself, was a phoenix made of emeralds and pearls rising from a nest of diamonds.

Wasey wondered how much the dealer would value this one at, and what fabulous sum the original would be worth.

He turned as he heard a step behind him, thinking it was the maidservant, but the girl had gone. Another woman stood there, and Wasey had never seen anyone like her in his life. At first he thought she was wearing a mask, but then he saw that it was just makeup she wore, although it had been applied with mathematical precision: the forehead was dead white, the white powder continuing in a straight narrow strip down over the bridge of her nose to its tip. Each side of this strip her face was painted bright pink, starting from under her eyebrows, which were heavily accented in black. The pink coloring rouged her cheeks, shaded slightly around her jawline, and became the white powder again at her chin. The mouth was tiny and painted a brilliant glossy red, and her eyes were outlined in black, their slant accentuated by paint applied in sharp splashes.

Her costume was magnificent. The headdress was a shimmering cluster of cut green glass and red and white beads. The front part was made of heavy blue felt worked in a silver-thread fish-roe pattern, the top part like a flat crown from which dozens of mauve paper fuchsias cascaded down in a pastel waterfall. Yellow bead tassels, easily twelve inches long, fell from her ears to the lapels of her gown, which was turquoise silk, heavily brocaded with chrysanthemums and fluttering black butterflies. Her fingers and wrists were weighted with ornaments: finger rings, thumb rings, shiny bangles, and flashing bracelets. And her hair beneath the headdress was caught by long flat mahogany pins inlaid with mother-of-pearl.

Tall, elegant, with perfect posture, the woman was like

a figure from the Chinese opera, but Wasey knew that that wasn't what she was supposed to be—he was looking at an imperial concubine of a hundred years ago.

She spoke to him in spaced, hesitant English; a firm, deep voice, but wholly feminine. "I speak . . . words . . . of your language."

Wasey replied in rapid Shanghai. "I speak words of yours."

She answered him in the same dialect; the only time she used English again was to pronounce her name. "I am called China Doll."

"I'm called Wasey."

She repeated the name, not quite able to get her mouth around it. "Way-see," she said. Her eyes were roaming over him, taking in his sandy-colored hair, the well-structured face, his lean frame. She said, still unmoving, "You were afraid?"

Wasey didn't understand what she meant till he saw her looking at his hand. He was still holding the gun. He slipped it into his jacket.

"A little," he replied.

She looked up at his face; her eyes were beautiful, a deep liquid brown. "The brave man has no fear," she said. "The fool admits to none. So you are neither brave nor foolish, Wasey."

"I would like to be the former, but I'll settle for not being the latter."

The answer seemed to please the woman, although her masklike face remained impassive.

Wasey held out his present. "For you."

She took it, turned, and moved to a table. With the makeup, and the heavy brocaded gown, there was no way he could tell what China Doll looked like, but he got the impression, by the way her gown swayed when she walked, that she was full-figured.

With small deft movements she unwrapped the outer paper and opened the tissue inside. She brought out the doll and recognized it instantly. "Yu Hsuan-chi."

"You like her?" He still couldn't penetrate the heavy makeup. He wondered if that was its original purpose, to hide from the emperor any negative emotion a woman might feel in his presence.

"She is beautiful," China Doll replied.

"The dealer, the old man on Pig Alley, said she would be of special significance to you, although he didn't say why."

"Because Yu Hsuan-chi was a concubine. As I am." It was said simply, in a matter-of-fact way with no trace of affectation, and Wasey realized that she really believed it.

"Do you know her story?" she asked. She carried the doll to the cabinet that housed the rest of the collection, Wasey following.

"I'd like to hear it."

"She was a mist and flower maiden in a brothel in Ch'ang-an, the old capital, where she was known as Sweet Orchid. She would sit with her favorite lover, Li Tzu-an, and watch the mandarins strutting along the Street of Heaven, wealthy men of the T'ang. Hsuan-chi told herself that when her lover was as rich and famous as these she would catch the reflection of his glory and be a great lady herself. But a great lady was not what she became."

Wasey, who knew that in China a response was required by a storyteller, dutifully supplied one.

"Why not? What did she become?"

"Li Tzu-an's concubine at first, then when he ceased to favor her, a novice at the Nunnery of Boundless Contentment in the hills above Ch'ang-an. There she wrote poems of sad beauty which soon attracted the attention of important poets and scholars. She took many of them as lovers, including one whose mistress she became, a scarfaced eccentric who taught her the ways of debauchery. She left the nunnery and returned years later, her looks tarnished, and little better than a drunken wanton, but still writing poems of abandonment."

China Doll paused a moment, then recited. "'South of the River, north of the River, wandering comfortless, Remembering you, longing for you, sighing in loneliness.'"

She opened the glass doors of the cabinet, placed Wasey's gift carefully on a shelf, then stepped back and gazed at the new addition.

"Her influential friends of old were embarrassed by her and complained about her presence, and not long after her maidservant was found murdered. The police claimed that Hsuan-chi had been jealous of the girl's fresh beauty and accused her of the crime."

"But Li Tzu-an, her original love, heard of it, returned, and stole her away," Wasey said, sure of a romantic ending.

"No. She was tortured until she acknowledged her guilt, and was executed. She was not yet thirty. Her most famous poem is called, 'Selling Wilted Peonies.'"

Wasey looked at the doll in the cabinet and for the first time understood the meaning of the white gown and the Taoist cap of feathers, and the calligraphy brush in her hand. He said, "I'm sorry to have brought you so tragic a figure."

"Tragic? Many do not feel so. Hsuan-chi wanted to be known as a famous concubine, but instead is remembered as a fine poet."

Wasey noticed that the woman didn't say which way she felt about it, and he wondered which way that would be. He switched his eyes to the gem of the collection, the doll he'd been admiring earlier.

"She's fabulous," he said, pointing. "Who is she?"

"Yehonala. The favorite of Hsien Fêng, the Dragon Emperor."

"He must have adored her. I thought she was an empress."

"She was. She became the Dowager Empress, Tzu Hsi, the Buddha of the Great Within."

"I've forgotten. What's the name of the emperor the old man has, the one in the yellow gown?"

"That is Huang Ti, the Yellow Emperor. I will own him soon."

Saving up? Wasey didn't say it, but he wondered about it. He wondered how many of the dolls she'd bought herself and how many had been bought as presents by her clients, and whether the money she made from him would go towards the emperor doll. He reminded himself that he didn't care if she spent the money on chewing gum just as long as it bought him some information. He also reminded himself that she had to accept him before any of that happened. But she'd accepted the present; would she do that and still turn him down?

She closed the cabinet door, turned to face him, held his eyes for a few seconds, then swiveled gracefully and moved towards a door in the far side of the room. She'd almost reached it before she turned again and said in her low, even voice, "My maidservant will attend you." Then she was gone.

Did that mean the maid would show him out, or take his coat? He was left to wonder for a few minutes until the maid appeared at the same door and stood waiting for him. Wasey crossed to her, followed her into a kind of anteroom and through a sliding screen partition. He almost walked into the steaming wooden tub that was sunk into the floor.

The maid began to unbutton his coat.

"I can do it," he said.

"Thank you, sir," the girl answered, "but there is no need," and proceeded to undress him.

He'd been undressed by Chinese women before, dozens of them, but, he reflected, this would be the first time one had given him a bath since his old amah had done it when he'd been a kid.

Naked, he tried the water, stepped into the tub, and sank down in it up to his neck. It had been a long evening with a lot of wine, and it seemed to be catching up with him. At the same time he knew that the evening was far from over, and he felt a curious excitement when he thought about China Doll, about the prospect of sleeping with her. She seemed so remote, so aloof that the idea appeared faintly ridiculous, and yet it was going to happen.

He wondered about her, about what made her tick. All this business about being a concubine, and living in this weird place, what kind of a woman did something like that?

The little maid poured a liquid into the bath, colorless and spicy-smelling, frothed it with a sponge, then began to soap him down. She worked her way all over him. The girl was quite pretty yet her touch was strangely sexless, and Wasey was lulled rather than aroused. When she'd finished she left him soaking, then returned shortly carrying a tray. There was nothing on it except a bowl containing something that looked like a soft pink candy, chopsticks, and a thimble-sized cup of tea.

He told her that he'd already had a lot to eat but the maid said that it wasn't food.

"What is it?"

"It will assist you," she said.

He thought she'd chosen a funny word; assist him to do what? But he took the chopsticks and popped the thing into his mouth. It had a chewy texture not unlike a marshmallow, and a flavor like toothpaste. He washed it down with the tea and decided it was a Chinese breath mint. The maid shook out a big white towel and he stepped out of the tub and let her wrap him in it. She took another one and dried him vigorously, getting down on her knees to do his legs and feet and toes. She'd also shampooed his hair, and she tousled that dry, then, with a brush, swept it straight back and down in the Chinese manner. She helped him into a white silk gown that came to his ankles, and tied it with a black sash, slipped clogs onto his feet, wooden ones that curled up at the front like the bow of a junk, then asked him to bend down so she could put a hat

112

on his head. It was a hat like those worn by the ancient emperors, a little like a chef's cloche but made of black bamboo and with wide sideboards that came down over the ears. He felt more than a bit silly in the outfit, but he went along with it, partly because the maid had a politely subservient way of ignoring his requests and partly because he was intrigued to see what it was all in aid of.

The maid crossed to the opposite wall, slid open another screen panel, and guided him through into a bedroom.

He'd never seen a room more deserving of the name: there was nothing in it but a bed, and the bed was a dazzling, piece of furniture. It was an enormous four-poster fifteen feet square with a base of black walnut with feet carved in the shape of horses' hooves. The sheets, coverlet, and pillow slips were of a filmy glazed fabric that looked iridescent in the glow of the wall lamps. But the main feature was the painted panels that hung from the top of the high frame. They ran all the way round the bed, two to a side, each one about six feet by three, and each carrying a painting of a dragon. All of the beasts were different; they were gold, crimson, green-striped, crouched in caverns, perched on clouds, thrashing in a rolling sea. They were whiskered, winged, horned, hornless; they had scales of fish, claws of a hawk, and paws of a tiger, but all were fierce and breathed hot tongues of fire.

He made a circuit of the giant bed, marveling at it, wondering when he was going to get a chance to try it out. China Doll hadn't put in an appearance yet, and he supposed that it was her turn in the tub. He had time for a few more circuits before anyone arrived, and it was the maid who entered first. He noticed that she'd changed from her workaday clothes into a pale blue gown, and that her hair, which she'd worn in the Manchu style with a pigtail, was now braided in a rosette behind each ear. She carried a tray, different from the one she'd had before, with a container of ink on it and a writing brush. She placed the tray on the floor, went over to him, pincered his sleeve in her fingers, and led him round to the end of the bed that faced the door.

She stepped back and remained very still, waiting.

Wasey waited, too.

Then China Doll came into the room.

Wasey was astonished. He wouldn't have recognized her but for the regal way she carried herself. The makeup had been like a heavy disguise pinching her features, sharpening them. The white powder had made her nose appear thin and long, the graduating red color had fattened her cheeks, and the painted mouth had made it appear prudishly narrow.

The real face was lovely: oval, high-cheeked, full-mouthed; a slight notch in the upper lip and a round, full lower one. The nose was a fine broad Chinese nose that made no apology, and the eyebrows, heavy thick slashes before, were now fine delicate lines arcing over eyes that had lost their accentuated slant and looked almost Western. Her hair was fringed across her forehead and fell to her shoulders in an ordered tumble, glossy black. The rings had gone, too, and the bracelets and the bangles. She wore no ornamentation save for three fingernail protectors, long ones, made of white jade, on her left hand. As for her costume, she'd swapped the turquoise gown for a plain one which was the exact opposite of Wasey's: black with a white sash.

It was a piece of symbolism that he understood: they were the Yin and Yang—the active male standing for vigor and penetration, the passive female representing repose and absorption.

She stopped several feet away and stood facing him, her expression serious, solemn almost. When the maidservant went to her Wasey thought it would be to beg permission to withdraw, but instead the girl untied the sash of her mistress's gown, and slipped the gown off her.

It was so unexpected Wasey started, and he might have

said something if his voice hadn't suddenly dried up. The woman was wonderfully, superbly naked, and she stood there like a diver on a springboard, arms and legs together but with the palms of her hands turned frontwards.

Her body was the only perfect one he'd ever seen. It was almost as if a master retoucher had painted out any faults—there wasn't a sag or a wrinkle on it.

Her flesh gleamed, not a honey gold as he'd expected, but a pale cream color, light-skinned like the women of Soochow, where she was probably from. It wasn't a slim body, yet there wasn't an ounce of excess anywhere. The arms and legs were long and cleanly muscled; her breasts jutted and hung with a firm fullness; spread wide, they were like melons near her underarms, beautifully proportioned. Her figure notched at the midline sharply, then flared out again at the quick angle of her hips. Her tummy was a soft marble slab curving over a deep-lipped navel that sloped away to the trim black triangle dotting her crotch.

She was a glorious sight, and he felt himself reacting to her, the blood and the juices beginning to flow.

She bowed to him, a deep bow that swung her breasts forward in a languorous glide.

He swallowed and looked at the maid, impatiently wondering what she was hanging round for. He got a partial answer when the girl picked up the brush and bowl from the tray, went to her mistress, dipped the brush in the ink, and began to write on her body.

It was the last thing Wasey expected; all the other prostitutes he'd been with had simply lain down on a bed. He watched the maid write in a spidery character he couldn't recognize, moving the brush carefully on China Doll's perfect skin. She wrote on her chest, on both breasts, and all the way down her belly, including her vagina.

Then she turned to Wasey.

He'd never been shy about his body—it hadn't troubled him when she'd bathed him—but in his present state he wasn't just nearly naked, he was clearly and unmistakably very ready for sex, something he was old-fashioned enough to regard as a private pursuit for two people. The thin gown he wore did little to hide his manly condition, but at least it was something, and he took a step back as the maid approached.

Then China Doll spoke. "It's a Sanskrit prayer. To ensure good fortune, an emperor would have it painted on a new concubine, and on himself as well."

The little maid, as irresistible as ever, peeled his gown from him, and set to work with her brush.

It made a shivery tickling sensation on his chest and his stomach that did nothing to dissipate his roaring erection. She wrote on that, too, which made him wonder if the maid hadn't undressed her mistress first so as to ensure herself a larger canvas when she got to him. Finished with the brush, she took his wrist and led him to the far side of the bed. She sat him down, removed the tall black hat, then, with gentle pressure, pushed him back onto the bed, turning him on his side so that he faced away from the room.

Wasey went along with it. He thought it was part of the same prayer ritual, but he was wrong.

The sex he was so ready for had begun.

He felt the bed depress on the other side, then nothing for a few moments. Then he heard a tiny rustle as China Doll—it had to be her—moved on the shiny material of the sheets.

He waited, wondering. Nothing seemed to be happening, and he couldn't figure out the significance of the slight movements he could feel. He turned his head to look.

China Doll, facing him, and with her eyes shut, was lying on her side about twelve feet away with her arms held stiffly along her flanks. She was creeping sideways toward him, her body undulating slowly like a beautiful white serpent as she slid forward.

The maid turned Wasey back again and remained standing near him, a servant in attendance.

He waited. He could feel China Doll getting closer—she was taking an age.

The sheets rustled, the weight shifted. He breathed faster and swallowed dryly.

Very close now; he could feel her breath raising the tiny hairs on the nape of his neck, swore he could feel the warmth of her body radiating out to him. He was quivering, the skin on his back tingling with the expectancy of touch.

There was another heavy moment, then he jumped with a shock that was almost electric as her nipples, hard and warm as coals, touched up against his flesh.

He expected her arms, or a hand, to curl round and grasp him, but she just kept coming forward in that same agonizingly slow way, shifting closer bit by bit, her breasts beginning to flatten against him. He felt her tummy then, touching against his bottom, and that was when the maid knelt down at the side of the bed, placed one hand on his chest and the other on his thigh, and braced him as her mistress pushed her body against him from behind.

He felt her thighs against the backs of his legs, her knees tucking into his, then her shins against his calves, toes against his ankles, her chin on his shoulder, the breath at his cheek sweet like scented ginger. She was plastered to him now, pressed hard against almost every inch of his back, yet the sensation seemed to be drifting through his flesh and registering on the *front* of his body; it was tingling in the same unbearable way that his back had been a minute before.

And still she hadn't touched him with her hands.

He didn't think he could stand it much longer, but he didn't have to.

China Doll peeled herself off him.

The maid waited a few moments, then got him to turn over on his other side. He groaned when he saw that China Doll was twelve feet away from him again. It was worse this time because he could see that superb body gliding towards him in slow sections: thighs, hips, tummy, breasts flowing forward in liquid movement. But there was one consolation, he was happy to note: there was no way she could flatten herself against him in this position, she'd be stopped eight inches away.

He should have realized that they'd take something like that into account. When China Doll had almost reached him the little maid simply leaned over and pressed his penis down for her mistress to straddle.

Wasey hadn't entered her, he was sandwiched harmlessly between her thighs, and although the position was a marvelous one that carried its own delights, it wasn't where he wanted to be.

China Doll came closer in that same sinuous motion, flattening against him. He flung his arms around her, but the maid, who was bracing herself against his back, retrieved his arms and returned them to his side.

Once again he found himself trapped between servant and mistress in a human iron maiden. He'd lost all reticence about performing in front of a third person; if the maid was part of the deal, as she surely seemed to be, then so be it. At the point he was at he wouldn't have cared if a hundred people holding tickets had been in the room.

Having pressed herself against him to almost intolerable levels, China Doll backed off, and the maid turned him onto his stomach, making sure, with another deft touch of her hand, that he was able to lie flat. He lay there awaiting the next move in this mind-wrenching performance, not sure how much longer he could last. It looked like being his first encounter with a woman where he spent himself without actually doing anything.

And what happened next only helped stoke the fires.

He felt China Doll's knee brush against the outside of his left thigh, then her other knee scrape against the outside of his right thigh. He could have wept; what was she trying to do to him? There she was above him, with her legs open, and once again he was facing the wrong way. When she lowered herself onto his bottom, and began to move up and down against it, he was half convinced that he'd have to have a talk with her mother. But again the sensation was marvelous. She moved on him in a series of lazy circles, each one ending with a sharp forward thrust of her hips. She did this a number of times while he moaned beneath her, then she was gone and the maid was turning him over. Groggy with desire, Wasey wondered what they'd do next—lie down with the soles of their feet touching, maybe—but that wasn't what they did. Before he knew it she'd popped him inside her, made a single, fast, thrilling, downward stroke, and was gone.

Wasey felt that his mind was hanging by a thread. Was that it? The world's longest foreplay followed by the world's shortest copulation? He pushed himself upright, but the maid was there restraining him with those polite firm hands of hers. She maneuvered him to the end of the bed and into a kneeling position, then he watched her as she joined her mistress at the opposite end.

He knew he wouldn't live through another slow advance, but he saw that he was to be saved that, because they were getting ready for something else—just what, he couldn't be sure. The maid had climbed onto the bed and was sitting with her legs crossed and leaning back on her elbows. Then China Doll—he blinked to make sure he was seeing right—China Doll sat down in her lap and put her hands behind her to support herself. He wouldn't have thought that he was capable of being surprised anymore, but what he saw next floored him: the two women, in an amazing feat of acrobatics, were bumping in tandem towards him. They moved together in strict harmony, bouncing up and down on the mattress and advancing at least twelve inches each time.

He might have found the sight funny if it hadn't been so sexy—it was awesomely thrilling because China Doll's marvelous breasts jiggled, jumped, and swayed, and with each bounce she opened her legs just a little bit more, widening them further and further apart.

Bounce, bounce, bounce she came. Jiggle, jiggle, jiggle, her perfect thighs revealing more of her pinky black treasure that was coming at him like soft hungry jaws.

Three feet away, then two. Then she was on him—literally—because with breathtaking precision, and just a little guidance with her hand, she bounced right onto him and swallowed him whole.

Her legs locked round him and her arms came up under his, and without missing a beat she drew him towards her, sliding her legs up around his neck as he assumed an ascendant position. She was still in the maid's lap, very much so, because both of them were clutching him; he could feel the silk of the maid's gown as her feet pressed against the back of his thighs. She was now directly underneath China Doll, moving her body in unison with the woman and catapulting her into him in a pounding rhythmic drive. Wasey had never known such delight, and couldn't understand why he wasn't climaxing. He wondered if the wine he'd drunk was doing it. Then his pleasure-fogged brain remembered the marshmallow the maid had given him. That's what was doing it; it hadn't been a breath mint at all. It was some kind of drug with a retard effect.

He blessed the Chinese and their cunning inventions, closed his eyes, and let himself sink into an ocean of pure, numbing ecstasy. But he found that even the Chinese pharmacists had a limit to their cleverness as, four or five minutes later, an express train started somewhere around his knees and roared up through him until, with a cry that was near to being a shout, his body jerked several times and he felt as if everything he'd ever owned had shot out of him. Released from two pairs of arms and legs, he sagged back onto the sheets and lay in a semi-conscious heap. He was vaguely aware of the maid doing things—the touch of a towel, and something else he was too tired to even think about. He felt the nub of a quilted comforter being tucked round him, then the wall candles were blown out and he was left by himself in the bed, and was sound asleep a minute later.

He woke in what must have been the early hours of the morning, warm and drowsy, and aware only of a sweet fatigue in his body. He heard a soft bumping noise coming from somewhere beyond the wall and knew what it was: the little boat moving in its endless circuit on the artificial stream. He got a quick image of it drifting on the waters, tripping the relays on its lonely voyage, the displays lighting up as it passed, empty.

He turned over, and like the boat outside the wall, drifted off into blackness.

8

When Wasey awoke the second time, the lamps had been relit, so he assumed it was morning. It certainly felt like morning; he knew he must have been asleep for hours because all of the tiredness had gone from his limbs and, apart from a little stiffness in the nether regions, he felt pretty good.

He saw the reason for the stiff feeling when he threw off the comforter and sat up: his penis was wrapped in a thin layer of cherry wood and tied with a ribbon.

It looked like the maid's handiwork.

Just what was meant by it, he couldn't imagine—some kind of award of merit? Or was it supposed to serve a more practical purpose? A splint perhaps?

Something else caught his eye, something equally curious. There was a breakfast tray on a low table that had been pulled up to the bed. On it was a peeled banana resting upright on two nectarines; the tip of the banana had been inserted into an oval notch cut into a melon.

More of the maid's handiwork.

Normally Wasey would have been a touch disconcerted to find, first thing in the morning, that his member had been made up like a chocolate box and that breakfast was a pornographic fruit display, but because he was in Shanghai he merely shrugged it off.

He discarded the cherry wood, hopped out of bed, and went looking for a latrine, which he found in a nook off the bathroom. The tub was steaming with hot water, a pot of tea beside it.

He soaked for a good long time, finished the tea, climbed out of the bath, and dried himself on the fresh white towel that had been left there. His clothes had been laid out, too, the shirt pressed like new. He dressed, put the Baby Nambu back into its box, and walked out into the main room. There was no sign of anyone; he assumed that the two women had rooms through the door in the end wall.

Passing by the doll cabinet, he was stopped again by the empress. She looked every bit as stunning as she had last night when he'd first seen her—the glass-stone cape and the phoenix headdress were wonderful. The doll he'd brought looked back at him from out of her sad eyes and made him wonder if her new owner would remember in a week or two who had given it to her.

He crossed to the door, the one that led to the hall, picked up the candle that was burning there, and went to the landing. He arrived as the maid was stepping out of the boat, a basket of vegetables in her hand.

She bowed and said, "Sir, I have arranged for a taxi. It is waiting at the gate."

"Fine. Tell your mistress thanks. And, um, tell her good-bye."

He stepped into the boat and pushed off, let it drift him into the black tunnel. It took him past several more displays, all of them as enchanting as the ones he'd already seen.

A faint edge of daylight showed ahead of him, then the boat barged through the exit doors and he jumped out onto the landing. He went down the walkway, came out into bright sunshine, and had to squint after the flickering darkness of the River Caves.

He strolled through the carnival, noting that his earlier impressions of the place had been correct; it was a blackened metal junkyard with weeds growing through the broken asphalt. He wondered if the fire had been at night, patchy wiring maybe, overloaded by all the lights. He got a quick picture of people pouring off rides, stampeding for the exit; it wouldn't have been nice.

The cab was waiting at the gates as the maid had said. She'd got him a good one, and twenty minutes later he was back in his hotel room, where he found Miss Tatlock waiting for him.

She rose quickly from a chair. "Mr. Wasey. You're here."

He wondered if there was a note of mild relief in her voice.

"So I am. Why, were you worried?"

Miss Tatlock sat down again, straight-backed and correct. "Of course not. I didn't think you were in any danger, but I naturally wondered why your appointment with Mr. Tuttle went on for so long. Your bed hasn't been slept in."

"You're right. I'll have to complain to the management." He took off his jacket and loosened his tie.

"I'd like a complete report, if you'd be so kind."

Wasey kicked off his shoes and stretched out on the bed. "What, do you mean my whole evening?"

"Yes. After all, Mr. Burns and I are employing you, in a manner of speaking. I think I'm entitled to ask how you spend your time."

"Well, let's see," Wasey said. He plumped up a pillow behind his head and got comfortable. "I met Tuttle and we had drinks in a teahouse."

"That doesn't surprise me."

"Then we went to a wineshop and got drunk by moonlight with goblets flying. Then we went to a sporting house run by a White Russian named Beulah Belle Lovelace, where we saw Sheena, the queen of the jungle, ravished by Mandrake's assistant. Then we saw a kind of fashion show and went back downtown and bought a Victorian china doll. Then I met an absolutely exquisite prostitute and went to bed with her and her maid in an abandoned amusement park." Wasey appealed to her. "You see? Just a typical night out in Shanghai."

Miss Tatlock was anything but pleased. "Besides meeting with Mr. Tuttle, Mr. Wasey, there are only two things I believe of that ridiculous story. One, that you got drunk. And two, that you spent the night with a prostitute."

"Now why is it you're only prepared to believe the worst about me, Miss Tatlock? The reason I went to the sporting house wasn't because of insatiable goatish desire. Tuttle took me there because, according to him, the madam, Miss Beulah, the belle of the Kremlin, knows everybody in town and might be persuaded to help us."

Miss Tatlock's face relaxed a fraction. "That's excellent news. Mr. Burns was certain Mr. Tuttle was our best chance. When do you see her, this Russian woman?"

"Tuttle was going to speak to her last night, so I guess—"

He stopped speaking when the desk clerk, knocking tentatively on the door, shuffled in. He bowed to Miss Tatlock, spoke to Wasey in rapid Shanghai, then shuffled out again.

Wasey swung himself off the bed. "How's that for timing?"

"What did he say?"

Wasey was over at the window looking down at the street. "A summons from Miss Beulah."

Miss Tatlock was on her feet, too. "She wouldn't want to see you if she didn't have some information, surely."

"You're right. It's a little early for business."

Miss Tatlock joined him at the window. Down on the street a shiny brown Nash was parked at the curb, a uniformed chauffeur leaning against it smoking a cigarette.

Wasey started to slip on his shoes. "I'll check with you later."

"I'm coming, too."

"It'd be a waste of time. They have all the girls they need."

"Mr. Wasey!"

"Miss Tatlock, you don't take ladies to a sporting house. It just isn't done."

"But this is different."

"Even when it's different. I can assure you they wouldn't let you in."

Miss Tatlock bit her lip. "Very well. But you must promise to come straight back."

Wasey picked up his jacket. "Yes, dear."

He went out of the room and down the stairs to the street. When the chauffeur spotted him he dropped his cigarette and smartened up.

"My name's Wasey."

The man's shoulders snapped back. "Sir!"

"Miss Beulah send you?"

"Yes, sir." The man jerked open the rear door and stood by it ramrod straight, an ex-military man Wasey judged. Wasey got in, the door slammed like a gunshot, and the man jumped into the front seat and took the car away.

Wasey was in high spirits; he'd meant what he'd said about it being too early for business. The only reason Beulah would want to see him at that time of day would be to give him some information, perhaps a real lead. And then it would be so long Shanghai, hello L.A.

The prospect made him feel good all over; he felt a genuine physical tingling in his hands and arms, and he wondered if he should have had something to eat. Maybe he should have eaten the fruit the maid had prepared for him. He chuckled when he thought of it, almost giggled. He moved his legs to another position—one of them seemed to have gone to sleep. Sleep, he told himself, was something he could probably use a bit more of, and he made a mental note to get back to the hotel early and hit the sack, catch up a bit.

Boy, he was tired; the smooth ride of the big car was lulling him like a baby. Fresh air, that's what he needed. He didn't want to be snoozing when he got to Beulah's.

He reached for the window, wondering why his hands felt so heavy, but the window winder was broken or jammed or something. The other window was closed, too.

He leaned forward to knock on the glass partition that separated the front and rear seats, but it all seemed like too much effort. He put back his head and closed his eyes, deciding to get in forty winks.

The last thing he remembered thinking, as he dropped off, was that the car's previous occupant had been carrying flowers—there was a high sweet smell in the air.

The driver glanced over his shoulder, then reached under the dash and pushed in the knob he'd pulled out a few minutes after Wasey had got into the car. He slowed and took a left at the next turning, then drove towards another section of the city.

Whether the trip took five minutes or fifty, Wasey had no idea; the first thing he knew when he came around was that the soft seat of the automobile had been exchanged for a much harder one, and that he was shivering. He thought he was back in the River Caves—he could hear the drip of water and could see a flickering light—but then he found that the flickering was his eyelids reacting to a bright electric bulb. And the water noise was coming from a leaking pipe. He was in a high-ceilinged basement, a dark smelly place whose naked cement walls oozed moisture. There was no daylight, no windows for it to enter, just a sharp glare thrown off by lights suspended on long ugly cords. His clothes had been dumped onto a plain wooden table several feet away—somebody had stripped him to the waist and sat him in a hard-backed chair.

As his eyes focused more, and the singing in his head subsided, he got a look at the people who no doubt had done it: two men, neither of them a pretty sight. Both were compact and solid-looking in quilted jackets and pants, but Wasey only noted this when he was able to tear his eyes away from their faces. One man had no ears and wore a leather patch where his nose should have been. The other had Chinese characters tattooed across his forehead and on both cheeks of his flat mean face. They said "I am a coward."

Wasey's stomach flip-flopped. He'd thought the two heavies at the dance hall were hard cases, the two in the George Raft suits and the yellow ties, but alongside these two they were jokes. What kind of people tattooed a person's face, or cut off a man's ears and nose? And what did you have to do to deserve such punishment?

He shaded his eyes to look past the light above him. There was some kind of harness dangling from a pulley sunk into a ceiling beam. Directly underneath it the floor sloped to a drain.

He didn't understand the function of either thing, but their juxtaposition bothered him. In fact, everything bothered him, most of all the realization that he was at last a guest of one of the secret societies. He was damn angry at his situation, he forced himself to be. He knew that if he stopped feeling mad he'd start whimpering with fear and blubbering all over the place. Goddamnit, he'd let down his guard and allowed himself to be maneuvered, if that's what you could call being gassed and waking up in a dungeon.

He was certain about the gas now; he'd experienced the same kind of benevolent feeling, and smelled the same sweet smell, only a few months back when he'd had some dental work done. The dentist had given him the same stuff the driver had given him: nitrous oxide. A tank of it in the trunk, a lead going under the rear seat . . . it wouldn't have been hard. He slid his eyes over to his clothes. The box containing the Baby Nambu was sticking out of his jacket. The tiny grenade was in there, too. The only problem was, he'd have to get past the two uglies to reach them. He remembered telling Miss Tatlock that he was no good at fisticuffs, which was true. But what he hadn't told her was that on at least two occasions when he'd had to defend himself—once in a poker game in Batavia, the other time in a fancy fake French restaurant in Macao—he'd compensated for his lack of a classic left jab by delivering a sharp kick to the kneecap and, in the other instance, by braining a guy with an ice bucket.

He shifted in the chair, testing his body. It felt fine, the heaviness gone, his head clear, too. Nitrous may have been a sneaky gas but at least its immediate effects were quickly dissipated.

He looked at the two men, who were looking back at

him stone-faced; they hadn't yet said a word or moved a muscle.

He got his game plan together: he'd go after the guy on the right first, the one with the nose patch; get him over on some pretext, then take him out with the only weapon in immediate proximity, the chair he was sitting on. That would bring the tattooed man running at him, and a running man was always wide open to a well-aimed kick.

Wasey jackknifed forward and clutched his stomach, his face contorted.

The two men stayed where they were.

Wasey groped at his pants pocket with a feeble hand, looked up at the man with the nose patch. *"Wan chi,"* he groaned.

He staggered to his feet, turned, and grasped the chair for support. The man started towards him to get the pills he'd been asked for. Wasey whirled round, the chair already swinging through the air, crashing down at the thug's head.

It never landed.

With phenomenal speed the thug snatched at it, grabbed hold, and redirected its flight with a savage jerk.

Wasey went with it, tumbling over on the cement floor in a painful tangle of arms and chair legs.

His assailant grabbed Wasey and, helped by his partner, pulled him to his feet, righted his chair, and dumped him back into it. They stepped away and resumed their previous positions. They weren't mad, they didn't appear to be upset at all, they'd merely acted to correct an abnormal situation.

Five minutes of nothing followed, a period which Wasey used to get his head back in working order. The buzzing gradually subsided and his eyes resumed single vision, but one side of his face was still going off and on like a siren.

Then a door in front of him opened and a man bustled into the room. He sat down at the table, sweeping the clothes to the floor, opened a note pad, took out a fountain pen, checked the ink supply, then said, "Your name is

Wasey and you speak Shanghai dialect. If you don't, you're not understanding a word I'm saying."

"I understand you," Wasey replied, checking the man over: short and thin in a drab blue suit, a sad bloodhound face, a gold tooth starring in a mouthful of uneven teeth. He didn't look like a gangster, he looked like an unpaid civil servant with too big a work load.

The man consulted his notes, scanning them as if he were looking for the right place. "You've been seeking information, is that correct?" He had a high narrow voice and a way of rolling his tongue around his words that showed he was from the north.

"Who are you? Where is this place, and what am I doing here?" Wasey was amazed that he'd got it out without a break or a wobble in his voice.

The man peeked at him over his notes and said, a bit prissily, "I am not interested in your questions. Only your answers. You have been asking about someone named Faraday. Why?"

"He owes me ten dollars."

The man closed his notebook. He looked weary, as if he were about to go into something he'd been into many times before. He said, "You have been asking about something that was in his possession. Yes or no?"

"Why the hell should I tell you anything?" Wasey demanded, pumping himself up. "I don't even know who you are."

The response was chilling.

"All you need to know about me," the man said, looking up at the harness thing near the ceiling, "is that I am someone who can cause you intense pain."

Wasey couldn't help it; he looked up, too. The thing hung from the beam like a rope of tree moss, black leather straps and a wire of some kind, very thin. It spooked Wasey, that and the drain underneath it, and he could feel himself beginning to lose control.

He tried his best not to let it show. He knew that the

threat of torture was just as effective as torture itself, so there was a chance that the man was just bluffing. Tuttle had told him what a stink there was when an American got into trouble in Shanghai; maybe this guy was just playing the boogey man, hoping to scare him into telling what he wanted to know. Well, he was damned if he was going to be faked out by a shoe clerk and a couple of scary-looking heavies. For all he knew, this could be the basement of some police precinct. Maybe this was the Shanghai equivalent of being taken downtown back home while the cops all stood round looking tough and mean.

Wasey started a reply, then began it again to keep the quiver out of his voice. In most of the Chinese dialects fear showed a lot faster than it did in English because the tones all went to hell and the wrong syllable stress could turn a normal sentence into nonsense. "You're a man who can cause me pain, and I'm a man who can cause *you* a lot of trouble. My passport is registered at the U.S. Consulate, and I have—"

In a bored, casual way the interrogator checked his watch and cut Wasey off, talking about something completely different. "There was an emperor named Cheng Wang who lived during the Ch'in. A peddler stole a rose from his garden one day and the police caught him and cut off his head on the spot. When the emperor heard about this he was furious at the leniency of the sentence."

Wasey stopped talking. With an anecdote like that the man had his complete attention now.

He went on in his high voice, weighting his words in all the right places. "One of the penalties for such a serious crime was called the Crow." The man flicked his finger towards the ceiling. "You can see the apparatus up there."

Again Wasey was forced to look at the harness; it had become a hideous thing hanging from the rafters, a giant squid trailing its tentacles, waiting.

"The offender was strung up outside the city walls. The leather thongs secured his arms and legs, and the string of gut—that's the thin wire you can see—was placed around the waist. The thongs were always slightly looser than the gut." The man paused so that Wasey could get a mental picture of a loop of needle-fine gut slowly slicing through a body. "A strong person took about an hour to die, although after about five minutes they couldn't be heard. Do you know why?"

Wasey didn't reply. His insides had iced up and, in a companion reaction, sweat had broken out over his eyes.

"Because," the man continued, "their constant screams made them hoarse."

Wasey coughed for lack of saliva, swallowed, and tried a reverse of the Br'er Rabbit trick. "Go ahead. String me up. I can yell all day."

It didn't work.

With a single nod of his head the interrogator set loose his two dogs. Nosepatch grabbed Wasey and jerked him out of the chair while Tattoo worked the block and tackle, bringing the harness swinging down from the beam. Together they clamped the leather thongs around his arms and legs, and looped the gut, not round his waist, but underneath his left armpit. Then they both began to pull on the rope, hauling him, bit by bit, up towards the ceiling.

The interrogator went on speaking. "I am told that you Westerners have an expression for something expensive. You say that it costs an arm and a leg. Most appropriate, because that will be the price of your continued stubbornness. The present record for stubbornness is held by a beggar in the Old City. He's quite easy to recognize, he's the man with no arms and only one leg."

Wasey had nearly reached the rafters, the leather thongs taking his weight, the gut not yet brought into play. He kept telling himself that it wouldn't be—this was 1940, not 1240, and he was in one of the world's most cosmopolitan cities, not some barbaric Mongolian outpost. They'd never do it, he told himself, sweat stinging down into his eyes. They were bluffing.

The interrogator was standing, gathering up his note-book and pen. "Are you prepared to answer my questions?"

Wasey, swept along by his own hype, shouted an expression he'd picked up from the rickshaw coolies, the Shang-hai equivalent of "Fuck you!"

His inquisitor gave a nod, and his two henchmen did something with the rope they were holding, then the man began to walk towards the door.

Wasey felt the pressure ease round his ankles and wrist, and the gut string press up into his armpit. His arms were held at right angles to his body, and there was no way he could grab the leather thongs. Whatever the men had done to the rope, it had altered the harness so that now most of his weight was supported by the gut, which had already started to cut into his flesh.

It was like a razor slashing into him, not just the quick shock of a cut but the continued burning pain of slitting skin.

Jesus Mother of God, they were doing it to him! They were going to take off his arm! "No!" Wasey cried. "Wait!"

He'd called out in English, but the interrogator pre-tended not to understand and just kept walking towards the door.

The gut was slowly slicing through his flesh like a wire drawn through cheese. He could feel the blood on his ribs. The pain was hideous.

"Get me *down*! Get me *down*!"

With his hand on the doorknob the man turned and said conversationally, "You will cooperate?"

"Yes! Yes!"

He twisted the knife.

"Fully?"

"YES! GET ME DOWN!"

By the time they'd done it, Wasey had passed out.

For the second time in less than thirty minutes he came to in the hard-backed chair, but he was in a lot worse condition than he had been before. His armpit was a solid ball of pain, his side was damp with blood, and there wasn't an ounce of fight left in him.

Smelling salts brought him around, waved under his nose by a woman who seemed to be a doctor. She dabbed spirit on his arm and gave him a shot of something from a porcelain syringe, then roughly began to clean the wound.

The interrogator was back at the table, his notebook open, his pen poised. "So," he said. "You have been asking about this man Faraday. About something that was in his possession. Is that correct?"

With his good hand Wasey wiped sweat from his forehead. The pain was receding quickly but he was still groggy.

"Yes."

"What exactly?"

"Opium poppies."

"Explain, please."

In a dull, flat voice Wasey answered. "I was hired to find the opium poppies he had when he was killed."

"What do you know about these poppies?" The man was taking it all down, scribbling in his notebook.

"There is half a ton of them. Hidden somewhere in the city." Wasey winced at a sharp pain; the woman was stitching his wound as if she resented the work. He wondered dimly why they were bothering to fix him up and decided that they were playing nice guys now so a grateful victim would be even more willing to talk. Wasey wasn't grateful, he just didn't want to go up in that harness again.

The questions continued.

"What else do you know about them?"

"People call them Faraday's flowers."

The man's pen stopped, and he looked up from his notebook. "Repeat that, please."

"The poppies are known as Faraday's flowers."

"Who told you about them?"

"A guy in Manila. He said if I found them we'd go fifty-fifty."

"His name?"

"George," Wasey said. "George Dartmouth."

The man went on looking at Wasey for a moment, then snapped his notebook shut. "You have been wasting your time. You have been searching for something that does not exist."

He got out of his chair and walked from the room.

The thugs stayed where they were.

The woman finished bandaging his arm and was now improvising a sling. She searched in her bag, took out a small bottle, shook it, uncorked it, and handed it to him to drink. "For the pain," she said.

Wasey put it to his lips, a pink, bitter medicine that stank.

The woman picked up her bag, stepped away, and grunted at him. "You feeling sleepy?"

"A bit," Wasey said as he passed out.

9

There were many people in Shanghai who'd been furious when the refugees had flooded in from Hongkew and Pootung, and a lot of these people still regarded them with great distaste. But not everyone; certainly not the two elderly brothers who were trundling their handcart down a dark alley off Rue Cardinal Mercier. They were delighted that the refugees had come because it had supplied them with a steady job, which was picking up their corpses.

Most of the refugees only just scraped by from day to day, and when they died, from hunger or exposure or simple desolation, the Benevolent Societies arranged for burial. All they asked of the impoverished relatives was that they wrap the body in a reed mat and leave it on a convenient street corner. As far as the two brothers were concerned—they were both in their seventies—the job was a good one, secure and well paid, and with little prospect of their ever being made redundant. If there was a drawback it had to do with the fact that some of the corpses were heavy, like the one they were puffing and pulling at now, half carrying, half dragging the thing across the sidewalk to their cart. They stopped when a groan came from beneath the reed covering.

The younger brother said, "There is something wrong with this corpse."

The older brother, a little deaf, hadn't heard the groan. "There is something wrong with all of them," he said. "They're dead."

"This one isn't."

There was another groan, loud enough for both of them to hear this time. They untied the mat and peeled it open.

Wasey sat up, shook his head, winced, and took in the nighttime alley and the corpse cart, and the two elderly Chinese watching him. He climbed shakily to his feet, moved on wobbly legs across the lane, staggered, and sat down on the cart to recover.

The elder brother had seen everything in his seventy years on the streets of Shanghai; he merely put his hand to his aching back and said, "If only they'd all do that."

Wasey had another try at standing. He steadied himself, then began to put one foot in front of the other. He felt more dead than alive, his arm was throbbing, he was stiff all over, he had a raging thirst, and his head felt as if it were coming apart. He would have paid a cabdriver a hundred dollars to take him to his hotel room, where there was a bed and a bottle of aspirin, but he was in no shape to dart into the road and try to flag one down. And he knew he couldn't have withstood the jouncing and the sudden stops and starts of a rickshaw. He'd just have to get somebody to find a taxi for him and hope for the best.

He went into the first shop that showed a light, with both good and bad results. Bad because, as he went through the door, a red and yellow parrot in a cage shrieked into his ear, *"K'e lai liao! K'e lai liao!"* Which meant "Customers have come!"

He stumbled into the store and collapsed in a chair. The owner came in from a back room carrying something in a large glass vase. It was probably the last thing Wasey wanted to see at that moment: a black and yellow snake in methylated spirits.

He looked around him and found that he'd blundered into a herbalist's shop. Dreadful and obscene things confronted him: gnarled and misshapen roots trailing anemic streamers floated in etched-glass jars; dried alligator skins, pieces of coral, and velvet-covered antelope horns rested in giant canisters stacked on a shelf. There were fat tins labeled Fritillaria Extract, Korean Red Ginseng, Tien Ta Wan (for bruises and strains), and something called Bao Zhen Gao made by the Shanghai Nature Medicine Works. There were dried roots, dried bones, dried seaweed, dried orange peel, dried chalk, and a thousand other dried things mercifully hidden away in an entire wall of drawers. There were strange and terrible mixtures: licorice root, grated soapstone, and scallion hearts to cut fever and make the urine flow; an eyewash made of dried beetles; dog rose, knotgrass, and steamed peach pits for liver complaints; oxlip, white lotus, and raspberries fried in wine to stop a nosebleed; hot sun-dried *yengge* fruit for bellyache; *hsu-tuàn* for arthritis; and *t'ung-kuan* powder for blowing into the nose, a sure cure for a cold.

The owner put down the snake vase and attended his new customer previously announced by the parrot.

"Sir, may I assist you?" he bellowed. He had no French or English and hoped by speaking loudly that the foreigner would understand.

"I need a taxi. Could someone get me a taxi, please."

"With the utmost ease, sir." The man called into the back of the shop, and a small boy came running. He hardly paused to get instructions from his father, then he was out of the door and gone.

The herbalist moved closer to Wasey, looking concerned. "Sir, you seem unwell."

It was the most tactful and, at the same time, the dumbest remark Wasey had ever heard. He was sitting slumped over with his head in his hands, wearing only the right half of his shirt and jacket, the left side dangling free on account of his slung arm. Blood had dried in a dark brown stain on his pants leg, there was a broad white bandage in his armpit, and a large lump over his ear from his tussle with Nosepatch.

Wasey forced himself to reply civilly; after all, the man had sent his boy for a cab. "My host has made a statement I cannot quarrel with."

"Then, sir, I would advise you to keep away for the cold and rough foods, and avoid goose and fish. Fowl, mutton, and pork should be boiled or steamed but not roasted. I advise a diet of one bowl of millet a day taken with pig's-foot jelly without pepper."

Wasey left his head in his hands. "It's not my stomach."

"Ah. Your shoulder joint, then. I note that you have it wrapped. I suggest a hot poultice of white honey alternated with steamed ginseng plasters."

"It's my head."

"Your head? Sir, you are indeed fortunate. The head is the easiest part of the body to treat." The man hurried away, leaving Wasey wondering how long it would take the kid to get a taxi; his head felt like it was coming off at the neck.

The proprietor was back in a minute with a tall wooden jar and a steaming kettle. He bustled behind his counter, opened a drawer, and sprinkled some white herbs into the jar, matching them with some chalky gray powder taken from a big brown bottle. He cautiously poured in boiling water, then brought the jar round to Wasey and handed it to him along with a kitchen towel. "Here you are, sir. A most effective inhalation against clogged antra, blocked ears, and other disorders of the head."

"What's in it?"

"Mugwort and powdered oyster shell."

Wasey didn't argue. He even allowed the man to drape the towel over his head. The towel smelled awful but the inhalation smelled worse. Still, the steam and the warmth were soothing on his face and he breathed in the stuff until the boy came running back with the news that he'd secured a taxi. Wasey got up, gave back the inhalation, and put some money on the counter, an amount the herbalist told him was most generous.

On his way out Wasey was amazed to find that his headache was receding, although it wasn't helped when the feathered doorbell in the cage, evidently unable to distinguish direction, screeched in his ear, *"Customers have come!"*

Wasey fled the bird, found the cab, gave the driver the address, and sank back into the seat. He felt drained, physically and emotionally. What the hell was wrong with this town? All the people in it were either sadists or shit worshippers or sex maniacs. Everybody was crazy. Even the fucking parrots were crazy.

He felt so many things he couldn't count them: anger, confusion, fear, and frustration. What an idiot he'd been! Nobody had had to sap him to get him into that car, he'd climbed in all by himself; jumped to a conclusion without a moment's thought and paid the price.

He felt the box in his pocket, rattled it. They hadn't taken the gun, or the grenade, which was almost insulting. They were treating him like a rookie, which was exactly what he was. Well, no more. No more looking for those damn, stupid flowers. From now on the only time he'd think of flowers would be on Mother's Day.

He closed his eyes, leaned back. His arm ached and he felt chilly. Probably, he thought, a little shock creeping in. He would have killed for a drink, and some hot food, and a warm bath, and some tender loving care. So why, he wondered, was he going back to his hotel room, where there was none of those things?

He leaned forward painfully and spoke to the driver, and the taxi changed direction.

He was sure the gangs were finished with him, at least for the moment, but the dark still scared him as he walked down the path through the twisted wrecks. He moved on his toes when he reached the entrance to the River Caves, but nothing moved in the blackness and there was no sound save for the splash and squeak of the waterwheel.

He crept down the walkway to the stream and waited, perfectly still, till he heard the doors bump open and saw the boat drifting towards him. He held it as it drew level, stepped in, and let it carry him into the blackness of the tunnel. The displays charmed him all over again. Lighting up in their silent splendor, they were even prettier than he remembered, and he felt soothed by them, lulled by their fairy-tale quality. His tense watchfulness drifted away, matching the slow flow of the boat.

The ride seemed shorter this time, and sooner than he expected he saw the flutter of a candle and the maid waiting for him on the landing. She hadn't known he was coming, so there had to be a buzzer of some kind at the entrance.

The maid bowed as he stepped out of the boat, mumbled a word of greeting, then picked up her candle and led the way down the corridor into the living area. She slid open the screen partition and admitted him to the tub room.

It was as if he'd been expected: frothy water smelling of rose petals and glycerine steamed in the tub, and the gown he'd worn before was folded and ready on a chair. Wasey supposed that it was the Chinese version of leaving a light in the window, but, whatever it was, it was nice to come home to.

The maid helped him out of his clothes and, with great care, untied the sling on his arm. She pinned a towel around the bandage, then put a little footstool in the tub for him to sit on so that the water came up only to his chest.

He sank back into the tub for a blissful half hour, relaxed and almost dozing, his headache fading away completely, and when he'd had enough of the hot water, got out and allowed the maid to dry him. His arm felt much better, so he left off the sling and stuck his left hand in the tie string of the gown she helped him on with. Then he went into the main room, crossed the swimming fish on the Ninghsian rug, and stood in front of the doll case.

He was becoming a fan of the dolls; the empress was a knockout. He couldn't get over that phoenix headdress. It reminded him a little of the ancient Egyptians he'd studied at school, the pharaoh's wives with the vultures in their high caps.

"You like her, don't you, Way-see?"

He spun round. The woman seemed to have the most

alarming way of suddenly appearing.

"I was wondering how much the original would be worth."

"It would be priceless."

"Where is it, do you know?"

"Vanished. Stolen years ago."

"Who stole it?"

"The palace guards," China Doll said, coming further into the room. She moved with a soft, cottony swish, the folds of her gown reaching all the way to the floor. The gown was a striking crimson color with long, green-stemmed lilies woven on the lower half, the bright red color accenting the paleness of her face and the jet black of her hair.

"The guards?" Wasey repeated automatically, struck once again by her poise, and the regal way she carried herself.

"They stole from the Ch'ing vaults and sold the treasures to the antique shops in Ti An Men Street."

"Did they get away with it?"

"No. The emperor asked for an inventory and found them out." China Doll came closer. "This happened only eleven years ago."

"That recent?" Wasey said. "Then he's the emperor the Japanese took to Manchuria."

"Pu-yi. The last of the Ch'ings, and the last Manchu," China Doll said. Then she added, in an apparent non sequitur, "He chose his empress and his consorts from photographs when I was only eight." The note of wistful bitterness in her voice was unmistakable.

Wasey said, "I assume they were girls from palace families?"

"Yes. Chosen by two of the High Consorts who had been concubines to the Emperor T'ung Chih." She nodded at the empress doll. "Her son." She brought her eyes back to Wasey. Her expression had not changed; the lovely features were still in repose, but there was a tension in her body and an edge to her words, and it was clear to him that she was speaking about something that pained her.

"In the old days everybody had a chance. Each city and town would send its loveliest girls for the emperor's approval. Then it was up to the talents of the girl to advance herself within the palace."

"How would she do that?" Wasey asked, fairly sure of the answer.

China doll put it beautifully. "By mastering the art of blandishment and dalliance."

"Ah. I see."

"And music, dance, and the preparation of food. But mainly by the secrets and mysteries of her sex that were taught her by her male tutor."

"Male? Didn't the emperor want a virgin?"

"For his empress, yes. The Four Properties were required: chastity, quiet work, gentle speech, and modest demeanor. But a concubine had to be—"

"Skilled in blandishment and dalliance," Wasey finished for her.

"Skilled. Exactly," China Doll said, her marvelously deep eyes eating into him.

Wasey smiled, wondering if it was possible to tease her. "I imagine the job of tutor was much sought after."

"It had its drawbacks. The tutors often fell in love with their students. A hopeless love, because a concubine lives only for her master." She brought her eyes down to his arm. "My maid tells me you are hurt."

"I cut myself."

"Have you eaten?"

"No."

"Sit," China Doll said, and walked from the room.

The maid scurried in a few minutes later with a small iron brazier, scurried out again, then returned carrying a pan of hot coals, which she poured into the brazier's mouth.

She was back again in a moment setting down a tray of food and utensils, then vanished once more as her mistress re-entered.

China Doll knelt before the glowing coals and began to prepare a meal. Wasey enjoyed watching her do it; he found it astonishing the way she turned a chore like cooking into a ballet. The long chopsticks in her hand went from chopping board to pan in a single unbroken movement. Oil sizzled, and a delicious aroma began to fill the room. Wasey wanted to ask her about herself, wasn't sure how to do it politely, so began by asking her the first thing a man usually finds out about a woman.

"What's your name?"

"China Doll."

"I mean your real name."

"My real name is Yehonala."

She stressed the word "real" in a way that made him wonder what she meant by it. It was as if it, too, was different from the name she'd been born with. And there was another thing: the name Yehonala pinged off the edges of his memory.

"Where are you from?"

"Wusih."

"Did you grow up there?"

China Doll didn't reply.

"I apologize. It was impertinent to ask."

"No, you have a right to know. A concubine's life must be an open book."

She said nothing more till she served the dish—*lapacho,* she called it—a sweet, crunchy soup of red, green, and yellow beans, red and brown dates, lotus seeds, chestnuts, almonds and peanuts, watermelon seeds, walnuts, raisins and fresh lichees. She poured him a cup of warm rice beer and told him some things while he ate. She told him that she'd been sold at six months to a *mui-tsai* dealer, someone you went to if you wanted to buy a little girl. At five she'd been sold again, to a man in the neighboring town of

Soochow, and had grown up in a floating world of canal markets, mirror-smooth lakes, big summer moons, and stepped stone bridges like white rainbows in the sky.

When she was nine she'd been put to work as a singing girl in the city's finest brothel and had loved watching the pretty ladies in their satin gowns and the loud, boisterous men who swaggered in, patting her cheek and tipping her with real brass coins. She'd been entirely happy until she'd learned that another man had bought her and was taking her to Shanghai, a huge city with no lake, no canals, but a smelly river instead.

During her early time there, singing in a house on the Hungjao Road, her only joy had been a now and then treat, a river ride in an amusement park which reminded her of the tiered pagodas and hidden lagoons of Soochow. On her twelfth birthday a tutor had been chosen for her and she was taught the six blown-breath stimulants, the eight shallow penetrations, the nine minor and the eleven major positions, as well as the various techniques of passive acceptance, forceful dominance, contortion, and mobile intercourse. There were the ceremonial acts to be learned as well: the West Wind, the Wounded Tiger, the Falling Star, the Willow Tree, and a dozen more suited to time and circumstance. When she'd passed the practical tests, given her by inspectors, who graded her progress, her owner introduced her at the brothel he owned as Soochow Flower.

It was a banker-gangster who'd renamed her when she was twenty. He'd brought her a doll one night and she'd loved it so much her new name had followed. The gangster bought her away from her owner and she went to live with him in his penthouse on the Bund. But when the man had been gunned down several years later, she'd suddenly found herself free for the first time since infancy.

It coincided with an event that drastically changed her life.

She'd come across an old sepia photograph of a woman

flanked by two men in ceremonial robes, a lotus grove in the foreground, a painted canvas river in the background. The woman, dressed as Kuan Yin, the goddess of mercy, had a rumpled baggy face and looked to be in her sixties, yet China Doll had instantly recognized herself in a previous existence. As she read about her former life—she'd been famous—the memories had seemed to flood back, and the way she felt about herself and her situation underwent a dramatic change.

No longer content to return to the house on Hungjao Road, she'd gone to the owner of one of the biggest houses in the city, Miss Beulah, and made an agreement. The madam had been surprised when China Doll told her where she wanted to live; the Great World Amusement Park had burned down two years previously, but the River Caves had survived. And Beulah, who had as a customer the director of the firm which had insured the park, was able to arrange for China Doll to reside there.

She'd loved the new arrangement. The caves not only reminded her of her Soochow childhood, but also took her back to the lakes and waterways of her former existence.

Wasey wanted very much to ask her about that but had to resist the temptation; it would have been poor manners to inquire any further. He finished the meal, drank more of the rice beer, and sat back and watched her. She held his gaze for a moment, then rose.

"Come."

She moved in a languid glide towards the bedroom, and after a moment's hesitation Wasey followed.

The dragon bed gleamed in the lamplight, a shining promise of future delights that Wasey didn't think he could handle.

"I'm, er . . . my arm . . ."

"Of course," China Doll said, a polite statement of agreement and understanding.

There were several pillows on the bed, big brocaded cushions that hadn't been there before. China Doll gently pushed him down against them, slipped the knot of her gown, and stepped out of it, her skin like pale perfect fruit, ripe and glowing.

As she knelt on the bed Wasey eased his bad arm out of the gown and let her gently slide the garment off him. She began to run her palm around the outline of his body, starting just under his right ear. To Wasey it felt as if she were leaving a trail of fire behind. With his heart hammering he said, "What we did the other night, the three of us. Is there a name for that?"

"It's called the Chair. There is a name for everything."

Her hand traveled down his neck and along the line of his collarbone.

He coughed and gulped. "I, um, I can't do much. Is there something..."

She correctly anticipated the rest of his question. "Eight Horses. It is for when the man is ill or otherwise handicapped."

"Eight Horses? What's involved?"

"A whip and eight horses."

He was well aware that the language he'd mastered was probably richer in symbolism than any other in the world, but there were still times when any possible meaning escaped him. The Chair, he could see; it *had* been like a chair, for both parties. But this one... Very cautiously, not sure how she'd react, he tried a joke. "Where are we going to get a whip at this time of night?"

China Doll's soft mouth curved the tiniest bit. "At the end of the horse's tail."

She leaned over him, turning her head so that her long black hair hung down, then began to flick her head from side to side. Her hair whisked back and forth across his stomach, swishing and licking at the sensitive skin below his navel. It produced a quivering electric feeling that tingled his flesh and rushed his blood, which in turn produced, he noted, looking down, the whip they'd been looking for. Once again she surprised him by the ease and swiftness with which she mounted him, and Wasey assumed that he was the horse, but where the other seven were, he couldn't imagine.

China Doll showed him.

"You know the character for horse?"

Wasey knew it as well as he knew the five thousand other characters of modern Chinese: it was like a big figure five with a vertical stroke crossed by two horizontals in the top half and four short slant marks in the bottom half.

China Doll began to trace the character with her finger on his chest. She made a broad five, put in the two strokes at the top, then began to add the four slant marks underneath them.

She counted them out. "One, two, three . . . four."

"Hunh!" Wasey cried out.

It had been so unexpected. Instead of adding the fourth stroke mark on his chest, China Doll, with amazing muscular control, had contracted herself around his penis in a quick fast-sucking squeeze, without moving on him at all.

"That's the first horse," she said.

She began the slow tracing on his chest again, drew the broad stroke first, the two top strokes, the three bottom ones, then added the fourth stroke in her own exciting way.

"Hunh!"

"Two," China Doll said.

Wasey had been ready for it but it still made him gasp. With his eyes closed he said, "Why eight? Why do they call it Eight Horses?"

Her reply sounded naughty but he knew that it was ancient Chinese symbolism and wasn't designed to be rude.

"Because eight is all it takes to pull the cart."

"For me, or . . ."

"If the rider is skillful, it should take no less and no more than eight. For all men."

He disliked being lumped into this category and was

148

determined that it would take a dozen horses to pull his cart.

China Doll traced the word on his chest again.

Maybe eleven horses.

By the time she'd got to the fifth horse he was hanging on for ten, but was willing to settle for nine.

The sixth horse was a shock of pure pleasure.

The seventh drained his brain.

But he was still in control. He was still good for two more horses.

China Doll, with no change in her movements, drew the eighth horse on his chest and added the last marvelous stroke.

Wasey started to smile, a word of triumph forming in his mouth.

He didn't get a chance to say it.

His eyes suddenly opened wide and he cried out as fireworks went off inside his body.

Five minutes later she'd left him, and once again he slept by himself, guarded by the dragons around the bed.

10

Wasey was back at his hotel, undressed and in bed, by ten the next morning. He was just dropping off when, after rapping on the door, Miss Tatlock came in.

"Good morning, Mr. Wasey." Ice tinkled in each syllable.

Wasey, the sheet drawn up to his chin, opened one eye and sighed. "Miss Tatlock, is this my room or yours?"

Miss Tatlock marched further into the room. "I waited for you yesterday morning for three hours, right here in this chair. I came back in the afternoon, in the evening, at eleven last night, and at nine this morning."

"I was unavoidably detained."

"You promised you'd come straight back from seeing that madam woman. It's obvious where you've been, of course, but I'd like to hear it from you, Mr. Wasey, if you have the nerve."

"You'd like a rundown on my movements, is that right?"

"You may start from when you got into that car."

Wasey moved under the sheet onto his back and blinked up at the ceiling. "Well, let's see. I got into the car and was enjoying the ride until I found I was sharing the back seat with a cloud of nitrous oxide. I woke up semi-naked in a basement run by Lon Chaney and his brother and a ribbon clerk who kept asking me questions. When they didn't like the answers they tied me to a wire, ran me up, and flew me from the rafters for a while. Then they brought in a seamstress to practice her hemstitching on me. I felt lousy, so she kindly gave me some knockout drops, and eight hours later I woke up in an alley dressed as a corpse. I then went to a herbalist, which wasn't too bad except an attack parrot tried to deafen me. By this time, sorely in need of aid and comfort, I decided to repair to the Great

World Amusement Park, where I was bathed and fed and introduced to eight horses. I slept like a log and arrived back here just in time to be woken up by Miss Tatlock, brilliant young missionary. And, so help me, that's the God's honest truth."

Miss Tatlock breathed in heavily. "I am waiting, Mr. Wasey."

With a weary gesture Wasey pulled the sheet down from his chin.

Miss Tatlock looked at his bandaged arm and her mouth tightened. "Well, that's the limit! Wrapping your arm in a sling to support that ridiculous story!"

"The only thing this sling is supporting, Miss Tatlock, is a sliced shoulder. Go ahead, take a look if you don't believe me."

"You don't think I will, do you? Well, that's where you're wrong." She was across to the bed in two strides but stopped dead when she saw the dried blood on the bandage beneath the sling. She flicked her eyes to Wasey's face, then turned quickly and marched towards the door.

"Sore loser," Wasey called.

She was back in fifteen minutes carrying a small canvas suitcase which turned out to be a pretty comprehensive first-aid kit. She brought it to the bed and, with a skillful hand, began to cut away the bandage.

"Who did this to you?" Her delivery had softened but there was still an edge to it, as if she were mad at him for getting into trouble.

"They wouldn't tell me, so we have a wide choice of suspects. It could have been the Red Beards, the Red Spears, the Society of Brothers and Elders, the Society of the Buddhist Way, the Righteous and Harmonious Fists, the Big Knife, or our old buddies the Red or the Green Society. And they're only the gangs I know of. Maybe it was some other group, the Puce Society, or the Dirty Chopstick and Noodle Association. It's anybody's guess."

"What did they want to know?"

"Why I've been asking about Faraday. They claim the flowers don't exist."

Miss Tatlock stopped her work for a moment and said quickly, "Then that proves they do. Otherwise they'd never deny it."

"Same thing occurred to me, I'm happy to say. I prefer to think I've been wasting my time on something that does exist rather than on something that doesn't."

"How can you say you're wasting your time when you're making such progress?"

Wasey drummed the fingers of his right hand. "You and I see things differently, Miss Tatlock. I almost lost a limb. How can you see that as forging ahead?"

She didn't answer, concentrating on removing the last piece of bandage. She caught her breath softly as she exposed the wound.

Wasey looked down at the crude stitches under his arm. "Jesus, I've seen neater work on potato sacks."

Miss Tatlock brought her eyes up. "They tortured you."

"A lot of good it did them. I held out for at least three seconds."

Miss Tatlock reached into her bag for a tube of salve. "Mr. Wasey, I can't ask you to put yourself in danger again."

"I can understand that," Wasey said generously.

"You're going to have to volunteer."

Wasey closed his eyes and pressed his head back into the pillow. "Miss Tatlock, I don't even volunteer to pass the salt. And even if I'm asked I often say no. So get this straight. I am not going out on the street again. Not as a volunteer, not as a mercenary, not as a conscript in chains. I'm not moving from this bed for a week. And you and Burns are paying the bill."

"But look at it this way—"

"No, you look at it. You were certain I wasn't going to have any trouble. Mr. Burns was certain I wasn't going to have any trouble. Tuttle didn't think I'd have any trouble. The only person who thought there might be a wee bit of risk was the only person who was right. Me."

"Very well, I admit I was wrong. You were hurt. But you were hurt because they thought you might know something about the poppies that you didn't. But they didn't tell you to stop, did they? They merely tried to make out that they didn't exist. They didn't threaten you if you went on looking, did they?"

"Miss Tatlock. They hung me from the goddamn roof beams. They don't need to pay Western Union to send me a message. I got the message while I was up there."

Miss Tatlock took a lot of care with the bandage she was winding around his arm. "You can't quit now, Mr. Wasey. We're getting closer and closer."

"Believe me, Miss Tatlock, the only thing I'm getting closer to is the front porch of an old folks' home on the Jersey shore."

Miss Tatlock made an exasperated sound in her teeth. "Must you always think of yourself? Think of all those soldiers lying wounded in pain."

Wasey stabbed a finger at himself. *"I'm* lying wounded in pain. Let them think of me."

Thirty seconds went by in which the only sound was the precise click of scissors.

"They should never have given you a sling," Miss Tatlock said. "It will heal faster if you keep the arm straight."

She finished and began to put her things away, taking her time over it. "You still haven't spoken to the Russian woman, have you?"

"I didn't get a chance. It wasn't her car, remember?"

"She may have the key to this whole thing. At least go and see her before you quit."

"No, ma'am. I'm not budging. I'm going to have a nice quiet rest, rob a nice quiet bank, grab my ties, and sail out of your life forever."

Miss Tatlock got up off the bed, crossed to the bureau,

and put down the case. With her back to Wasey she said, "Then there's only one thing left for me to do." She reached up and began to pull the hairpin from her bun. Wasey sat up in alarm. "Wait a second! Hold it! You can't do that! Not a second time."

Miss Tatlock's hair came loose.

"Miss Tatlock. I'm in no shape for an obligation right now."

Miss Tatlock unbuttoned her jacket.

"I'm a sick man," Wasey protested.

Miss Tatlock finished undressing and turned.

Wasey shut his eyes tight. "I'm not going to look. You're wasting your time."

Miss Tatlock approached the bed.

"Have a heart, lady. I can't perform with a wounded arm."

"I am taking into account your handicap, Mr. Wasey. So let us say this. If you touch me I will deem it an expression of desire on your part and you will therefore be under obligation to me."

"Then I'm in absolutely no danger. You may fire when ready, Miss Gridley. It's not going to do you an ounce of good."

Miss Tatlock climbed onto the bed and Wasey opened his eyes. The sight of her naked body surprised him all over again. With China Doll it was hardly a shock that the magnificent gowns she wore clothed a superb figure. But to see Miss Tatlock's luscious body emerge from her strict uniform was something he found curiously exciting. And his feeling was very much in evidence when she pulled down the sheet and his pajama pants with it.

"Disregard that," Wasey ordered. "We're independent of each other. The opinion expressed below is definitely not that of the management."

With an awkward movement, clearly unused to what she was doing, Miss Tatlock straddled him and, after considerable fumbling, eased him into her. Then she sat there looking straight ahead at the wall. Wasey was watching the ceiling. After a moment he said, "This is the most fun I've had in bed since I caught the mumps."

Miss Tatlock experimented. She moved forward a little, moved back again, repeated the action, then settled into a hesitant rhythm.

Wasey grunted. "That's close, but no cigar."

Miss Tatlock's movements began to grow in confidence.

Wasey pressed his hands to the sheets. "Note my hands, Miss Tatlock. They're keeping strictly to themselves."

Miss Tatlock embroidered on her movement and began to sway her hips in a circular motion.

Wasey swallowed. "They're not going anywhere."

Miss Tatlock took up the tempo.

"I'm not putting a single—ooh, do that again—finger on you," Wasey said. Then his eyes started to get big in his head. "Miss Tatlock—ooh—in spite of everything—aaah—I think I'm getting . . . close. So pay particular . . . particular attention . . . to my . . . HANDS!"

She locked her arms around him and suppressed a whimper as they rocked together and released at the same time, then lay panting.

Wasey, his eyes closed, tried to get his wind back. "Oh boy . . . oh wow . . . Miss Tatlock, you are definitely my favorite missionary."

With her head on his chest she breathed shallowly and said, "I followed your advice, Mr. Wasey."

"Advice?" He was almost dozing.

"I paid particular attention to your hands."

"That's nice," Wasey said dreamily.

"And they're on my bottom."

"WHAT?"

Wasey's eyes shot open. He looked down and saw that it was true. He brought his hands up in front of his face. "Rotten traitors!" he said. Miserable, he let them flop back.

As Tuttle was the contact with Miss Beulah, Miss Tatlock decided that he should be the first person they should talk to, and they arranged to meet him that evening. It gave Wasey most of the day to rest up and although Miss Tatlock didn't like the delay it did give her time to report back to Mr. Burns.

So at 9 P.M., in a taxi in fair condition——it was raining and they'd inspected the tires before getting in——Miss Tatlock said, "Mr. Burns was very sorry to hear about your ordeal."

"Which ordeal? The one with the gang or the one with you?"

"Mr. Wasey, you will please not mention that."

"Why? You embarrassed? Did you tell Burns how you roped me in again?"

"I merely told him that I'd persuaded you to continue helping us."

"Persuaded." Wasey dwelt on that for a moment. "Miss Tatlock, since you and I started wandering around asking people about opium, I figured there was a chance we'd end up in the river together. Or in the cemetery together. But I never thought we'd end up in bed together."

"I've said I don't wish to discuss it, Mr. Wasey. Your help is vital in this matter. It was a necessary sacrifice I was prepared to make."

Wasey slumped in his topcoat. "I was the one who was sacrificed."

He looked sideways at her but she was pointedly watching the rain on the window. Wasey had noticed something about her lately: a return to her former cold manner. There'd been a time when she seemed to be warming to him a little, but lately she'd been very cool indeed. It seemed to him that the frost had reappeared the day after he'd first met Tuttle. Which was the morning after he'd come back from his first visit to China Doll. It was almost as if she was mad at him about something, but what? She was getting her own way. Why should she be mad at him? He flirted with the idea of asking her directly but his attention was diverted by the cab's engine blowing up. Fortunately they were only a few yards from their destination, so they were able to complete their journey without getting wet.

The place they entered was a club called the Zig Zag on the Avenue Joffre, a nitery modeled after the intimate little boîtes of Paris, as it turned out, except the club was a lot bigger and even darker. There was a circular padded bar at the entrance, Dufy prints behind it lit by portrait lamps, and a chanteuse in a spotlight on a small stage singing in French about lost love. The crowd at the tables looked to be regular nightclub-goers; the women wore everything from long sequin-studded evening dresses to tailored suits with fox pieces round the collars complete with snout and claws. The men wore navy blue suits, with a few dressed formally in black tie. Everybody was chattering in the usual Shanghai mix: English, French, Russian, Japanese. The only Chinese to be heard was spoken by a girl in a brief costume and black net stockings who was selling cigarettes and fluffy toy bears from a tray.

The maître d', who was Swiss, greeted Wasey in English, then looked doubtfully at Miss Tatlock and her uniform.

"It's okay," Wasey said, "she's not collecting."

A hatcheck girl took Miss Tatlock's cloak and Wasey's topcoat, then they wandered in and found Tuttle behind a bottle of cognac in a banquette.

"Hi, Glenn," he said. He unwound his thin body and climbed to his feet.

Wasey made the introductions.

Miss Tatlock said, "I'm very happy to meet you, Mr. Tuttle. I appreciate your helping us."

Tuttle shook her hand. "Thanks, but I haven't done very much."

As they settled themselves Tuttle nodded at Wasey's arm; he could see that he was favoring it.

"What happened?"

"Cut myself shaving."

Miss Tatlock turned the empty glass in front of her upside down as a waiter arrived to pour drinks. "Mr. Tuttle, yesterday morning Mr. Wasey had an unfortunate experience."

"This morning wasn't so hot, either," Wasey said under his breath.

Tuttle asked him what had happened and Wasey took a drink.

"You know those gangs you said I didn't have to worry about? One of them hooked me up to something they said was called the Crow. Invented in the Ch'in dynasty, so I was told."

Tuttle grunted, almost making a laugh out of it. "Glen, as they say in the antipodes, you get into more strife than Flash Gordon."

"Who do you think they were, Mr. Tuttle?" Miss Tatlock asked.

"Did they pick you up in a big brown Nash?"

"Right. Big brown Nash, smelly back seat."

"The MBIS," Tuttle said.

"Who are they?" Wasey and Miss Tatlock asked together.

"The Military Bureau of Investigation and Statistics."

When they both looked blank Tuttle said, "Chiang Kai-shek's Gestapo."

"He's got a Gestapo?"

"You better believe it. Chiang's fascinated by the Nazis. Hell, right this minute his son, Wei-kuo, is at a military academy in Berlin. He's been received twice by Hitler, and was in the front line when the Germans marched into Austria."

"What would they want with Mr. Wasey?" Miss Tatlock asked.

"They like to know what's going on. They've got a finger in a lot of pies. They're counterespionage, they run the secret prisons, and they have a network of spies and agents as thick as a phone book." Tuttle took a drink. "One of them obviously told them you were asking about illegal opium and they wanted to know what was up."

"The chauffeur," Wasey said, "the guy who drove me, he told the hotel clerk he was from Beulah's."

"They've probably been following you for a couple of days."

"The Gestapo, huh." Wasey massaged his shoulder. "Sounds about right. They sure had ways of making me talk."

"Anyway, now that they know what you're doing," Tuttle said, "they won't bother you again."

Miss Tatlock wanted to know why. So did Wasey.

"Because they don't care about opium. Or any other gang-related business. They're kind of like Hoover's FBI: as long as you're a patriot, they're not going to get too excited."

Wasey, reaching for the cognac bottle, didn't look like a man convinced. "What do you hear from Miss Beulah?" he asked.

"I can't approach her until you've become a steady customer."

"Believe me, I'm steady."

Tuttle glanced at Miss Tatlock.

"It's okay. She knows all about it and approves."

"I do *not* approve, Mr. Wasey. I accept your arrangement with this woman as a necessary evil."

To hide a smile Tuttle dabbed at his mouth.

Wasey said, "I've seen China Doll twice. How many more times will Beulah expect me to be evil?"

"Oh, I think one more visit should suffice."

"I don't know." Wasey looked like a man racked with doubt. "I may have to see a priest."

Tuttle chuckled, then looked round and spotted something he didn't like. "Duck," he said.

"Why?"

"Kronk's coming our way."

"Who's he?"

"A professional Jap hater. Also a terrible bore."

Tuttle stopped speaking as a short, jowly, nervous-looking man appeared at his elbow. Tuttle introduced him, then excused himself, telling Wasey he'd talk to him later. The jowly man sat down, nodded at Miss Tatlock, then paid her no more attention.

"You here on business, Mr. Wasey?"

"That's right. Import-export."

"You deal with the Japanese at all?"

"Now and then."

"Keep your ears open, Mr. Wasey."

"What will I hear?"

Kronk wet his lips, glanced furtively around, and brought his stale breath closer. "The Japs are planning something."

Wasey was already bored. "Like what?"

"A surprise attack on the United States. A sneak attack. That's how the Japs start their wars. That's how they started their war against China in 1895. And Russia in 1904." Kronk inched forward, reveling in his subject. "There were two books published about fifteen years back written by a man named Bywater. He was naval correspondent for the London *Daily Telegraph*. They're called *Sea Power in the Pacific* and *The Great Pacific War*. Have you read them?"

Wasey didn't bother to answer.

"No? Well, I have. And I'll tell you who else has read them. The general staff of the Japanese Navy. They had them translated for distribution among all senior naval officers, and also made them required reading at their Naval War College. Do you know what those books postulate, Mr. Wasey? A surprise attack on the fleet in Hawaii and the Philippines, and a simultaneous attack on Guam. Pearl Harbor, Mr. Wasey. They're going after Pearl Harbor."

"I see. Well, I'll certainly keep my ears open, Mr. Kronk.

Now, I'm afraid you'll have to excuse us, we have an appointment."

Guiding Miss Tatlock towards the door, Wasey said, "Pearl Harbor yet. I tell you, this town is full of nuts."

They waved goodbye to Tuttle sitting at the bar and went out to the sidewalk. They were pounced on immediately.

"Sir, I have a message for you."

It was a young man barely out of his teens. His face was brightly animated and full of teeth, his clothes a Chinese approximation of an American college student's.

"Who from?"

"I don't know, sir. I was only paid to fetch you. I came to your hotel but you were just getting into a taxi, so I followed."

"What's he saying?" Miss Tatlock asked.

"Who paid you?"

"Another taxi driver like me. He was unable to do the job because his vehicle broke down. He offered to go halves with me."

"What's the message?"

"I am to take you to a man who has information for you."

"What's he saying?" Miss Tatlock insisted.

"He's trying to get us into his cab. Claims a guy has information for us."

"I knew it! I told you we were making progress." Miss Tatlock made a move towards the car parked at the curb.

Wasey stopped her. "You crazy? You'll end up swinging from the rafters with the Chinese Gestapo looking up your skirt."

"Mr. Tuttle said they wouldn't bother you anymore. And besides, this is nothing like the car you got into yesterday morning."

It was true; the car she'd been moving towards had newspaper pages covering both front fenders sprayed with brown pre-Duco paint. The rest of the car was shiny black except for the hood, which was white. The legend on the door said *Yellow Cab Co*.

"I don't care what Tuttle says, or what that car looks like. Ten seconds after I get in it the windows roll up and the gas comes on."

"Ridiculous! There *are* no windows."

Wasey checked and saw that she was right. "I'm still not getting into it."

"I'm going, and you have to come with me."

"Not going."

Miss Tatlock breathed in sharply through her nose. "Must I remind you of your obligation, Mr. Wasey?"

Wasey, recognizing a no-win situation, gritted his teeth and swore softly.

He moodily asked the cabdriver his name.

"Te-hai, sir."

"Where are we going, Te-hai?"

"The Old City, sir."

They got in and the young driver slipped in behind the wheel. Wasey, suspicious as a cat, inspected the plush interior. There was an acre of legroom, and the seats were wide and overstuffed.

"What kind of car is this?"

"An Austin-Buick," Te-hai answered. "A 1938 Buick body, a 1934 Baby Austin engine." He started the car, floored the gas pedal, and the big automobile dragged itself sluggishly away from the curb and dawdled down the avenue at its top speed.

11

The Old Chinese City was under Japanese control, which made it even less like the original Shanghai it had once been. The Japanese sentry who stopped them wasn't interested in the passengers but studiously examined the pass Te-hai had to show him. He grudgingly admitted them. They drove on and were immediately plunged into a puzzle of narrow winding streets.

The rain had washed the cobblestones but there was no glistening reflection; even though it was early the streets were dark, the houses locked tight. They lumbered through a deserted central square, then past a row of shuttered ivory shops, then a street of bird shops, the cages hooded and quiet.

A wooden bridge, lit by a pitch torch burning at one end, zigzagged across a small lake that appeared out of nowhere, part of an open area stuck right in the middle of the ancient city. There was a double-storied structure with exaggerated swept-up gables and, beyond this on the far bank, the faint silhouette of a small pagoda climbed against the sky.

As they approached it another building appeared at its base fronted by what turned out to be an open grassy court. The taxi stopped at its entrance, and Te-hai turned in his seat.

"The man is waiting for you. In the pagoda, sir."

"I warn you, Te-hai, if this is a trap, and I get killed in here, I'll come back as a goat and eat your upholstery."

The young man looked alarmed. "No trap, sir. Only a man with information."

Wasey got out of the car, Miss Tatlock with him. "He says our man's in the pagoda."

Miss Tatlock set off immediately, Wasey lagging behind.

They crossed the courtyard to the first building, whose stone statues marked it as a Buddhist temple. Beggars, barred at sunset from its interior, slept in ragged bundles along its wall, waiting for daybreak and generous worshippers. They moved quietly by them, climbed the steps, and entered the main hall. It had a narrow oblong shape filled almost entirely by a statue of a reclining Buddha, its worn gilt paint glowing in patches where rapier-thin candles, most of them gutted, had been placed beside the figure. The high sweet smell of incense came down from the blackened walls, one or two sticks still smoldering, their thin smoke trails spiraling upwards, flattening out against the low ceiling. There was no wind to rattle the gongs or flutter the chimes, no sound at all save for their footsteps as they went across the floor to a side door leading to the pagoda. They could see its main room at the end of a hallway that joined the two buildings. It held another statue of Buddha, a seated one, lit by a tin lamp that was too weak to illuminate any part of the pitch-black hall they'd have to traverse.

Wasey balked in front of it, listening, trying to stare into the blackness.

"Come along," Miss Tatlock said crisply.

"Miss Tatlock, the last thing in the world I want to do right now is move another inch forward."

"You have to come. I can't go by myself. I don't speak the language."

"Just point."

"Very well, I'll go ahead. If it's safe, you can follow." It was said with frigid disdain, although Wasey was relieved to hear a slight tremble in her words.

She retraced her steps and picked up a votive candle that was almost extinguished by a pool of melted wax. She brought it back to the hallway and held it high, but the flame was too feeble to penetrate more than a foot in front of her. Nevertheless, she took a step towards the inky hall.

"Wait," Wasey said. "I'm too scared to be left alone."

"Then let's go down the hall together."

Wasey took her hand; his other one held the automatic, which he'd taken out of its box. He had the tiny grenade in his topcoat, too, although both weapons were cold comfort; you couldn't defend against something you couldn't see. The darkness was incredible, so thick and sweet he felt he could scoop out a handful of it.

He took a step forward, then stopped, struck by the obverse side of the previous thought: you *could* attack what you *could* see, and there he was with a candle over his head.

He blew it out.

Miss Tatlock started. "What did you do that for?"

Wasey didn't trust himself to answer; he knew he wasn't going to last.

The darkness licked at them, tasted them, got ready.

There was no way he was going to get down that tunnel by creeping along it one step at a time; he'd have a heart attack.

So he did the reverse. He sucked in his breath, jerked Miss Tatlock with him, and bolted down the hall yelling as loud as he could.

"YAAAAAA!"

They raced down the hallway and charged into the pagoda, caromed off the seated Buddha.

The echoes of Wasey's shout rang around the room but nothing stirred; there was nothing there except the Buddha smiling at their entrance. They recovered themselves. Wasey wiped the palm of his gun hand on his topcoat and took a fresh grip on the pistol.

Then somewhere on the floor above somebody moved.

"Upstairs," Miss Tatlock whispered. "He's waiting for us upstairs."

"Maybe with a knife in his hand," Wasey whispered back.

"Don't be so dramatic." It sounded brave. She looked

up at the ceiling, then around the room. There was a staircase on each side, both in miserable condition, a rope stretched across them, forbidding entrance. Miss Tatlock stole a second candle, a bright one from in front of the statue, crossed to the nearside staircase, and swung her leg over the rope. Reluctantly Wasey followed.

The ancient wooden staircase creaked and sagged under their weight as they began to climb it. It curved up following the shape of the inner stone wall, giving them away at every step.

With no way to disguise their approach they just kept going until a soft glow began to sift into the darkness, and they paused when they saw the stairs opening out onto the second-floor landing above them. They creaked their way up again, then, with three steps to go, Wasey edged by her, gathered himself, and took the steps in a fast burst. He sprang out onto the landing, the gun waving.

Nothing.

Just the echo of his own plunging charge.

Miss Tatlock joined him. "Put that gun away," she hissed. "You'll scare him off."

"Fine by me."

There was a shrine in the center of the room, smaller than the one on the floor below and with a smaller Buddha, but it grinned at them with the same superior smile.

Fat candle stubs threw light in their last minutes of life against the hexagonal walls. Each section of wall had an arched doorway cut into it opening onto an outside parapet that could have sheltered a dozen men. There was no movement and no sound except for the creak of the stairs over their heads.

The person they were following had climbed again.

Miss Tatlock started up the stairs. Wasey called softly to her but she ignored him and he was forced to follow.

As before, he went by her, rushed up the last three steps, and froze, his gun covering the room, but it was empty except for another statue. The only sound was the groan

166

of a board on the floor above.

Holding the candle high, Miss Tatlock moved towards the third set of stairs.

Wasey leaned against the wall, flicked a trickle of sweat away before it could sting his eye.

"Miss Tatlock. A word with you."

"What is it?" she whispered.

He whispered back. "I don't think you realize something. We are being enticed up a pagoda. And as you may have noticed, pagodas taper. A few more floors and it will be very easy for someone to just reach out and push us over that crumbling stone parapet."

"Mr. Wasey, if you're trying to scare me, you're doing a very good job. Now come on."

"No. This is as far as I'm going."

"Come *on!*"

"Okay, But you're only going to get one more floor out of me. Then I quit."

He took the candle from her, led the way up the stairs, treading them very carefully, willing them not to squeak. Halfway up he halted, strained to listen, tried to bore a hole in the blackness that swamped the candle glow. Whoever was up ahead had stopped moving.

Miss Tatlock pressed a hand against his arm, urging him on, and together, just inches apart, they continued their slow climb. The stairs, midnight black, curved round, then a low radiance nibbled at the dark. Wasey snuffed out his candle and got ready. He didn't charge this time; they crept up the last few steps, hugging the cold stone wall, paused for a second, then eased out into the room.

Nobody rushed at them. Everything was still, quiet, serene. The room was different from the others; there was no Buddha statue. Instead a little shrine flickered in the shadows, its central feature a large intricately carved wooden screen. Stuck all over it were red and yellow paper charms, some bearing incantations written in florid calligraphy, others containing swallow ashes with replicas of the bird drawn on the paper. Dozens of hooded candles had been burned in front of the screen in tin and clay holders, and the remains of incense sticks lay in front of it like crumbled brown leaves.

There were fresh candles burning, quite a few of them, so they were able to get a good look at the figure seated in front of the shrine. It was a man in a black brocaded gown, the gown open on his chest and tummy. He was incredibly old and very fat, his flesh falling around him in layers as if he were made of wax and melting in a hot sun. He was totally bald yet even his scalp was wrinkled, and his face was concertinaed in rolls of skin so that the features were almost lost. The eyes weren't there at all, and the mouth could have been any one of a hundred lines.

They went towards him, still tiptoeing, and it was a moment before Wasey spoke.

"Where are Faraday's flowers?"

Thirty seconds went by, then Wasey repeated the question.

When an answer finally came from that crushed-paper-bag face it was in a voice like a slow wind moaning through wires.

"Mei Gan will lead you to them."

"Who is Mei Gan? Where can I find him?"

"Mei Gan mimicked the last phoenix."

"What do you mean? Where can I find Mei Gan?"

The old man coughed; it sounded like dead things rubbing together.

"Who is Mei Gan? Who sent you?" Wasey asked.

The seated man could have been made of stone.

Wasey took Miss Tatlock's arm, guided her down the stairs to the floor below, where she burst out with questions.

"He said someone named Mei Gan would lead us to the flowers," Wasey answered.

Miss Tatlock was bubbling with excitement. "I knew somebody would help us. How do we find this person?"

"I think that's going to be the hard part. I asked him who Mei Gan was and he gave me some kind of riddle. He said Mei Gan mimicked the last phoenix. That's all I could get out of him."

"Does that make any sense to you?"

"Not at first blush."

"Why give us a riddle at all? If someone wants to help us, as they clearly do, why not tell us straight out?"

Wasey moved her towards the steps and they talked as they descended. "The Chinese will do that, they can drive you crazy. They love games and riddles and puzzles. Whoever sent that old man wants us to earn our information."

"Then I suppose the first step is to find someone named Mei Gan who knew Faraday."

"We can ask around but it'll be a long shot. It's a pretty common name. I think our best bet would be to start with the riddle."

They didn't say anything further till they were out in the open air and crossing the courtyard.

Wasey said, "The last phoenix sounds like something from the legends. We need a Chinese scholar. Or at least access to some pretty heavy reference."

"If we could find a library open you could check the Chinese encyclopedia."

Wasey had his hand on the cab door. He stopped with it half open. "We don't need a library. I know where we can find a Chinese scholar. And a Chinese encyclopedia."

He ushered Miss Tatlock into the taxi and said, "Tehai, take us to Pig Alley. And drive like a bullet."

The big cab blundered through the tight streets, passed the Japanese checkpoint, joined the traffic on the Honan Road, and, at maximum revs, howled down the boulevard at better than twenty miles an hour.

In the rear seat Wasey knew that, sooner or later, he had some explaining to do about their destination, and chose to take the bull by the horns. "Um, Miss Tatlock. You know I've been seeing this woman who works for Miss Beulah. The one who lives at the old amusement park . . ."

"What about her?" The ice was tinkling again.

"She likes china dolls. She collects them. That's how she got her name, China Doll."

"How quaint."

"The first night I went to see her Tuttle took me to this place we're going to now. To buy her a doll."

"Why on earth do you think I'd be interested in knowing that?"

"Just that if we want to hold on to Miss Beulah as a possible source of information, I have to see China Doll one more time. Tuttle told us that tonight. So as a way of getting a favor from this scholar we're going to see, who runs an antique shop, I'm going to have to buy her another doll."

Miss Tatlock's mouth was the thinnest of thin lines. "It's no concern of mine, Mr. Wasey. I certainly won't be footing the bill."

Wasey, who'd been counting on her paying, said, "Of course not. I just wanted to put you in the picture, that's all."

Te-hai knew the street well enough and pulled up outside the window Wasey pointed to. Wasey escorted Miss Tatlock inside the shop, where the old dealer was haggling with a customer, a broken-nose type who could have been on his way to a costume party dressed as an American gangster. The man turned away at their approach, disassociating himself from the Shen Yeh statuette on the counter, a sure tip-off that the old dealer also handled stolen goods.

The shop owner recognized Wasey and greeted him in his excellent English. "Young sir, you are welcome once again. And you too, young mistress. You will take tea?"

"Thank you, Feng, another time. This evening we must bargain quickly."

170

"The briefest are always the fairest."

"Agreed. So I make my offer only once. Twenty-one dollars for the emperor doll."

"Sold," said Feng instantly, letting Wasey know he'd offered too much.

"I may have credit?"

"Of course. You are a friend of Mr. Tuttle."

Feng scuttled into his back room, returned a minute later with the doll, and said exactly the wrong thing. "It is for the young mistress?"

"No, it is *not*," said Miss Tatlock.

Wasey could have throttled him. "It's for China Doll," he said bravely.

"Ah!" Feng said. "It is not fully completed, as you can see. However, I think she will be well pleased." He packaged the doll and laid it carefully on the counter along with something small wrapped in cloth.

"The stones for the cloak and headdress."

Wasey pocketed them and took the doll.

Feng smiled and looked naughty. "And now perhaps a gift for your *mei mei?*"

"I am *not* his *mei mei*," Miss Tatlock declared.

"Oh, come on, Miss Tatlock," Wasey said, "let me buy you something." He turned to Feng. "What do you have for fifty cents?"

"Mr. Wasey. I suggest we get to—"

Wasey cut her off with a surrender sign and addressed the shop owner again. "Feng, I would like to ask you a question."

"I would be honored."

"What can you tell us about the phoenix in Chinese legend?"

"An animal we accord every benevolent quality. It was only supposed to appear during times of peace and during the reign of a just and good emperor."

"How about the last phoenix? What did the last phoenix do?"

Feng, testing his memory, stroked his thin, wispy mustache. His black mandarin hat bobbed as he reached under the counter and brought out the shoe-box-shaped encyclopedia. He found a page in the fat book, adjusted his wire-rimmed glasses, and strained to read in the dim light. "The first phoenix appeared during the reign of Huang Ti, the Yellow Emperor, the doll you have just bought. It showed itself again"—he paused to convert the date—"over two thousand years before Christ when two of them nested in Yao's palace." He ran a finger down the entry and continued reading. "The next time it was recorded was during the Han. Then it was seen off and on for fifteen hundred years until"—his voice picked up—"until it was seen for the last time when it scratched at the grave of Hung Wu, the first emperor of the Ming."

Miss Tatlock was looking at Wasey. "So the last phoenix scratched at an emperor's grave. Does that help us?"

Wasey said, "Feng, we're looking for a person who we've been told mimicked the last phoenix. The name is Mei Gan. Do you know a Mei Gan who"—Wasey shrugged—"scratched at a grave?"

"Mei Gan . . . Mei Gan . . ." Feng worried the name on his tongue. Then he called to the broken-nosed heavy, who had wandered to another part of the shop. "Sir, perhaps you could help us," he said in Shanghai dialect. "This gentleman and lady are looking for a person named Mei Gan."

The man mooched over, glanced suspiciously at Wasey, then spoke in street slang. "Who is this guy?" he said to Feng.

He got a small shock when Wasey answered him in the same language.

"The Mei Gan I'm looking for probably knew Walter Faraday."

"He a Westerner, like you?"

"With a name like Mei Gan?"

"Meegan," the man said. "I think you're looking for Meegan, not Mei Gan."

172

Wasey thought about it; the old man in the pagoda had been awfully hard to understand. Maybe he *had* said Meegan.

"Would this Meegan have known Faraday?"

The padded shoulders of the man's chalk-striped suit rose and fell. "Maybe. This Meegan guy, he don't exactly collect for the church."

Wasey found out from the man what Meegan looked like and where he could find him, said goodbye to Feng, picked up the doll, and hurried Miss Tatlock out of the shop. He waited till they were in the cab and moving before he translated the conversation.

"It sounds right," Miss Tatlock said. She spoke quickly, excited again. "Mei Gan and Meegan are very close. And if this Meegan has something to do with graves—" She stopped and clapped her hands together. "Gravedigger. He scratches at a grave. He's a gravedigger."

"That's not bad," Wasey said. "Miss Tatlock, I think you've solved it."

The taxi joined the jam of traffic on the Szechuan Road, a bustling avenue ablaze with the lights of twenty-four-hour shops and stores and huge neon signs that carved bright-colored chunks out of the night sky. The address Wasey had been given was a cafeteria. It was easy to find, being right next door to a movie house called the Grand, an ornate picture palace whose marquee flashed Clark Gable's name every few seconds.

Helping Miss Tatlock out of the cab, Wasey said, "According to Broken Nose, Meegan conducts his business at a table inside. Now the trick is to spot him."

It wasn't as hard as Wasey thought. The cafeteria was busy, all harsh lighting and dish clatter, but at one table against the wall a man sat by himself with a newspaper and a pencil in his hand. He was the only person in the place who wasn't eating.

"Mr. Meegan?"

"Yeah, that's me."

173

"We were told we might find you here."

"Yeah? Who tolja?"

"A man with a mashed nose. Chinese. Chalk-striped suit. Peddles hot antiques."

"Sounds like Chen Ya. He's a mate a mine."

Meegan had a strong Australian accent that strung the words out in the wrong places. He was about forty, short and stringy with a bouncy, birdlike quality to him, his face creased and tanned the color of light tobacco.

"May we join you?"

"Go ahead. It's a free country." He put his paper down and checked over Miss Tatlock. "You with the Sally Ann, miss?"

"I'm with the Door of Hope."

"They got a band?"

"No."

"I like a band," Meegan said. "All them tangerines bangin' away." His hair was roached back in glistening furrows. When he ran his hand through it the smell of old brilliantine rose in the air. "So. What can I do yer for?"

"Did you know a man named Walter Faraday?"

"Know 'im? I'm wearin' his socks." Meegan's laugh showed uneven stained teeth. "Sure I knew 'im. Real bludger he was, too."

"We're looking for something he used to own."

"Like what?" Meegan used the eraser end of his pencil to scratch at his neck.

"His flowers," Wasey said.

The pencil stopped moving. Meegan slowly stuck it behind his ear. "How about some tucker?" he asked. "Dunno about you, but I'm famished. You like Chink food?"

"You go ahead."

Wasey's answer was covered by a sudden shouting that had resulted from the kitchen doors bursting open. Several young girls carrying covered silver trays, deep heavy trays supported by straps around the neck, fanned out into the restaurant. As each called out the contents of her own

174

particular tray, she was answered by a horde of hungry diners calling for their favorite dish.

Meegan was halfway out of his chair, throwing his arm in the air like a schoolboy. *"Tsungtse! Tsungtse!"* he cried, then sat back with a happy grin as one of the girls stopped by their table and plonked down two plates of glutinous rice dumplings. A waiter arrived, paused to set down chopsticks and a teapot, then flew off. Meegan snatched up his chopsticks, picked up the bowl, and expertly flicked a dumpling into his mouth. He said through a mouthful, "Why arsk me?"

"We were told you might know."

Miss Tatlock spoke. "Mr. Meegan, are you, by any chance, in the funeral business?"

"Why?"

"Because we're not entirely sure you're the person we should be talking to. According to our information, the person we want has something to do with graves."

Meegan poured tea, swallowed it, then attacked his bowl again. "If you're lookin' for the flowers, you got the right joker."

Wasey and Miss Tatlock traded looks.

"You can tell us where they are?" Wasey asked.

"Yeah. But I'm not goin' to."

The shouting started once more, and without missing a beat Meegan cried out, *"Chiaotse! Chiaotse!"*

One of the girls, back from the kitchen again, flipped up the lid of her steaming tray and put down two more plates. Meegan spoke to her in rapid Shanghai, his accent crunching the tones and making him hard to understand. "Wouldn't you know it," he said to Wasey, "it's off. They have a real bonzer dish here usually, lemon-steamed duck."

Miss Tatlock pressed him. "Why won't you tell us?"

"Because this is a flamin' tough town." Meegan made three syllables out of the last word, all of them through his nose. "I don't wanna go down the mine for bein' a bigmouth." His chopsticks flew as he gobbled more food.

175

"Tell ya what I'll do, though. I'll give ya a name of a bloke. Although he ain't really a bloke, he's a Chink. But he's on good terms with the gangs, and I'll betcha me boots he knows where the flowers are. In fact, he knows bloody well where they are. If ya arsked him nice, and threw a bit of squeeze around, he'd be a moral to tell ya. Then it'd be up to you to get 'em."

"We'll settle for that," Miss Tatlock said.

Still chewing, Meegan took the pencil from behind his ear, tore off a piece of newspaper, and wrote on it. He passed it to Wasey.

"Wan-li's his name. Runs a card room. Tell him I sent ya soon as you get there. You'll hafta play a few hands, a course, so watch yerself, because Li's liable to ring in a crook pack a cards on ya. In fact"—Meegan took back the piece of paper and scribbled on it again—"better take yer own pack. He's gotta accept it, it's the law. I'll give ya a shop that's on yer way. Mention me name and they'll sell ya a good American pack."

Wasey took the piece of paper and stood, Miss Tatlock doing the same.

"Mr. Meegan," she said, "I still don't understand why our informant referred to you as, well, as I understand it, a gravedigger."

Meegan drank from his teacup, then thumped his chest. His cheeks puffed as he belched softly. "I'm a bit sensitive about that. I've gone part shares in a graveyard up in Chapei. I reckon that makes me a gravedigger, in a way."

Miss Tatlock started a reply, but the kitchen doors burst open again and the Australian jumped to his feet and loudly competed for dumplings.

Wasey maneuvered her out of the cafeteria and onto the sidewalk. "My, how the game has changed," he said. "When we started off, nobody knew where the flowers were. Now, everybody knows where they are."

Te-hai opened the cab door for them, and Miss Tatlock, settling into the rear seat, said, "That's because we stuck at it. I knew it would happen if we did."

Wasey passed Meegan's piece of paper to Te-hai, who found the first address a few blocks away. It was a small grocery that also sold engine oil, cosmetics, and fencing wire. When Wasey mentioned Meegan's name and asked for a deck of cards, the owner produced a crisp new Bicycle-brand poker deck, hard to get in China.

Wasey got back into the cab and Te-hai drove to the second address, down in Nantao, the Chinese section south of the Old City.

They could hardly believe the place they pulled up outside, but they knew the moment they saw it that their search was over. It had a floridly carved doorway painted in crimson and gold with rivers of electric light flowing the length and breadth of its gaudy façade. It was as bright and cheerful as a penny arcade and appeared to promise heaven.

They were still in the cab at the curb yet the cloying scent reached them. Wasey put both their thoughts into words. "An opium hong. The first place you'd think of and the last place you'd look."

Miss Tatlock was still a little stunned. "It just never occurred to me."

They got out. It had stopped raining and the night was warm. Wasey took off his topcoat and tossed it onto the back seat.

"Now that you've found the flowers," he said, "how will you get them?"

"Mr. Burns and I will buy them. The money will come from the two organizations."

"So it's the end of the line. You and Burns get your morphine and I get my ticket to L.A."

"Yes," Miss Tatlock said. For someone who'd reached her goal Wasey thought she sounded curiously flat.

They moved toward the entrance. The thick, sweet smell went up their nostrils and they coughed as they went through the throbbing pink door. There was a man behind a counter with a row of pipe stems in front of him, an open wooden chest, and some balance scales to the side. They moved by him into a long room, dim and cheerless, shrouded in smoke. A double tier of bunks lined each side with one or two men in each section sitting or lying on torn straw mattresses, the pipe stems in their mouths inserted into long rubber hoses. The hoses were connected to fat bottles bubbling over clay stoves on the stone floor.

At one end of the room was the second-class section for people too poor to rent a bunk and apparatus. There a man lay on his side on a bunch of rags clutching a pipe in a hand like a thin winter branch. A teenage girl, perhaps his daughter, was hovering over an alcohol burner pouring black powder into the bottom half of an English tobacco tin. She took a metal wire and dipped one end of it into the tin, twirling it slowly so as to collect a blob of the powder. She did this again, over the flame this time, but quickly enough to prevent the ball of opium from catching fire. She placed the glowing ball in the metal bowl of the man's pipe. The man sucked at the stem deeply, his thin chest swelling twice, then he faded away into the black rice dream.

Miss Tatlock, depressed and upset by the place, hurriedly followed Wasey in the other direction towards a door in the far wall.

Wasey rapped on it—it was steel painted to look like wood—and it was opened by a man who filled the hallway behind him. He was massive, a mountain of flesh, perhaps six and a half feet high, and with a huge tummy and fat sloping shoulders. In his gown and sandals he reminded Wasey of the photograph he'd seen of the old palace eunuchs.

"We are friends of Meegan," Wasey said. "We are welcome?"

The giant nodded, stepped back to let them pass, then preceded them down the hall. As they followed, Wasey said to Miss Tatlock, "If we get into a fight, you take him."

They came into a room lit by a single shaded bulb hanging from the ceiling. It illuminated the green baize of a circular card table and three men sitting around it.

The fat giant waddled across the room to where an elegant-looking man sat in a raised chair as if he were refereeing the card game. The giant had a word in his ear, and the elegant man glanced briefly at the newcomers, then went back to watching the game. The two other men at the table were a dealer, lean and hatchet-faced in a frogged silk jacket and quilted pants, and a business type in a suit who looked worried.

There was a single card on the table, a joker. Outside each corner of the card, painted on the green cloth tabletop, was a Chinese character. The businessman picked up some money and put it down against the character at the top right of the joker.

"Fan-tan," Wasey told Miss Tatlock. They stood a few feet from the table and talked in whispers. "Each of those characters is a number, one, two, three, four. You put your money against one of the numbers. The dealer cuts the deck, then deals out the cut four cards at a time. Whatever he's left with is the winning number."

"I don't quite understand," Miss Tatlock said.

"Say there are twenty-two cards in the cut. The dealer counts them into groups of four. Five fours are twenty. That leaves two cards over. If your money's on number two, you win."

"So it all depends on the number of cards in the cut."

"Right. And the dealer's controlling that. That's why the guy in the suit is losing."

"He's being cheated?"

"Sure. He should know he's in a crooked game by the way the dealer holds the cards. See? Flat in the palm of his hand. The sharper's grip. That way he can deal bottoms and seconds so you'd never know. But that doesn't help him in fan-tan."

"Then what is he doing?"

"Watch."

With the deck sitting in front of him the dealer turned his face away and cut them with his right hand about two thirds of the way down. He dealt them like bullets into seven neat piles of four, making twenty-eight cards out. He slowed as he dealt the next four, which made thirty-two cards out. Then he dealt the remainder. There was only one.

The businessman, who'd bet on number three, thumped the table as the dealer took his money.

Miss Tatlock leaned close. "How did he do it?"

"He's using a crimped deck. The edges of the cards have tiny little nicks that act as counters. He can recognize them by touch and get the exact number of cards he wants every time he cuts."

The businessman bet again and lost, pushed his chair back in disgust, and walked out.

Wasey addressed the man in the raised chair. "You are Wan-li?"

"Indeed."

"I may sit?"

"Of course." The man moved his arm and light winked off the black sequins in his dark gown. "Your pleasure?"

"Same game."

Wasey took the bettor's chair and watched the dealer's long slim fingers gather up the cards. He put a dollar against the number four.

"I am looking for something, Li. My friend Meegan said you might do more than just point to the right direction."

The dealer cut and dealt and was left with two cards. He took Wasey's money and gathered the deck together again.

"It depends," Wan-li said, "on what you are searching for."

Miss Tatlock bent to Wasey's ear and asked what the man was saying. Wasey shushed her with a gesture, then bet another dollar.

The dealer's cut came out even this time, leaving him with no cards at all, which counted as four. Wasey had bet on number three.

"I'm looking for Faraday's flowers."

Wan-li was silent.

Wasey bet again and lost again.

"Who else knows that you have come to me?" the gambler asked. His face was hard for Wasey to see; only the raised chair and the black-beaded gown were lit by the shaded bulb. The man's head and shoulders were obscured by shadow.

"Meegan. No one else."

"You can assure me of this?"

"May my tongue rot if I lie."

The gambler seemed to be studying him from his dark position. There was a short strained moment, then he turned his head to the fat giant standing behind him. The huge man lumbered out of the room.

"Very well," Wan-li said. "I have arranged for you to see the flowers. Try your luck a few more times. Then you may view them."

"Bingo!" Wasey said to Miss Tatlock. "A few more hands and he'll show us the flowers. Give me some money."

She thrust some bills into his hand, and Wasey bet another dollar.

"More," Wan-li said.

Wasey put down ten dollars, and lost it, as he expected to. He put down a second ten.

"Why not bet twenty," Wan-li suggested, "and recoup your losses."

Wasey bet twenty and lost, as he knew he would. He

asked Miss Tatlock for more money and she handed him another twenty.

"That's all I've got with me."

Wasey lost again.

"My luck is poor, Li. I am ready to see the flowers."

"Your luck may change."

"Alas, I have nothing left to stake."

Miss Tatlock, who could see that the gambler was proving more avaricious than they'd expected, told Wasey to ask for credit.

"They never give credit. Don't you have anything left?"

She rummaged in her purse. "A few coins. That's all."

Wasey patted his jacket, which was empty except for his passport and his wallet. But he found something in his wallet he could use.

"Five more hands, Li, and then you lead us to the flowers. A bargain?"

"Six more."

"Done!" said Wasey. He passed the paper to the silent dealer, who passed it to his boss.

"A receipt," Wasey said, "for a valuable shipment of apparel currently in storage at the Whangpoo docks. I bet one sixth of it."

The man in the chair held the document under the light and scanned it. "One fifth," he said.

Wasey tapped the table to indicate agreement, then, from his back pocket, took out the deck of cards he'd bought and tossed it onto the green baize.

"A fresh deck for a fresh bet."

"What was the paper you gave him?" Miss Tatlock asked.

He filled her in and she reacted uneasily. "But it's your shipment. You can't afford to lose that."

"I don't intend to lose it. I'm going to sit on the same number. This is a fair game now, and the odds against losing on the same number five times in a row in a fair game of fan-tan are so long you can forget about it."

At the table his new deck was being greeted by a hostile silence. The dealer stripped off the cellophane wrapper, held the cards under the light, reverse side up, and riffled them, looking for markings. Then he quickly broke out the aces and the picture cards and compared their width with a three of hearts, and tested their corners for pinhole pricks.

"No need," Wasey told him. "We're going to play the same game."

The dealer fanned the cards face up on the table, tossed out the joker and the two spares, fanned them together again, and set them down with an angry thump.

Using a coin as a token, Wasey bet on number one. The dealer brushed the old deck off the table, turned his face away, cut the cards deeply, then swiftly dealt into piles of four. He ended up with two cards over.

Wasey put down another coin against the same number: one.

This time the dealer had three cards left.

Miss Tatlock sounded worried. "What's gone wrong?"

"Nothing. I'll win this time."

Wasey lost.

"Oh no. That's three fifths of your shipment gone," Miss Tatlock said.

"Relax, will you. I can't lose four times in a row."

Wasey lost again.

"Hell. I've never seen such lousy luck."

"This is terrible," Miss Tatlock said. "You've only got one bet left."

"That's okay, a win pays three to one. I'll get my whole shipment back this time. I can't lose five times straight."

The dealer raked in the cards, neatened them, turned his face for the cut, and dealt.

The deal came out even.

"Jesus Christ!" Wasey was staggered. "I just lost all my ties."

Miss Tatlock had alarm bells in her voice. "You have to bet one more time. Wasn't that the arrangement? Six bets before he'll tell us?"

"I *can't* bet one more time. I've got nothing left to bet with. I don't believe it," Wasey moaned. "My whole entire shipment. I've gotta get it back. You must have something we can bet."

She showed him her empty purse. "I don't have a thing. You even lost the coins I gave you." She looked at the two silent men at the table; they sat unmoving, listening to the gobbledygook of the Westerners' unfathomable tongue. "Come on, think," Miss Tatlock implored. "We're only one bet away from finding the flowers."

Wasey nervously tapped a thumbnail against his teeth. "There's got to be something. It took me three months to get that shipment set up. One more bet. One more..." He got a sudden idea. "Hold everything!"

"What is it?"

Wasey leaned forward and spoke to Wan-li, who pondered for a second, then nodded an agreement.

Wasey fell back in his chair, blew out breath. "Oh, thank God."

"What's happening? What did you say to him?"

"He accepted the bet. I wasn't sure he would."

"But what did you bet?"

"I'll tell you in a minute." Wasey nodded at the dealer, who gathered up the cards, patted them into shape, and set them down squarely.

"I bet number one again," Wasey announced.

Miss Tatlock couldn't bear it. "Mr. Wasey, what did you bet?"

"It doesn't matter. It's academic anyway. There's no possible way anyone can lose six times in a row."

Under Wasey's watchful eye the dealer turned his head, cut the deck, dealt the cards in little piles of four, and held up what he had left.

He had two.

Wasey gagged for words. "What is this, a world record? Nobody loses six times straight at this game."

"This is appalling," Miss Tatlock said. "What did you lose this time?"

Wasey didn't answer her.

"Mr. Wasey." She sounded very firm. "What did you bet?"

Wasey raised his hands in a helpless little gesture. "Miss Tatlock, I don't know how to tell you this."

"What—did—you—bet?"

Wasey examined his hands. "You."

"Pardon?" she said immediately.

"I bet you."

This time her question was a long time in coming. "What do you mean, me?"

Wasey didn't know where to look. "I asked Wan-li if he'd accept you as a bet. And he said yes."

"YOU BET *ME?*"

"It's only for one night," Wasey said defensively.

Miss Tatlock's face was a series of circles and she had trouble with her speech. "You are the most contemptible, the most despicable, the most . . ."

"I had to do it, Miss Tatlock. You want the flowers, don't you?"

"And you want your ties! That's why you did it, for those dreadful ties. Admit it!"

"Look. I can solve all this. So don't get hysterical."

"You'd *better* be able to solve it."

Wasey had a few words with Wan-li, then nodded at the dealer, who gathered in the cards.

"It's okay," Wasey told her. "I've made another bet."

He thought that steam might come out of her ears.

"Mis-ter Wasey! What have you bet this time?"

"What's it matter? There's no earthly way I can lose seven times in a row."

The dealer cut, dealt, and was left with three cards.

Wasey slapped a hand to his brow. "It's not happening.

It can't be. This is a mathematical phenomenon. The odds against this are astronomical."

Miss Tatlock took several deep breaths and said, as evenly as she could, "What did you bet him?"

Wasey mumbled the words, but she heard him only too clearly: "Double or nothing."

Miss Tatlock looked as if she'd jammed her thumb in a door and was holding in a scream. "I don't care what you do," she said from the back of her throat, "or how you do it. Just get me out of this mess."

Wasey forced himself to concentrate. He knew he couldn't bet his way out of it; his luck was atrocious anyway. The only thing he could do was talk his way out of it.

"Wan-li. I have something to tell you." Wasey picked at his nails and looked sheepish. "I feel badly. You have kindly consented to guide me to the flowers. You are doing me a favor, and in return I am afraid I have not done you one."

"Explain, please."

Wasey's head sank a little lower. "The apparel that I wagered. It is not gowns. It is not jackets. It is not even slippers."

"What is it?"

"It is seventy gross of neckties."

"Neckties?" Wan-li was dismayed.

Wasey made a full confession. "Hand-painted. They glow in the dark."

Wan-li was horrified. "I cannot sell neckties in Shang-hai."

"I know," Wasey said.

"The stake is worthless." Wan-li tossed him back the receipt. "You have deceived me."

"I deserve death. Double death. For the second stake is faulty, too."

"Your *mei mei?*"

186

Mortified, Wasey confirmed it.

"What is wrong with her?"

"She wears false breasts."

"It is of no importance. There is no delight for me in the breasts of a woman."

"Oh."

"It is the cheeks of the buttocks that pleasure me."

"Alas, Wan-li." Wasey bit his lip. "These are false, too."

The gambler half rose from his chair; never in his life had he heard such a thing. "False buttocks?"

"Her figure is as flat as an ink stone. She had buttressed herself with foam rubber in all departments."

Wan-li was astounded, and not pleased. "Then this, too, is worthless."

Wasey wrung his hands. "I beseech you. Think of a way I may make redress."

"You must bet again."

"*Again?*" Wasey said it in English. He slipped back into dialect. "But I have nothing left to stake."

"You may stake your clothes," the gambler said.

Wasey smote his brow in genuine revelation. "My suit!" He turned to Miss Tatlock. "What an idiot! I could've bet my suit all along and I never thought of it."

"Forget your suit. What have you done about me?"

"You're off the hook. I got my shipment back, too. So at least we'll only be out the money we lost."

Wasey agreed to Wan-li's proposal, and nodded at the dealer to begin. "Number one," he announced.

This time the dealer slowed the action. He slowly gathered in the cards and patted them together, slowly turned his face away, slowly cut, slowly dealt, and slowly counted out the three he was left with.

"Oh no," said Miss Tatlock.

Wasey was beyond speech. He counted the little piles of four. They were all correct, seven piles, four cards each, twenty-eight cards out. Three in the dealer's hand made thirty-one. That meant there should be twenty-one cards in the rest of the deck. He counted it. There were twenty-one cards.

Like a zombie, he rose and began to take off his jacket. "Eight times straight," he breathed. "Un-bloody-believable."

He put the jacket on the table, retrieved his passport and his empty wallet, and, with little hope in his voice, said to Wan-li, "I may keep the pants?"

The gambler replied in the negative.

Wasey took off the pants, added them to the jacket.

"Now the shoes," Wan-li said.

"One moment. I only bet my suit."

"The wager was for your clothes. The shoes, please. If they are tight, Chao will be honored to assist you."

The fat giant, who'd come back into the room a few minutes before, took a half step forward.

Wasey, not wanting to have his feet taken off along with the shoes, slipped out of the moccasins and put them on the table. He said sarcastically, "You would like the socks?"

"And the shirt and tie."

Wasey looked at the fat giant, placidly standing there ready to break his arms, and took off his shirt and tie. And his socks.

"Now, about the flowers," Wasey began.

"First let us conclude this transaction," the gambler replied. "The little trousers, please."

"Surely not those. Wan-li, leave me something."

"Very well, you may keep the tie."

"Whatever is going on?" Miss Tatlock asked.

"Nothing's going *on*, Miss Tatlock. Look the other way."

Wasey added his shorts to the pile of clothes.

"This is extremely embarrassing," Miss Tatlock said.

Wasey faced the gambler, determined to get his end of the bargain. "Now, Wan-li. The flowers."

"Chao will take you to them."

The fact that Wasey was naked suddenly didn't matter

anymore; the overriding thought of the flowers gripped them both and made their humiliating situation superfluous.

The fat giant waddled over to the far wall, which was covered with a heavy curtain. He beckoned to them and they crossed to him. He slid back the curtain and revealed a door, which he partly opened. A wisp of air came to them, of a different temperature and smell. It was dank and garbagy, as if it had been locked up for a long time; the kind of smell, Wasey thought with a quickness in his pulse, that you might get in an underground storeroom.

The huge man waved them on, and they went together to the door. They pushed it open and went through into darkness.

There were three steps, which they could barely see, then the door closed behind them with a metallic chunk.

They stopped and waited for their eyes to adjust and, a second later, they saw where they were.

It wasn't a storeroom as Wasey had suspected. The air he'd felt was outside air, and the smell came from rotting fruit rinds and fish bones.

They were out in an alley.

But there were flowers.

Straight ahead of them, perched on top of an overturned oil drum, was a tin can holding a bunch of withered daisies.

Wasey stared at them. Miss Tatlock stared at them. Then they took in the alley and the steel door tightly closed behind them.

"Miss Tatlock..." Wasey didn't have much volume, and he sounded ill. "I think we've been had."

12

Meegan rushed at him, his ratlike face drawn back in a wolfish snarl. He feinted a punch then brought his shoe up in a vicious kick aimed at Wasey's groin, but Wasey had expected that. With superb timing he jumped back, grabbed Meegan's foot, spun him sideways, and dug a hard left into the little rat's solar plexus. As the little bastard whooshed out air Wasey crossed with a beautiful right, the full power of his shoulder behind it. It caught Meegan flush on the jaw, lifting the rotten grifter clear off his feet and sending him sprawling in a tangled heap, out for the count.

Wasey socked the pillow of his hotel bed and, for the umpteenth time, cursed himself for not seeing it sooner. He hadn't had the slightest inkling till he'd found himself out in the alley looking at the fish bones.

Then he'd understood everything.

Meegan wasn't Mei Gan; the broken-nosed heavy in the doll dealer's shop had innocently jumped to the wrong conclusion. But Meegan, the little toad, had grabbed his chance with both his dirty little hands once he'd discovered they they'd mistaken him for somebody else.

He didn't know anything about the flowers. He'd probably never even met Faraday, but he'd lied in his teeth and steered them to the fan-tan game, for which he would no doubt get a fat 20 or 30 percent commission. And the sonofabitch had made certain of a big win by sending him to buy a new deck from the owner of that little grocery store, with whom Meegan clearly had an arrangement.

Wasey socked the pillow again. The new deck had been new all right, but it had been unwrapped, crimped, rewrapped, and resealed before he'd bought it.

The hell of it was, he knew it would be pointless going back to the cafeteria in the hope of nailing the guy; the bastard would be doing business somewhere else for the next few weeks.

He got off the bed, hitched up his pajama bottoms, went to the open wardrobe, and examined himself in the full-length mirror.

"Hello, sucker," he said. He moodily checked his bandaged arm. At least that was one bright spot, it felt fine and wasn't even stiff. Miss Tatlock had done a good job on it.

Miss Tatlock . . .

Boy, she'd been crushed. She'd thought she'd practically had the damn flowers in her grasp. Her disappointment had made her all the more mad at him for losing fifty-four American dollars. And as for using her as a betting chip, she was never going to forgive him for that.

He looked gloomily at the cheap suit hanging in the empty wardrobe. They'd bought it on credit at a cut-rate all-night men's store, and it looked it: the lapels might have been tailored with a bread knife. And the shoes weren't much better. They called those brogues? They looked like a riveter had made them.

Wasey mooched over to the window to see what the day was like. It was pleasantly warm again, although the air seemed nervous and there'd be more rain sooner or later.

A quick movement caught his eye high up against the clouds; a flight of wild geese bursting through the sky.

"Wild geese, wild geese," Wasey chanted in dialect, "make us a man." He smiled, remembering how they'd say that when they were kids. They'd watch as the birds would change their formation from a horizontal line to a dignified vee, the same shape as the character *jen*, the word for man.

They'd been good days, his childhood in Shanghai. A lot better than the ones he was having now. But the sight of the geese had cheered him and he threw on a pair of pants and a shirt and went downstairs to the lobby to call Tuttle's office.

"John? Glen Wasey."

"Hi, there. What's up?"

"You know a guy named Meegan? An Aussie?"

"Sure. Stay away from him."

"I could've used that advice last night. The bastard steered me to a fan-tan game run by a charmer named Wan-li."

"Oh God! That game's as rigged as a clipper ship. Did he take you to the cleaner's?"

"I didn't have anything left to take to the cleaner's."

"How did you get mixed up with a chiseler like Meegan?"

"Case of mistaken identity. We got a tip that someone named Mei Gan could help us. Does that name ring a bell?"

"Not a very loud one. Mei Gan..." Tuttle played with the name. "Hey, you know, maybe it does. I've got an idea that Mei Gan was one of the warlords who threw in with Chiang. Chiang made him a general."

"When was this?"

"About ten years back—1930, '31, something like that."

"He's still on the scene?"

"Far as I know. He's an ex-gambler with a private army. And"—Tuttle's delivery quickened—"wait, you may be on to something. I think he also peddles opium."

"That part fits," Wasey said. "But the warlord part doesn't. The guy we're after is some kind of gravedigger. Something to do with cemeteries, anyway."

"Have you checked the records at the Council?"

"Miss Tatlock's doing that this afternoon."

"I'll check our files here and get back to you this evening. It sounds like things are starting to come together, Glen."

"Maybe. I'll talk to you later. And thanks for your help."

Wasey hung up and considered what Tuttle had told him. Most of Chiang Kai-shek's generals peddled opium, so that was no big pointer. And he'd be in Chungking anyway, with the rest of Chiang's officers, while it was ten to one that the man they were looking for lived in Shanghai.

Wasey wondered if finding out about Mei Gan, whoever he was, qualified as a lead. Burns had said that a lead would get him his ticket to L.A. But he'd also run up some bills; he owed Sing Sing for the gun and the grenade, he owed old Feng for the emperor doll, he owed Miss Beulah, although that expense was being incurred in the line of duty. Burns would pay that, and he'd probably pay the other two debts if he could track down this Mei Gan character. But debts or no debts, he wasn't going into any more midnight pagodas or gambling dens. No more adventures, and that was final!

Feeling as if he'd decided something important, Wasey went back upstairs, dressed, left the hotel, and spent a footslogging afternoon touring the various benevolent societies checking their records for Mei Gans. Nothing he came up with looked promising; there were no gravediggers or funeral arrangers or Mei Gans whose jobs suggested anything to do with illegal opium.

He got a rickshaw back to the hotel and was relieved to find that Miss Tatlock wasn't waiting for him. He didn't need the frosty reprimand that would have been his once she learned how he planned to spend his evening. What he did need was some rest and recreation, warmth, understanding, appreciation, consideration, and lots of tender loving care. And booze. He showered, picked up the doll he'd bought the night before, and left the hotel quickly.

He went first to the movies, seeking mindless relaxation, and watched Johnny Weissmuller wrestle a crocodile. He could sympathize with the guy; Faraday's flowers was a crocodile he'd been wrestling for the last five days. With just as many teeth snapping at him and just as much danger of being drowned.

The second feature had Deanna Durbin playing a singing Austrian pastry chef. Wasey left in the middle of a high

C and went for a drink. After that he dropped into a teahouse for some steamed mutton pies, hot fruit fritters, and plum flower wine. Then, with his recent humiliation pushed to the back of his brain, and feeling a bit happier about the world, he found a taxi that looked good for a few more miles, and went out to the Great World Amusement Park.

As he walked through the ruins under the dim bulbs strung over the path, he felt a twinge of fear. He wondered about the possible ramifications of his inquiries about Mei Gan, and the gangs' reaction to it, if any. But after riding the little boat through the River Caves it fled his mind when he saw the maid on the landing.

She greeted him and conducted him through the hall. He refused the waiting bath, accepting just the robe, then went into the main room. He realized how much he enjoyed coming back there: the charming boat ride, the candlelit welcome, and this room with the marvelous rug and the silver-bird walls, and the shining dolls in the bamboo cabinet.

But for Wasey it was all reduced to mere prettiness when China Doll entered. She looked ravishing.

Her gown was the palest of blues with two yellow storks so cleverly embroidered on it that as she glided towards him the storks appeared to be dancing round her. She had her hair lifted off her lovely neck and swept in curving rolls behind her ears in the Soochow fashion. A fine line of charcoal continued the slight slant of her eyes, and her lips had been touched with pink, fleshing their full roundness. As before, she wore the three jade fingernail protectors but no rings, no bracelets, no necklaces. She was her own stunning ornament.

"Way-see," she said in her deep, soft voice.

Wordlessly he handed her his gift, which she took and unwrapped.

"Ah." She ran her fingers over the doll's layered silk gown, then lifted her marvelous eyes to his face. "The

Yellow Emperor. Thank you."

Wasey searched his jacket. "I am a fool. There are stones for his cloak but I have left them behind."

"Perhaps next time," China Doll murmured.

Wasey doubted there would be a next time, but he said nothing.

China Doll opened the bamboo cabinet. "He will stand between Yehonala and Hsiang Fei, the Neglected Concubine." She put the new addition between a doll in a brocaded pink gown and the magnificent empress.

Wasey gazed at the new arrangement. "Neglected? By whom?"

"By the Prince of Wei, whose harem she lived in. She remained unvisited by him all her life. When Li Po heard of her plight he dashed his drunken face with cold water and seized a brush."

"Li Po?"

"One of the Eight Immortals of the Wine Cup." China Doll closed the cabinet door, then said softly, " 'The wind blows and the dust, tomorrow he swears he will come. His words are kind, but he breaks his trust. My heart is numb. All day the wind blew strong, the sun was buried deep. I have thought of him so long, so long, I cannot sleep.' "

She'd recited the poem simply, unselfconsciously, yet Wasey was astonished by the feeling she'd put into it. He knew she hadn't just been reading emotion into it, it was actually how she felt: China Doll also waited in vain for the call to the emperor's bed.

And right then he remembered where he'd heard the name Yehonala before. It had been she who'd mentioned it when he'd first seen the empress doll.

"Who was Yehonala?"

"Tzu Hsi."

"The Dowager Empress?"

"Yes."

"You were her?"

Ever so slightly China Doll moved her head.

Wasey understood now, it explained everything about her; she was trying to duplicate the life she thought she'd lived before. Hadn't she told him that Tzu Hsi had been a concubine before becoming the emperor's wife? That's why she was fascinated with the past. And it was another reason why she lived in this weird and wonderful place with its scenes of a China long gone.

The woman was aware of the effect her revelation had had on Wasey, and she moved to assuage it. She rose gracefully and went to him. "Come," she said.

Wasey followed her across the room. She picked up a candle and lit the way down the hall to the landing, Wasey wondering where she was taking him. But he understood a little while later when they were drifting through the blackness, floating by the perfect displays that flared up in silent greeting. She was sharing her world with him, letting him into her other life, and he was flattered and complimented by the gesture.

They sat together, the little boat moving them gently along. For Wasey the displays had never been so charming. They twinkled and glittered hypnotically, and he saw secret figures and hidden details that had escaped him before.

A bit timidly, he asked her a question. "How well do you recall your previous existence?"

The answer was immediate. "As if it were yesterday."

"What do you remember most?"

"Peking, the Violet Enclosure. And my Sea Palace in the western sector. I remember long summer nights boating on the Pei Hai, the loveliest of the three lakes, and the temples built on its islands, the Little Western Heaven, the Temple of the Two Bronze Pagodas. I remember the hissing sound the water lilies made as our boats glided by them, and the moon on the water, a moon so full you could see the hare that lives in it pounding out the drugs of immortality. I remember the little theater I ordered built for the Flower Drum Song plays. And my Throne Hall of

196

Kindliness and Tranquillity. And my collection of clocks and dolls and yapping lion dogs, lively little things with black faces and ears like the sails of a war junk.

"I remember my jewels and my beautiful gowns, my eunuchs, my son, my emperor, my ladies-in-waiting.

"And I remember my death with my face to the south, as custom decreed, and my mouth wide open."

The darkness was absolute.

The boat bumped against something in the stream.

A spirit grotto sprang into twinkling life, the soft illumination playing on the molded curves of China Doll's face.

He stared into her eyes, fairy lights reflected in their dark rich depths, then the blackness snapped back in again, and they drifted on.

The boat nudged through the doors into the bleak, colored glow that marked the start of the caves. The scoops of the waterwheel rose and fell in a lazy continuous arc, its slapping plunge following them as the boat took them through the entrance doors and on through the first half of the ride back to the landing.

They left the boat and went down the hallway together, across the main room and through the other door.

The painted dragons above the bed were shimmering in the light of a single lamp left burning. The flame on the short wick sent long snaking shadows that writhed on China Doll's body.

Her mouth opened like a perfumed flower, and her arms went around him, her pelvis moving into him with gentle pressure. Wasey was so weak-kneed he had to reach for the bed.

She introduced him to something called the Obedient Wife. She was passive, yielding, letting him take charge; responding in tiny thrilling ways—everything contained, warm, slow.

She didn't leave him straightaway; she stayed and showed him the Setting Sun ritual, an intimate regimen of hand

and mouth caresses that began at the pulse in the wrists, traveled slowly along the arms to the neck, then down the body to the scoop beneath the anklebone.

It was a while before Wasey could speak; she'd drained him, dazed him, emptied his brain. So when he did begin talking, some kind of mindless reflex made him ask her the question he'd been asking so many other people the past few days.

"Did you ever hear of a man named Walter Faraday?"

He got a mild shock; he felt her tense. In the three times he'd been with her it was the first involuntary reaction he'd known her to make. Realizing that she'd already answered with her body, she confirmed the query.

Wasey didn't have to ask the obvious question; there was something in her manner that told him that Faraday had been a client. Which was a little more than a mild shock.

"Since I came to Shanghai," he said, "I've been looking for something that belonged to him."

There was no answer.

"Did he ever talk of opium poppies? A great number?"

"No."

A one-word answer, yet it had been a long time coming. Her face was in shadow, hard to see in the flicker of the single lamp, but Wasey felt that her eyes were on him.

"I have looked all over the city. I cannot find them. Someone named Mei Gan might know, but I cannot find Mei Gan."

China Doll raised herself on one elbow, and this time he could see her studying his face. It was almost as if she was waiting for something to appear there—words, perhaps, that she could recognize and read out loud.

"He left me something," she said, "to look after. Of great value." Wasey was coming up from his supine position but her hand stayed him. "What he asked me to keep has nothing to do with opium."

He would have questioned her further but he knew it

would have been pointless. Whatever if was Faraday had left in her safekeeping was no business of his. And if she did know anything about Faraday's opium racket, she hadn't chosen to volunteer the information.

Five minutes passed during which they said nothing, then she kissed his cheek with her hand and slipped from the bed. She drew a quilted satin coverlet up to his chin, and padded silently out of the room.

Wasey gave it five minutes, then got up and went into the tub room, dressed quickly, took a candle down the hallway, and for the third time that night rode the little boat.

Clouds had covered the stars when he came out into the park, and the night was almost as dark as it had been in the caves.

He let himself out the gate and walked the silent, unlit streets for several blocks.

A car cruised up behind him.

Wasey fumbled the gun box out of his pocket and was tearing off the lid when he saw that the car was a taxi. The driver, no more than fourteen, sat on a sofa cushion and had a pet chicken beside him.

Wasey closed up the box, got in, and told the boy where he wanted to go.

All the way back to the hotel he thought about China Doll and Faraday.

13

"Mr. Wasey, wake up!"

Being shaken as he was, Wasey could hardly do anything else. He rolled over and blinked up at his tormentor. "Miss Tatlock, you spend more time in this room than I do."

"Get up, Mr. Wasey. Come on."

Wasey pushed himself to a sitting position. "I thought I locked the door last night."

"The desk clerk let me in. Do you know what time it is?"

"Two A.M.?"

"It's ten-thirty, and you have an important message from Mr. Tuttle."

Wasey got out of bed like a badly injured man.

"Where are you going now?"

"To take a shower. You can watch if you like."

He came back into the room fifteen minutes later, dressed and toweling shaving cream from his face. "So what's the big message?"

Miss Tatlock had already called Tuttle and had copied it down. She read from her notes. "According to his newspaper files, Mei Gan was a warlord-cum-gangster who joined forces with Chiang Kai-shek. In August 1928 he announced that he was going to conduct military maneuvers in the Malan Valley in Hopei, right next to the site of the Imperial Tombs. He cut all communications with the area and set a battalion of engineers to digging. They went at it for three days and three nights straight, and when they'd finished there wasn't a single thing left. Gold, silver, jewelry, jade, coral, ivory, they took it all." She looked up. "This has to be the Mei Gan we're looking for. He mimicked the last phoenix. He scratched at an emperor's grave."

"Jade and ivory? No mention of any opium?"

"No. But that doesn't mean it wasn't there."

Wasey doubted it. "I know the emperors were buried with all their treasures, including their concubines. But I've never heard of anyone being buried with half a ton of opium."

"But say it happened. Say it was a gift the emperor had received from some visiting Indian maharaja. Isn't it possible that Mei Gan took the opium as well, and then Faraday stole it from him?"

"You don't steal things from a man with a private army."

"Maybe he bought it, then."

"That still doesn't tell us where it is," Wasey said. "Anyway, what about this Mei Gan character? Does Tuttle know where he is now?"

Miss Tatlock looked down at her shoes. "After he robbed the tombs the whole country was outraged. He was executed."

"Then that's that. Case closed. We can't talk to a dead man."

"I don't think it matters that he's dead."

"Okay, but it'll be a one-sided conversation."

"Mr. Wasey, please be sensible. I'm thinking of what that old man said in the pagoda. He said that Mei Gan would lead you to the flowers. That was the word you said he used, lead."

"So?"

"So there's something about Mei Gan that we have to find out. Something that will tell us where the flowers are."

Wasey's hand moved in an iffy gesture. "It's possible. But where do we start?"

"The library perhaps," Miss Tatlock suggested. Then she brightened. "Or a historian. Could we go to the university? Talk to somebody there?"

Wasey considered it while he put on his shoes and

socks. "I think a street historian would be better for something like this. This thing only happened twelve years ago and a street man would be more likely to know all the gossip."

"What on earth," Miss Tatlock asked, "is a street historian?"

"I'll show you," Wasey said.

The desk clerk helped them locate one. He directed them to a side road near the South Station of the Hangchow-Ningpo Railway, a kind of market devoted to the mystical arts. There were fortune-tellers, soothsayers, diviners, and graphologists, several K'an Hsiang men, who maintained that a person's fortune was in his features, and several sages of the Pa Kua, the ancient Eight Diagrams the Emperor Fu Hsi had evolved from the markings of a turtle shell. And there were also a number of mole removers who offered to improve a client's destiny by improving his face.

Wasey stopped to talk to one of them who had set up a stand with a banner attached to it. It showed a face covered with good and bad moles, the good ones on the forehead and chin auguring long life and riches, the bad ones on the neck indicating an inglorious end. The man had a bottle of acid and some blunt needles with which to circumvent hanging, drowning, impotency, death by lightning, and mother-in-law trouble.

"Sir, we are looking for a historian. A man of boundless knowledge and superb memory. Perhaps you could recommend one."

The mole man pointed up the street. "Master Chung. He has seen the ocean changed into mulberry fields."

Wasey thanked him and, with Miss Tatlock in tow, continued up the street to a grimy shopwindow whose sole ornament, behind the smeared glass, was a painting of two tortoises holding up the columns of an ornate wooden temple.

An old man standing in the doorway spoke to them. Wasey had noticed that anyone under the age of sixty automatically assumed that he wouldn't be able to speak Chinese, while those older than that appeared to regard foreigners as capable of anything.

"The ancients believed that the tortoise could live for three thousand years without food or air, so they built on them to preserve the wood from decay."

"You are Master Chung?"

The man bowed. He was aged and wrinkled, completely bald, and had just a few straggles of mustache hair and a goatee like silk floss.

"We have a question, Master."

The old man's expression made it clear that everybody who came to him had a question. He ushered them into his shop, which was nothing more than bare boards and a table with a chair on each side. But the walls were graphic and interesting, covered with long lists written in a beautiful calligraphic hand—the Ten Celestial Stems, the Twelve Terrestrial Branches, the Thirty Dangerous Barriers, the Cycle of Sixty Years, plus a treatise on the misty geomantic science of Feng-shui, a system of finding the most favorable orientation for houses, temples, and graves.

They sat down at the table, the old man resting a long-nailed finger on a worn deck of cards. Near his other hand was a small bamboo cage, a bird chirping inside it. In his crackly voice he asked Miss Tatlock a question.

Wasey apologized for her lack of the Wondrous Tongue and said to her, "He wants to know your year of birth."

"I can't see that it's necessary but I was born in 1918."

Wasey translated.

"The year of the ox," Master Chung proclaimed. "Strength and stubbornness, then. The creature is deaf in the ears and hears with its nose."

"I think we've come to the right man," Wasey said.

Chung smiled at Miss Tatlock on a set of white-painted wooden teeth. "Now to your fortune. The little yellow bird has the answer."

He swept the cards into a semicircle, then let the canary out of the cage. It hopped halfway along the cards, then pecked one up in its beak and tossed it down, face up. It was done in brilliant-colored inks, a drawing of a man holding a big golden bracelet in his right hand and a spear in the other. Rays of shining light poured out from his head, and the chariot he rode had wheels of whirling flames.

"No Cha," the old man said. "A great hero who fought the Dragon King and defended the emperor."

He reached out and turned the card over. The sleeve of his long gown rustled as he gave the bird a grain of rice. "However," he said, a solemn note stiffening his voice, "the hero treads a perilous path, and his card augurs danger and discomfort, pain, torment, fear, and unease."

"He says you have a brilliant future."

Miss Tatlock shifted impatiently. "Ask him about Mei Gan."

"All in good time. You don't hurry elderly Chinese." Wasey was enjoying himself; he had no way of knowing that he was shortly to hear something that would rock him to his heels.

The old man told Wasey his fortune, then waited for the question Wasey had said they'd come to ask.

"Master Chung, there was a general, a warlord named Mei Gan. What do you know of him?"

"A thief. A tomb robber. A desecrator of graves. He plundered the tomb where Chien Lung is buried."

"What did he steal?"

The old man gazed into his memory. "Paintings, scrolls, books, swords, gold Buddhas, coral and ivory carvings. Porcelain dreams and jade fantasies, pale green Sung figures, baying T'ang camels, and wild-eyed horses of the Ming. Dragon-sided amphorae, and wine jugs with clawing lions, glazed pottery polo players and paper-thin stem cups. Lotus leaf basins, Chun ware shaped like ancient bronzes, and the ancient bronzes themselves. Monk's hat jugs, archaic stone wine beakers, perfect Hsuan-te jars with delicate rope-shaped handles. And jade, carved jade the size of cantaloupes—a horse and two monkeys, a reclining buffalo and its calf, an ancient fisherman with his catch of carp, a long-bearded sage floating in a hollow log."

"And opium? Did he steal opium from the tombs?"

"No. Chien Lung was buried only with his treasures," the historian said, then added, after a moment, "as was Tzu Hsi."

"Tzu Hsi?" Wasey asked. "Yehonala? The Dowager Empress?"

"The young master is well informed."

"She was buried in the same tomb?"

"It is a Ch'ing tomb. It was her right."

Miss Tatlock was watching Wasey, her eyes flicking between him and the old man. She wasn't getting a word of it yet she recognized the change in the pace of the questioning, and Wasey's sudden intensity. It was a second or two before Wasey spoke again.

"Master Chung, what was Tzu Hsi buried with?"

"Her Pekinese dogs, her mechanical clocks, her gowns, her capes, her jades, her gold, her silver, and her shining garden."

"That last, Master. What was that?"

"Peonies outlined in gold thread on a silk square. The stems were emeralds, the buds rubies, the leaves diamonds."

"Mei Gan took that, too?"

"Mei Gan left nothing."

Very slowly, and very precisely, Wasey put both hands flat on the table. He closed his eyes. "Oh my God!"

"What is it?"

Wasey turned his face to Miss Tatlock without seeing her. "Oh, *God!*"

"What, for heaven's sake?"

Wasey snapped out of it, jumped up, fumbled money onto the table.

"Come on."

Miss Tatlock had to trot to keep up with him. But he stopped once he made the street.

"Mr. Wasey, what on earth—"

"There's no opium. Not half a ton, not half a pound. We've been chasing the wrong thing."

She stared at him with zero comprehension.

"The flowers aren't opium poppies, they're jewels. Made in the shape of flowers. They belonged to Tzu Hsi, the empress who was buried in the Imperial Tombs."

She was shaking her head at something she didn't want to believe. "That can't be right. That's not true."

"Miss Tatlock. Listen to what I'm saying. I saw China Doll last night. She told me she'd known Faraday. I asked her about the opium. She didn't know anything about any opium, but she did tell me that Faraday left something with her for safekeeping. Something very valuable."

"But how do you know she was talking about jewels?"

"Because she wasn't talking about half a ton of opium. Because there wasn't any opium in the tombs. But there were flowers. Worth a fortune. And that's what we've been going around almost getting killed asking about. Flowers that are worth a fortune. Don't tell me you're going to say it's just a coincidence."

It had been too quick. She was floundering, grasping at understanding. "It doesn't make sense."

"It makes all kinds of sense. Faraday acquired the jewels from whoever bought them or stole them from Mei Gan. He gets into trouble with one of the gangs for cheating at cards, remember? So he has to get out in a hurry, travel light, swim the river, God knows what. So he stashes the things with China Doll, whom he'd taken up with. You're going to have to face it. Faraday's flowers are jewels."

"But . . . Mr. Burns was so certain."

"So was whoever he heard it from. Probably someone just like Burns who hasn't been here very long and doesn't know the language, except he knows that flowers can mean poppies. They're supposed to be worth a fortune, so somebody says there must be half a ton of them and bingo, bango, the rumor's off and running."

Miss Tatlock turned away and stood facing up the street, saying nothing, not moving. She allowed herself a single shuddering breath, and held herself very still.

Wasey reached out a hand to her, thought again, and dropped it. "I'm sorry," he said.

Still facing away, Miss Tatlock said, "I have to tell Mr. Burns."

"I'll come with you."

"He won't be in his office till five."

"I'll see you there, then."

She nodded and walked away.

Wasey let her go. She was crushed and embarrassed, and bitterly disappointed.

She wouldn't want company.

When Wasey arrived at Burns's office he could have cut the air with a knife. Miss Tatlock was over by the window, staring sightlessly out at the alley below. And Burns, sitting behind his desk, was hunched as if he were cold. He hadn't taken off his uniform cap, and with his dark beard it formed an oval frame for his face, which had lost its customary color. He looked up when Wasey came in, then immediately lowered his eyes. When he spoke it was without raising his head.

"As you can probably tell, Mr. Wasey, Miss Tatlock had already filled me in."

"I'm sorry it worked out this way," Wasey said.

Burns made a soft fist and dropped it onto his desk. "I'm still trying to get my mind around it. I heard about the flowers from an unimpeachable source. At least, I thought so. I was a fool. I should have checked it out thoroughly before involving you and Miss Tatlock."

"Don't be too rough on yourself, Mr. Burns. You haven't been in this country long. It's a mistake anyone could have made."

"Thank you, but I still could've . . ." Burns waved away the rest of the sentence. "Well, it's too late now." He lifted his head. "You did an excellent job for us, Mr. Wasey. You fulfilled your end of the bargain, and I'll be more than glad to buy you that ticket to Los Angeles."

"That's nice of you. I just wish I'd been able to bring you good news."

"It was better we found out sooner than later. Before we wasted any more time on this wild-goose chase."

Miss Tatlock spun round, her face a series of hard edges. "We don't have to have wasted our time. We were looking for something worth a fortune. Well, we've found something worth a fortune. The question is, can we do anything about it?"

"I don't understand," Burns said.

She looked at Wasey. "This woman you visit. What kind of person is she? I mean her nature."

"I'm way ahead of you. I've just been to see her."

It was a bombshell for Miss Tatlock. "You asked her?"

Burns looked from one to the other. "Please tell me what you're talking about."

"Did Miss Tatlock tell you about China Doll?" Wasey asked.

Burns nodded.

"I went out and talked to her. I explained how I'd been looking for Faraday's flowers thinking they were opium poppies. I told her why I'd been looking for the poppies, and about you two. I told her the flowers could still be used to buy opium."

"You mean buy the jewels from her?" Burns blew out breath. "We could have bought opium, if there'd been any, because it would have been at the black market price, which is a tenth of what it costs on the open market. But stolen jewels . . . We'd have to resell them to the underworld, at a huge loss, I'm sure, then buy legal opium. We'd lose a fortune in the process."

"I figured that," Wasey said. "I didn't bother to ask her because I knew she wouldn't sell the jewels anyway. But I had an idea that, if I put it to her properly, she might give them to us."

Miss Tatlock took a step towards him. "What did you say to her?"

Wasey reversed a chair and sat down on it, then patted his thoughts into shape. "I have to explain something. I told you that the jewels belonged to Tzu Hsi, the empress who died forty years ago. What I didn't tell you was that China Doll thinks she was Tzu Hsi in a previous life. I don't think Faraday knew that or he would've chosen somebody else to bank the jewels with."

"Why?"

"Because if he'd survived I think he might have had a hard time getting them back again. Anyway, I told her that the jewels were rightfully hers, and that they belonged to her. Except they belonged to China more. And that they weren't doing China much good lying at the bottom of a shoe, or wherever she's got them. I asked her to give them to us so we could trade them in for morphine."

The room seemed to be holding its breath. Then Miss Tatlock said, "What was her reaction?"

"She's going to give me an answer tonight. But I think there's a chance she'll do it."

Miss Tatlock almost went to him but stopped herself. The hard edges had fled from her face, and there was a look in her eyes he'd never seen there before.

Burns pushed his chair out. His back had straightened and he seemed like a different person. He said, "You're quite a salesman, Mr. Wasey."

Wasey brushed the praise aside. "We'll see."

"There's still a moral problem," Burns said. "Stolen jewels aren't quite the same as an evil thing like opium. But"—a ghost of a smile flickered at his mouth—"I think I can wrestle my conscience down."

Miss Tatlock hadn't moved her gaze from Wasey. "When will you know?"

"Ten o'clock tonight. And, Miss Tatlock"—Wasey blinked innocently at her—"this time I think you should come with me."

14

Wasey had been right about the rain coming back. It arrived in a hard burst around nine forty-five, making him regret they hadn't chosen a cab with a better roof.

He sat scrunched over next to Miss Tatlock and managed to keep fairly dry except for the right sleeve of his topcoat. He had a legitimate excuse for being so close to her, although he knew that, normally, that wouldn't have helped him a bit. She would still have barked him back to his own side of the seat under the dripping roof. But she didn't say a word now. He guessed she was probably too preoccupied to register a complaint. They were coming down to the wire on this one; in fifteen minutes' time they'd know whether they had a hell of a something or a whole lot of nothing.

"Tuttle called me a couple of hours back," he said, partly to break the nervous silence. "Wanted to know how we were doing. I told him I might have a scoop for him tonight."

She nodded, not wanting to talk, so Wasey didn't press it and remained quiet all the way to the old amusement park.

Wasey waited till the cab had gone before he opened the gate. He could see Miss Tatlock reacting to the desolate area, the sagging wire fence, the shadows of the wrecked Ferris wheel, and the twisted roller coaster against the sky.

"This is where she lives?"

"I asked the same question myself," Wasey said.

The rain, easing, sprinkled down on them as they walked through the ruined carnival, through puddles yellowed by the feeble bulbs strung above the path.

When Wasey stepped off it and went towards the entrance of the River Caves, Miss Tatlock balked.

Wasey took her hand and led her forward into the wedge

of darkness. She didn't respond to the first chunk and splash of the waterwheel, but he felt her jump when the little boat barged through the doors. He stopped it, stepped in, and held out a hand to her. She got in without a word and he wondered how she could keep from tumbling out a dozen questions.

The boat drifted them through the door. She had the same reaction to the first display as he'd had: a shock at the sudden light bursting in on them. But, as with him, the scene of the ancient Chinese village, with its pavilions and parks and river willows, charmed her once she recognized what she was seeing. She turned her head to take in all the detail as the boat floated by and the lights winked out. She was ready for the other displays, understanding the ride, and was as soothed and calmed by their soft, shining appeal as he had been.

There was no maid to welcome them at the landing, just a candle fluttering in a holder. Wasey picked it up and lit the way down the shadowy hall and into the gorgeous room.

Still saying nothing, Miss Tatlock took in the swooping silver birds, the ancient woodcuts, pictures, and prints, the swimming fish on the scarlet rug, and the silky glow of the dolls in their bamboo cabinet.

"Way-see."

China Doll startled her with her sudden appearance.

"Yehonala," Wasey said. "I have brought the person I spoke of."

The two women studied each other, both straight-backed, head high, and still. Wasey was struck by the contrast: Miss Tatlock in her dark rain cape and correct, long-skirted uniform, the strict hair, the fresh natural prettiness of her face. And China Doll, dahlias and winter plum blossoms embroidered on her magnificent yellow gown, her hair a blue-black cascade, her perfect lemon-dark skin, her radiant, classic features.

"Please tell her," Miss Tatlock said, "that she is very lovely."

"My friend compliments you on your beauty."

China Doll gave a small bow of her head, and the formalities were over. She spoke to Wasey but watched Miss Tatlock. "Ask her this. If the jewels brought a million American dollars, how many men would that keep alive?"

Wasey translated.

"Tell her—"

"I think she wants to hear it from you. She only has a little English, so she won't understand it all. I think she'll judge you from your tone of voice."

Miss Tatlock spoke directly to her. "It will keep none alive. Morphine only stops pain. It doesn't cure."

In her own language China Doll said, "Then would it not help China more if the money was used to buy more guns?"

Wasey continued to translate for Miss Tatlock.

"More guns would only bring more suffering. More soldiers wounded. More soldiers dying."

"Then the opium drug benefits those who can no longer fight?"

"Yes. That's why the generals hold it in so little regard."

"There are many soldiers dying?"

"One hundred thousand a month. The opium drug would let them die without suffering. And it would keep the wounded out of pain."

China Doll was still watching Miss Tatlock's face, but her searching look dimmed as her mind shifted time.

"When I held the Peacock Throne, I backed the I Ho Ch'uan against the foreigners. They claimed their magic boxing art would turn aside bullets. One hundred thousand of them were killed in three weeks." Her eyes focused again on Miss Tatlock's face. "I will give you the flowers."

She turned round, clapped her hands sharply once, and the little maid appeared, went straight to the bamboo cabinet, and took out the empress doll.

"Yehonala," Wasey said. "I don't understand."

Neither did Miss Tatlock.

But it became exceptionally clear when they saw what the maid did next: she placed the doll on a side table and produced two things from the folds of her gown: a square piece of soft cloth and a pair of scissors. She laid the cloth flat, picked up the doll, and began to snip away the colored stones that adorned the doll's clothes.

"I had to have a hiding place," China Doll said. "I stripped the empress of the original glass stones, painted the jewels, and sewed them on."

Wasey moved across the room for a closer look. It was a beautifully simple idea: the red stone he picked up off the cloth was a ruby, but there was no flash of brilliance to give it away; the red lacquer paint had dimmed its fire so that it looked like dull glass. The green-painted stones had to be emeralds. And the pale yellow stones, diamonds.

The maid snipped with swift efficiency, and the cloth square filled up with glassy, cheap-looking glitter. She cut the stones from the shoulder cape and the phoenix head-dress, added them to the pile, then folded the cloth in a little bundle and handed it to her mistress.

China Doll held it out to Miss Tatlock, who accepted it with dignified grace. She nodded her head once, smiled at China Doll, and said, with a simple warmth and sincerity, "Thank you."

Wasey had something to say to her, too, but his thanks were cut off by the noise of a buzzer sounding somewhere.

China Doll turned to her maid, asking her a question with a glance, but the maid, with the smallest of frowns, said softly, "No one is expected."

It suddenly didn't feel right. To any of them.

Miss Tatlock, assuming correctly that the buzzer had announced an arrival, had the same thought as Wasey: that a fortune in jewels was out of its hiding place and in the open.

214

China Doll's face changed the merest fraction, the fine line of her eyebrows lowering slightly. "You should go," she said.

Wasey didn't argue. He took Miss Tatlock's arm and hurried her down the hallway, the little maid trotting ahead with a candle held high.

They spent a nervous minute waiting on the landing.

"I don't know why we're being so jumpy," Miss Tatlock said, not very convincingly.

Wasey told her exactly why. "Because of that little bundle you've got in your hand. Which, incidentally, is a bad place to have it. Better give it to me."

She handed it over just as the little boat came out of the dark towards them.

The maid stopped it, held it steady for them as they got in, then shoved it off. Wasey called a soft thank-you as they vanished into the blackness. The stream wafted them along, no sound coming to them, their eyes trying to adjust after the candle glow.

Miss Tatlock expected to see an illuminated display, and Wasey knew there was one coming up, but what neither was prepared for, when the boat triggered a relay and the display lit up on their right, was the flat-faced gangster who was traversing it.

The man reacted fast to the light bursting over him, but he either didn't know about the boat or wasn't prepared for it, because he stopped in his tracks and looked wildly around before he saw them.

The big Luger he was carrying jerked up and pointed, but he didn't get a chance to use it.

With a noise like the popping of a giant firecracker, a gun exploded on their left, the echo cutting into the man's scream as he clutched at his belly and fell backwards into the display. He crashed into a white river of stars, smashing through delicate painted cardboard and a hundred tiny light bulbs.

A hanging half-moon and a flight of silver storks broke

up with a tearing paper noise, and bulbs burst and wooden frames snapped as the whole sugar-spun display fell in on itself, dragged down by the man's weight.

The light blinked out as the gun roared again, two bullets thunking into the border of the stream inches behind the boat.

Wasey pinned Miss Tatlock down, the sound of the shots still ricocheting through the caves.

"Oh my *God!*" he said. He fumbled for the box in his pocket, got the Baby Nambu into his hand.

Miss Tatlock slowly raised herself. "What happened?" The words wobbled in her mouth.

"Two guys waiting for us. One of 'em missed us and got his buddy." Wasey was having trouble getting words out, too.

They listened. They heard the clump of receding footsteps.

Miss Tatlock let out the breath she'd been holding in. "He's not coming after us."

"Yes, he is. He's gone the other way. Back to the entrance. We're still going to have to get by him."

They both felt the boat bump a relay beneath its keel and ducked instinctively as a Ming city came to life on their right. The sudden illumination caught a man straddling the town walls like some legendary marauding giant.

Wasey came up fast with the automatic, but the man fired first and Wasey ducked, realizing almost at the same time that he wasn't the target.

Gunshots crashed out and bullets zinged over their heads, then the man pitched forward, grasping at a paper pagoda, snapping it in half as he carried it with him into a courtyard full of tiny figures, destroying an archery contest, a pond and a bridge, and a Purple Light hall.

As the display blacked out, Wasey heard, in loud Chinese, "Boat! They're in a boat!" Then gunfire right on top of it. There was a high scream, the sound of a stumble, and a thick, heavy splash.

216

He hissed at Miss Tatlock. "Into the water! Quick!" She didn't question it. She tumbled out after him into the stream. The water, surprisingly warm, was no more than three feet deep, and they waded through it, holding on to the little boat and following it.

They both knew what was happening now: there were two groups in the cave.

On their left, a few yards in front of them, a flashlight popped on, a gun went off in three red blasts, and wood chunked out of the boat, sending water and splinters spraying against their faces.

It was answered immediately by the shattering din of a machine gun, very close and incredibly loud. Then another gun joined in, and there were a few uninterrupted moments of riotous noise, of yelling and smashing, and the punch and chatter of continuous gunfire.

Then it ceased abruptly, and they pushed through the water and the cordite smell, and a blackness which dissolved a second later when a dragons' lair lit up, a dozen of the beasts, red-eyed, red-breathed, all sharp claws and lashing tails.

They bobbed down instantly behind the boat, water up to their necks, but there was nothing fiercer than the dragons there, nor in the tunnel beyond, the final stretch that led to the double doors of the exit.

They waded the remaining distance, moved in front of the boat, and eased open the left-hand door.

The waterwheel chunked around, the only thing moving in the bleak red glow.

In a fragile whisper Miss Tatlock said, "What are we going to do?"

Wasey could feel the fine trembling running through her body, so he tried a little bravado. "Listen, I've been in tough spots before and I always got out of them."

"How?"

"I ran like hell."

He grabbed her arm, climbed onto the boardwalk, stumbled up the ramp, and dashed out into the park.

The first thing they saw was a man running towards them. They veered to their right, the sound of a bullet clapping past their heads obscured by the blam of a gun. The dark swallowed them, but there was no way they could silence their running footsteps. Water squelched in their shoes as they slapped down wetly onto the broken asphalt, their soaking clothes clinging like grasping hands.

Wasey ran with no plan in his head except to somehow slip by the man who had changed tack and was racing to cut them off. But they were making too much noise. Their footsteps drummed as they rushed across a warped metal floor on which bumper cars lay smashed together in a colossal pileup.

Wasey jumped off it onto grass, pulling Miss Tatlock with him, circled round the crippled horses of a wrecked carousel, and stopped when he caught a flash of movement in front of them.

He changed direction again, darting to his left, running into the entrance of a funhouse.

The doorway was a gigantic clown's mask twenty-five feet high, its red-lipped face burned away on one side, the huge eyes heat-peeled and blackened. They crouched behind it, hearts hammering, breathing fast.

Fifty yards away the man was coming towards them, bent low and moving at a half run.

Wasey fiddled clumsily with the gun, making sure he'd pushed the safety catch off.

"It won't . . ." Miss Tatlock fought for breath. "It won't do you much good."

"This is the wrong time"—Wasey had to breathe twice before finishing—"for a lecture."

"I took . . . I took the bullets out."

"You took the *bullets* out?"

"In your . . . hotel room." She snatched at air and ran three words together. "Youwereasleep."

218

"Miss *Tat*lock!" It was a cry of anguish. "Say it isn't so."

"Killing people . . . is wrong."

There was a burst of gunfire at the entrance of the River Caves, and Wasey waved his hand wildly in that direction. "Tell them that." He dropped the useless gun and felt in his pocket for the cigarette-lighter grenade. At least that had been safe from Miss Tatlock. He tried to remember what Sing Sing had told him about it: just turn the little wheel; the first notch meant a five-second fuse, the other notch twenty minutes. But he knew he couldn't use it now, not on just one man when there were God knows how many coming any second.

He looked up at the back of the giant mask: thick, heavy papier-mâché bonded to several layers of strong chicken wire. The crisscross of wooden joists that had held it in place were nothing but blackened sticks, and now the mask was attached to the façade of the funhouse by a single metal bracket at its base.

Through a crack in the mask he watched the man creeping closer. He was almost level when Wasey raised his right foot and stamped down hard on the bent metal bracket. It came away with one kick, its rusted screws popping out. He pushed with all his weight, and with a creaking groan, the mask began to topple.

The man on the other side never had a chance.

He whirled at the noise, but shock nailed him to the spot as the huge face came to life towering over him, the scarred, blind eyes staring down at him, the grotesque, horribly burnt mouth open to swallow him up. At the last moment he turned to run, but the mask caught him as it fell, knocking him down and pinning him.

"Come on!" Wasey grabbed Miss Tatlock and they sprinted for the gate. They ran parallel to the lighted path, skirted the crashed wreckage of a Jack and Jill slide, and slipped through the blistered framework of the teetering roller coaster, its stanchions as bent and buckled as the looping track above them.

They cut across the skeletal remains of a hall of mirrors, glass splintering under their shoes, a few large pieces of mirror still in place, stretching their running figures to preposterous lengths.

They could make out the gate ahead, and two big automobiles parked outside it, and movement as someone got out of one of the cars and stood uncertainly, pointing a gun into the park.

Wasey jerked Miss Tatlock into a little wooden ticket booth, all that was left standing of a ghost-train ride, the track still in evidence, some tumbled cars spilled across it, the rest of the place just torn canvas and naked metal supports. A stiff wind would have blown the booth down; it was smoke-scorched and listing, and the roof had been burned away, but it was a hiding place and Wasey latched the door and they stood there panting, holding on to each other.

They heard the gate squeal, then heavy, measured footsteps.

Wasey was certain the man hadn't spotted them, sure he'd go on by and give them a chance to run for the car.

He was wrong.

The man had seen where they'd gone and knew he had them trapped. He came round the back of the ticket booth and leveled his gun at the door they were leaning against. His voice was without tremor, flat and professional. "Come out now or you're dead." He spoke tough Shanghai slang.

Wasey knew he'd have to use the grenade; there was no way to improvise a weapon as he'd done before. He dug it out, got it between thumb and fingers.

"We're coming out," he called. "Okay?"

"Let's see it," the gunman said.

Wasey lobbed the grenade over the roofless top, pulled Miss Tatlock down, and huddled over her. "Block your ears!"

"What's happening?"

He didn't answer. He squinched his eyes shut, ready for the blast.

Several beats later the voice outside said, "I'll count to five."

Wasey had already counted to five. He didn't understand. Was the grenade a dud? Had Sing Sing . . . ?

"Oh, Jesus!"

"What is it?" Miss Tatlock wasn't getting any answers to her questions.

"Nothing." Wasey didn't see any point in telling her that it was a miniature grenade he'd thrown and that he'd forgotten to set the fuse.

"Three," the voice said, counting.

He was right outside the door and Wasey could see only one thing to do: burst through the door and hope it would knock the gun out of the man's hand.

He straightened, backed up the two paces to the front wall, then launched himself forward, grabbed for the latch, missed it, and plowed into the door with his shoulder. The door buckled and took the frame with it, which pulled down the rest of the rickety structure, the whole thing collapsing around them like a house of cards.

The gunman, with plenty of time to jump back, started firing, but Wasey and Miss Tatlock, stretched out flat and sandwiched between the wooden walls, were an impossible target. The man, however, was an easy one, revealed as he was by the demolished booth, and shots from somewhere back in the park dropped him where he stood.

Wasey struggled out of the debris, hauled Miss Tatlock to her feet, snatched up the tiny grenade, and dashed for the gate. They jumped into the first car and Wasey took it away in a screech of rubber, made the corner, and had to swerve wildly to avoid the big black Hudson that came wheeling around it. Its headlights washed over them, and whoever was driving made an expert skidding turn and came back on their tail a mere hundred feet behind.

Miss Tatlock, in wailing dismay, said, "Not a third gang, surely."

"I think it's a backup car," Wasey yelled over the roar of the engine. "I only spotted two men. How many do you make?"

Miss Tatlock scrunched round in her seat. "Two. One of them has—"

A bullet took out the rear window, fanned between them, and smashed the right-side windshield. "A gun," Miss Tatlock finished.

Wasey risked a glance over his shoulder and got a glimpse of the car behind as it flashed under a streetlight. The man who'd been riding in the passenger seat was now out on the running board and pouring shots at them. And he was going to get them if he was allowed to stay there. Wasey stamped on the brakes and swung the car into a screaming left turn. It caught the car behind by surprise. When it swerved violently to follow, the man on the running board was catapulted off the car and sent crashing into some suburban garbage cans.

Wasey barreled into an avenue and bored the car along, knowing that the professional wheelman behind was going to make mincemeat out of them any minute. He had to reach the comparative safety of the narrow, twisting downtown streets.

He did insane things, drove like a maniac, mounted sidewalks, scattered pedestrians, passed a tram on the inside, and swerved fifty yards through traffic in the oncoming lane.

Behind them the big Hudson duplicated every move.

"Where are the police?" Miss Tatlock shouted. "Why don't they stop us?"

"Probably think we're a couple of cabs," Wasey shouted back.

He checked the rearview mirror and saw that his problem was about to be solved, although he wasn't crazy about the solution. The other car that had been parked outside the gate at the park, a dirty gray one, was swinging alongside the black Hudson.

It was all over in a minute. The driver of the Hudson only got off one shot before a machine gun raked his car, popping glass and bursting tires.

With a tremendous screech the Hudson spun one hundred and eighty degrees and, with no loss of speed, traveled backwards for an incredible twenty or thirty yards before it peeled off and whacked into a telephone pole.

The exchange bought Wasey a few precious minutes, enough time to make the junction of the Hunan Road and the ribbon-thin side streets which ran off it.

He slammed the car to a howling stop, shoved Miss Tatlock out, scrambled after her, snatched at her hand, and ran.

They didn't have to turn to know that they were being chased on foot, two or three of them, doing what they were doing, rushing down the narrow street, brushing by people, going over them.

Wasey at least knew where he was heading: the Bund and its taxis and its long, wide sweep that led to the Garden Bridge and Burns's office. Not because Burns could help them, but because it was located in Hongkew with its puzzling maze of twisting side streets and corkscrew alleys. They might lose their pursuers there and hide.

His breath was pumping in his throat and his legs felt funny, and beside him Miss Tatlock was making choking noises as she struggled to keep up. They pounded down an alley into another street, and ran an obstacle course of sidewalk stalls and peddlers who cursed and spat at them as they rushed rudely by, bouncing through them. There were rickshaws here, some with fares, some cruising, and Wasey grabbed hold of one pulled by a young man with some flesh on his bones. He bundled Miss Tatlock into it, climbed in after her.

"Keep going!" he yelled. He brandished money. "Down to the Bund! Fly!"

The rickshaw man doubled his pace, the American dollar a fine persuader. A hundred feet behind very much the same thing was happening: rickshaws were being commandeered—the pursuers were running out of breath, too. There were many rickshaws in the street but only three of them were racing, their passengers hunched forward like jockeys in trotting sulkies, urging on their pullers, promising, cajoling, threatening. The threats proved the most powerful goad. Wasey, looking behind him, saw two rickshaws pull out of the pack and begin to gain.

And he saw something else: the man in the lead rickshaw was the one with the submachine gun. He was half standing, moving his head, trying to get a clear shot.

"An extra two cash!" Wasey cried. "Faster! Let's go!"

He knew if he'd offered another U.S. dollar the coolie might not have believed him. Yet his offer didn't do much good. Wasey had been unlucky in his choice; the man he'd picked had had a good day and had just eaten a bowl of lard-fried mustard greens, and a cramp was forming in his side. He began to slow, shaking his head and leaning to his left, while back up the street the two rickshaws came on fast.

Wasey sneaked another look, saw the second man, a big, broad-faced thug, leap from his rickshaw and start running towards them along the sidewalk, sprinting like a football player down a sideline, bowling over people, belting into peddlers, leaving a trail of rolling fruit and spilled tea and crushed flowers. He jumped up onto and over a table, sending pans of swimming goldfish crashing down, bounded back into the jammed street, and came at their rickshaw from an oblique angle.

He leaped onto the footboard and tried to climb over Miss Tatlock, who didn't have enough breath to scream. He was halfway into the carriage when Wasey lashed out with his foot and caught him in the chest. The thug reeled back, swung away like a hinged door, but didn't let go his grip on the side rail.

He swung back again, tried once more to climb in, and would have made it if Miss Tatlock hadn't acted. With a fast, fluid movement she waved her hand behind her head, whipped out her long, sharp hairpin, and jabbed at the man's stubby fingers.

The man clutched his hand, took a second kick in the chest from Wasey, lost his balance, and soundlessly fell away. He landed on his feet, stumbled, caught himself briefly, then went down hard.

He fell right into the path of the other puller, who tried to leap him, couldn't do it, and spilled over.

The rickshaw nose-dived and stopped dead, and the machine-gun man was pitched out of it and thrown into the road. But he landed beautifully, touching with his feet and rolling over on his shoulder. He came up on his knees, the machine gun whipping up, and got off a quick wild burst that shredded the canvas top above Wasey's head and sent the lower half of a big neon sign sharding down onto scattering pedestrians.

Wasey threw money at his flagging puller, dragged Miss Tatlock out, and fled. He knew what he'd see if he looked back: crowds parting like a wave for a running man with a machine gun, and the crowds were the reason why he couldn't pull the miniature grenade from his pocket, fuse it on the run, and lob it behind him. So he just ran, hauling Miss Tatlock into an alley that brought them out into another cross street. They raced down it, slowing every step, their legs beginning to feel like somebody else's, little breath left in their bodies.

Wasey hated the idea of another rickshaw, but it was either that or stop and face a tommy gun.

He stopped a group gathered round the entrance to a bar. The pullers turned as one when they heard his shout, and rushed toward him already bargaining. But he thrust a bill at every one of them, hoisted Miss Tatlock into the first rickshaw in line, and jumped in himself, yelling instructions. The pullers didn't question any of it. They ducked into their traces and moved their vehicles away fast, Wasey's leading, the rest following. It gave the machine-gun man a confusing multiple target, and he wasted his aim.

A moment before the volley came Wasey peeked back and saw him vault into the seat of a pedicab, stand up, and shove the butt of the gun into his shoulder. The burst was too high again, ripping through the canvas tops and demolishing shopwindows beyond them. The exploding gun, the crash of shattering glass, and the bullets rocking their rickshaws was too much for the pullers and they tailed away, wanting no part of a gang war. But Wasey bullied and threatened his man, kept him moving for another fifty yards, until exhaustion stopped him in his traces. They leapt off and took to their heels again.

The street curved and opened up, and they saw at the corner ahead the glorious bulk of two big granite buildings.

They'd reached the Bund.

They rushed by people, weaving in and out, dodging, darting, not giving the man behind a single clear chance. They charged into the wide boulevard and jumped at a cab stopped for a red light. It was occupied, but that didn't halt Wasey. He leapt inside, startling a man and a woman in evening dress, pulled Miss Tatlock in after him, and threw a ten-dollar bill at the driver.

"Hongkew! *Now!*"

The driver recognized authority when he heard it, and American money when he saw it, and didn't hesitate. He gunned his cab through the intersection and sped up the Bund.

Wasey darted a look through the rear window, squeezing the man against the woman. Miss Tatlock collapsed on the floor, gasping. Like Wasey, she was sodden and still dripping water.

"Sorry," Wasey said, apologizing for the intrusion.

The man was English. "Bit irregular," he said huffily.

Wasey didn't hear; he was watching the corner and the

machine-gun man who came sprinting out of it. And the dirty gray car, which had arrived by a circular route. It screeched into the curb, picked up the man, zoomed away, and immediately opened fire.

The English woman, a hand to her skinny throat, dramatically caught her breath as the side mirror disappeared in a shower of glass.

Her husband was affronted. "I say," he said to Wasey. "Do you know those chaps behind?"

They howled through the S bend of the boulevard, then straightened for the bridge that spanned the Soochow Creek, the bridge lights twinkling in its dark waters.

The taxi hummed over the metal roadway, made the far end of the bridge, then skidded into the blaze of blue mercury lamps as it reached the checkpoint.

Two Japanese Bluejackets, alarmed by the speeding car, had their rifles unslung, and two more were running towards a machine-gun nest.

"Passport!" Wasey called.

Miss Tatlock fished for it in her damp handbag, tossed it to him, then followed him out of the cab.

They flashed the passports at a Japanese guard, went by him on the run.

"American," Wasey cried, and kept going, betting they wouldn't be stopped; the Japanese were treating Americans with kid gloves, and he knew it. He also knew the cab wouldn't have made it through; the English couple would have refused to show anybody anything.

They had fifty feet to cross, all open space, the river on one side, the sanctuary of the alleys on the other. But he was banking on the dirty gray car being held up.

They put their heads down and ran.

He thought they were going to make it until he heard the sound of the car. Rubber squealed and an engine roared. The car was trying to charge through the checkpoint.

There was a long chattering concussion as the heavy Japanese machine gun opened up, and the bang of punched metal and exploding tires. The car, riddled low down, skewered around in a shrieking spin.

Only one man emerged, the man with the submachine gun, who hit the road running, zigzagging towards the alleys.

Hypnotized for a half second, they watched him come, then turned and bolted. They heard the Bluejackets fire again and weren't sure if they'd got the man until there was another explosion and bullets danced chunks of brick out of a wall a foot behind them.

Wasey pumped his legs, swung Miss Tatlock, who was half stumbling, half running, into an open corridor which twisted between two alleys.

His injured arm pained him, and there were flames in his chest, and he tried to think where he could use the little grenade.

The corridor finished at another alley full of people who scrambled out of the way, parting for the running couple. It was like leaving a trail of bread behind; all the gunman had to do was follow their wake through the crowds.

Miss Tatlock gasped something which Wasey didn't have to catch to understand. Her face was red, her eyes unfocused; she didn't have much left in her.

He slowed her, wheeled her into the first opening he saw, the doorway of a shop, which, he found a moment later, was gruesomely appropriate to their situation.

It was painted completely white, the color of mourning, and in the middle of the open floor, on a low platform, was an example of the shop's product: a brick beehive grave surrounded by plants and dwarf pines and bundles of firecrackers, with *fen-piao* sticks, fancy long spears bound with colored strips of paper, sticking out of the real grass that grew, freshly watered, on top of the grave.

An eighty-year-old man lacquering a coffin looked up startled at their flying entrance, and hobbled over to them where they sprawled behind the shelter of the brick display.

"You have come about death affairs?" he inquired.

They hardly heard him. They heaved for air, coughed, choked, thin breath rasping inside them. Wasey, chest thumping, peeked around the grave.

The gunman was right outside.

He'd lost them and was looking round wildly, panting like a dog, the submachine gun held loose but ready.

"You are wise," the funeral man complimented them. "Not many so young make arrangements before they ride the stork."

If the gunman looked in he'd see the old man talking to someone in hiding.

"Master," Wasey gasped. "Please . . . go away."

"We all go away one day. To the arms of Old Father Buddha."

The machine-gun man turned his brutal, panting face towards the shopwindow.

Inside, the funeral arranger was telling Wasey that Confucius had said when asked about the Great Beyond, "'I do not yet know life, so how can I know death?'"

Suspicious, the gunman moved towards the door.

Wasey couldn't stand it. He got Miss Tatlock to her feet, wrapped his arm around her, and ran for the back door.

The only thing that saved them was the same thing that had saved them before: the thug's inexperience with the tommy gun. He was still letting it kick up on him. The gun exploded and a row of china urns dissolved on a shelf above the door, showering them with ancestral ashes as they plunged through it.

The alley opened on a duplicate of the one they'd just left, a poorly lighted strip full of hawkers and street peddlers, open counters and lantern-lit stalls. But there was one point of difference, a lifesaving one: Wasey recognized the alley as the same one Burns's office was on. And, in a companion thought, he realized that that was the ideal place to use the grenade—they'd run in through the street door, take the stairs, then he'd lob it down as the thug charged up after them. A confined space with nobody else there to get hurt, it was perfect.

"The office!" he yelled to Miss Tatlock. "Not far!"

They both found something extra within and improved their pace, dodged through fabric tables, chicken cages, stacked baskets, noodle stands, blind men, children, and barking dogs. There was no way for the man behind to get off a clear shot, and he was forced to slog after them and wait his chance.

Wasey didn't give it to him.

They made it to the dilapidated building that housed the Helping Hand Society and pounded up to the second-floor landing. When they fell into the office Burns was there and he said immediately, "How many of them?"

Wasey was hardly surprised by the question; he knew what they must look like: exhausted, shattered, Miss Tatlock with her hair half down, and both of them soaking wet. So it was natural for Burns to instantly assume they were running from something.

"One," Wasey gasped. "Got a machine gun."

"He see you come in here?"

"Had to."

"Get down behind the desk." Burns spoke with an authority neither of them had heard before.

Wasey dug for the grenade. "I got..." He sucked in air. "I got a..."

"Behind the desk. Both of you. *Move!*"

The harsh order was totally uncharacteristic. And then Burns did something that was even more so.

Something that literally floored them

With a swift, easy action he reached under his uniform jacket and flipped out a big nickel-plated Smith & Wesson forty-four revolver. While they stared at him he opened the door, checked the stairs, closed it again, and said, in a voice that wasn't his, "Get over there and get down." He waved the revolver at them as if he'd been around guns all his life.

Miss Tatlock recovered from her surprise enough to try

to say something, but Wasey hustled her over to the desk and pushed her down.

They watched him as he opened the door again, left it ajar, slid behind it, and waited there, the gun at his side like an extension of himself. He didn't move the same way and he didn't look the same. He was taller, straighter, stronger. It was as if a stranger had put on a uniform and a beard and glasses and was impersonating Mr. Burns.

They heard the sound of the door banging back on the landing below, then the clump of heavy footsteps on the stairs.

Wasey and Miss Tatlock tensed together, but Burns looked relaxed, almost bored.

The door flew open, and the thug, taking a guess, jumped into the room, the tommy gun up and ready.

Burns stepped from behind the door and slammed the butt of the heavy revolver into the man's elbow. The gunman cried out and whirled round, the machine gun bobbling in his grasp. Burns snatched it from him with his left hand, his right hand slashing the gun butt across the man's head. The thug staggered, stumbled forward, and caught the full weight of the revolver as Burns brought it around backhand, shifting his weight like a tennis pro.

The thug dropped, unconscious before he hit the floor.

Awed, astounded, flabbergasted, Miss Tatlock breathed out two words, "Mr. *Burns* . . ."

Very quietly Wasey said, "I don't think his name is Burns."

Bewildered, panting, shaking her head, she looked from one to the other.

"Do you know who I think he is?" Wasey asked, still trying to come to terms with it.

Miss Tatlock, with no breath in her mouth, just went on shaking her head.

"I'll give you a hint." Wasey inhaled deeply, his breathing getting back to normal. "His initials are W.F."

Miss Tatlock froze, then swiveled her eyes.

"He's right," the man said to her. His smile was quite charming. He looked at Wasey. "When did you figure it?"

"When I saw kindly, milksop Mr. Burns pull out a forty-four."

Miss Tatlock, eyes wide, was a couple of beats behind. "You're Faraday?" She had trouble with the name.

"Born and bred." With a practiced ease Faraday disengaged the key spring on the submachine gun, slipped out the drum magazine, crossed the floor, and tossed the drum out of the window as if it were an apple core. They heard it bang and clatter in the alley, then watched him walk back and pull out a chair. He put the toothless machine gun at his feet, sat down, and watched them as they slumped against the wall. The heavy revolver sat on his lap like a silver-colored kitten.

"Figured it out yet?" he asked.

"It's coming," Wasey replied. "I'm slowly working up to it."

For her part, Miss Tatlock was still struggling with the basics. She said thinly, "Where's the real Mr. Burns?"

"There never was one. Although there is a Helping Hand Society, except they're in Africa. I was their first China Hand."

Wasey, way ahead of Miss Tatlock, began asking questions and answering them himself. "The two groups that chased us. You hired one of them, but they're not from the gangs, because you can't go near the gangs. They were free-lance hoods, correct?"

"Yes, sir."

"Why hire them if we were bringing the jewels to you anyway?"

"Because I was sure Tuttle would try a double cross. I knew he'd hire some boys to take the stuff away from you, so I had to hire men to keep him from doing that."

"Mr. Tuttle?" Miss Tatlock blinked. "He's in this with you?"

232

"I couldn't have done it without him. It would hardly have done for a Christian missionary to take Mr. Wasey to a cathouse."

"And I had to go there," Wasey said, "so I could meet China Doll."

"Top of the class, Mr. Wasey." Faraday pointed a finger, a kind of salute. "You read it pretty well this morning when you said that Faraday would probably have had a hard time getting the flowers back from her. I did. She wouldn't give them to me because she said they were hers." Faraday made a little circling motion at his temple. "She being Tzu Hsi, and all that. She'd hidden the flowers and I couldn't persuade her to tell me where they were. And, believe me, I tried."

"Ah!" Wasey said, making a discovery. "Could that be why she wears those fingernail protectors?"

Faraday shrugged. "There are some people who won't talk no matter what you do to them."

To Miss Tatlock, Wasey said, "Charming fellow, your ex-boss. He pulled out three of her fingernails."

Miss Tatlock looked sick. And she hadn't yet completely assimilated the enormous cheat that had been played on her.

"You are," she said to Faraday, "a foul, hideous person."

"And you're dedicated and dumb. Exactly the type I was looking for. I couldn't have done it without you either, Miss Tatlock. I needed someone to help me find a guy like Wasey, and you did a great job of keeping his nose to the grindstone."

"What made me so special, Faraday? The language?"

"Mostly. And the fact that you were an American. A couple of years back China Doll fell in love with a guy. Name of Paul Cusack. American, a personality kid, spoke the language passably. I went looking for somebody like that and came up with you. If I couldn't get the flowers by twisting her arm, I was going to have to con her out of them. Except a lady as smart as China Doll would've known if she was being conned, so whoever did it had to believe in what they were doing. Hence the story of the opium poppies."

Faraday was enjoying himself. Proud of his feat, he wanted recognition and applause.

"She's romantic and sentimental," he went on. "I figured she'd go for the hundred-thousand-wounded-soldiers routing. You can sucker anybody once you find the right approach. Isn't that right, Mr. Wasey?"

"You sure suckered me, Faraday."

"Where did she hide the flowers? Did you find out?"

"What's it worth if I tell you?"

Faraday moved the gun around. "I shoot you later than sooner."

"Not much of an incentive," Wasey said, "but I'll take it. She took the stones out of the embroidery and sewed them onto one of the dolls."

Faraday made a noise through his nose like a laugh. "Well, how about that. I turned that lousy carnival upside down looking for those things. I think I did more damage than the fire. And all the time she had them on display."

He mulled it over for a second, then said, mocking Wasey, "By the way, where are they?"

"I'll mail them to you."

Faraday sniggered, held out his hand, and clicked his fingers.

Wasey got to his feet and dug into his pocket.

Faraday took the cloth bundle from him, put it on the table, and unfolded it.

"She painted them with colored lacquer to take the shine away," Wasey said. "As you say, Faraday, she's a smart lady."

Faraday picked up a couple of the stones and jiggled their glassy brightness in his hand. "Which doll did she sew them on?"

"The empress."

Faraday said, "Of course, what else? Shit, I must've

234

looked at that thing a dozen times." The man was absorbed in the stones but not so much, Wasey noted, that he forgot to keep the big revolver pointed at Wasey's stomach.

"How much will you get for them?" Wasey asked.

"Why do you ask him a question like that?" Miss Tatlock snapped out. "However much it is, he'll keep it all."

"Don't be too hard on him, Miss Tatlock. Wasey's a businessman. When a guy loses something he likes to know how much he's lost, right, Wasey?" He tossed the stones back onto the pile.

"How much?" Wasey asked again.

"I guess I'll net half a million."

"I may throw up," Wasey said. He reached out and rolled up the cloth around the gems and handed the bundle to Faraday. "Better keep them somewhere safe."

"Wasey," Faraday said, "you have style."

He opened his jacket and put the bundle in his inside breast pocket. Then he got out of his chair. "I'll just wake up the sleeping beauty and we'll get out of here."

He went over to the thug, who was making mumbling noises and trying to sit up. With his body half turned towards Wasey, still keeping an eye on him, Faraday toed the man with his shoe, then bent down and slapped his face. He said, in Shanghai slang, "Snap out of it. The cops are coming."

The man was concussed, but Faraday got him standing and pushed him to the door. He nudged him through it and put the hood's fingers on the handrail. "Beat it," Faraday said to him. The man walked unsteadily down the stairs like a windup toy.

Faraday turned and waved his gun at them. "Let's go."

Wasey helped Miss Tatlock up. She was shivering with cold or fear or shock, or a combination of all three. He put his arm around her and moved her towards the door.

Faraday had put on his cap, and with the gun out of sight under his uniform jacket, he was back to looking like Mr. Burns. "We're going to take a little stroll," he

said. "I'll be right behind you. And if you try to run"—
he gave them a little grin—"I'll shoot you in the spine."
He motioned them out onto the landing, turned the light
off in his office, locked the door, then pointed down the
stairs.

When he came out into the alley a fine rain was misting
down, and the air was chilly.

"That way," Faraday said, and they began to walk, Wasey
holding Miss Tatlock's arm, Faraday very close behind
them.

"Where are we going?" Wasey asked.

"Sightseeing. Keep moving."

The crowds had waned, driven inside by the sprinkling
rain, and there were few people around. Most of the stall
holders were folding up for the night, the tables had been
cleared, and the extinguished lanterns made the alley that
much darker.

Wasey flicked a glance at Miss Tatlock. It was hard to
see her face properly, but she seemed to be looking straight
ahead, her jaw set and her head rigid, although the fear
still fluttered in her body.

Wasey spoke over his shoulder. "What about Tuttle? He
may be waiting for you."

"Not him," Faraday answered. "He's probably on his
way to the airport. Once he found out that his side lost
he'd know I'd be coming for him. I'll catch up with him,
one of these days. I'm the patient type."

He guided them into a side street, through an alley that
crossed it, and into a small square, deserted in the rain.

Wasey could hear the ripple of water, and saw a little
stone bridge arcing across a narrow canal. Halfway over
it, Faraday stopped them. "End of the tour," he said.

Wasey looked down at the water; it was black, flowing
fast, snaking along with a cold incessant mutter.

Faraday read his thoughts. "It flows into the Soochow
Creek. Too narrow for any watercraft, so there's nothing
to hold up anything you care to throw in. If the tide's right,

and it is, you should make it all the way to the Yangtze by tomorrow morning."

"You've used it before, huh?"

"Many times."

"Faraday, how can you kill people with soft brown eyes?"

The man laughed. "You've got guts, Wasey. At this stage people usually get down on their knees."

"I may make it there yet."

Faraday pulled out the revolver. "Then now's the time."

Miss Tatlock spoke up. Her words were strong but they were delivered shakily. "Faraday, you're the worst thing a person can be. A rotten human being."

"Sorry you don't approve, sweetie." Faraday took a quick check to make sure there was no one around.

Wasey coughed. Like Miss Tatlock, he was putting on a brave front but the nervousness was showing through. "May I ask you something?"

"What?"

"Why kill us at all? We can't hurt you."

"Sure you can."

"The police only write traffic tickets. We can't go to them."

"You could go to the gangs. They don't know I'm Richard Burns of the Helping Hand Society. I can walk down the street in this uniform and this beard and these nonprescription glasses and what am I? Walter Faraday? International crook and cold-blooded murderer? No, sir. I'm just one more Bible-thumping missionary come to bring the Gospels to the heathen Chinee."

"Okay, then, what if we promise not to tell the gangs?"

"Oh sure. I can just see Miss Tatlock here iiving up to that."

"I'd make absolutely certain the gangs found out," she hissed at him. "And take great pleasure in it."

"You see?" Faraday said.

"Then kill her. You don't have to kill me. I know which side my bread's buttered on."

Miss Tatlock swiveled her head and stared at Wasey. He didn't meet her eyes.

"Can't do it, sport," Faraday said. "What do you have to bargain with anyway? Your ties?" He laughed.

"I can raise some money."

"Come on, the rain's going to rust my gun. Let's get it over with."

Faraday shifted, backed to the low balustrade of the bridge. Wasey and Miss Tatlock were ten feet away from him on the other edge.

"Okay," Wasey said. "But if I'm going to die, grant me one thing."

Faraday waited.

"Very few people know the exact time of their death in advance." Wasey took hold of Miss Tatlock's wrist, brought it up close to his face, and peered at her wristwatch. "It's eleven-nineteen. Don't kill me till eleven-twenty."

"You're joking."

"No, I'm not. Come on, Faraday, let me feel superior to the rest of the world for the last sixty seconds of my life."

Faraday shook his head admiringly. "Like I told you, Wasey, you're some salesman. Okay, sixty seconds."

He checked his watch, then lowered the gun to his side.

The little square was still deserted, no movement in the alleys, few lights, no sound save for the rush of water bustling along the canal. The three of them stood looking at each other through a fine mist of rain. Faraday was relaxed, Wasey the reverse, and Miss Tatlock's trembling had been replaced by an electric tension that transmitted itself as he clutched Wasey's arm.

The seconds ticked by.

Then, from out of nowhere, a young woman appeared in the square. She carried a torn paper umbrella over her head, and she started across the bridge looking like a figure in a classical woodcut. Her sandals made a wet, slapping noise as she moved toward them, passed between them, made the other side, and disappeared into one of the alleys.

Faraday watched her go, raised his arm, looked at his watch for a moment, then said, "Time," and swung the gun up.

Hurrying down the alley on the far side of the bridge, the young woman heard the loud boom. She was from Woosung, but she'd lived in Shanghai long enough to know that you didn't mess in things which didn't concern you.

She huddled under her umbrella and kept on going through the rain.

15

There were only a handful of people in the teahouse. Most of the locals preferred the one in Double Dragon Alley, where the fritters were always freshly made.

The owner, thin and dyspeptic, poured wheat brandy into half a dozen cups that needed rinsing and took them to the far table. There were only six tables in all, so he didn't have far to walk.

"You'd better have one of these," Wasey said.

He put a cup in front of Miss Tatlock, who picked it up with a shaky hand.

Wasey's was none too steady either. *"Kan-pei,"* he said, drank, reached for another cup, and tossed that off, too.

Miss Tatlock tasted hers, hated it, but didn't care. She got it down in little sips, welcoming the kick it gave her body and brain. She shut her eyes, then opened them instantly. She didn't like what she saw behind her closed lids: a picture of Faraday reeling back, toppling over the low balustrade, flopping into the canal below. She could still hear the splash, still see the body emerge from beneath the bridge gripped by the dark waters which rushed it out of sight like something obscene that had to be hidden.

She finished the cup and asked the question she'd held in for the three minutes it had taken them to hurry from the little bridge and wander through the alleys until they'd found this place.

"How on earth did you do it?"

Wasey reached for his third cup. He still had the shakes, a delayed reaction, but he was getting them under control.

"When I bought the gun from Sing Sing, that department store? He sold me something else as well. A miniature grenade."

"That's what killed that man?"

"Yep."

"But how did it get into his pocket?"

"I put it in with the stones when I rewrapped them in his office." Wasey drained the cup. "It had two settings, a five-second fuse or a twenty-minute fuse. I couldn't use the short fuse in his office because he would've shot me before I had a chance to toss it in his lap, so I chose the long fuse and hoped I'd get a chance to slip it to him."

"That poor man," Miss Tatlock said. "I know he was a murderer and was horrible, and that he tricked us, but all the same . . ." She let the sentence tail off and tried to keep from closing her eyes again.

"You can't let people pick on you," Wasey said. "You can't let them bully you, and you certainly can't let them kill you, can you?"

Mournfully she shook her head. She examined the bottom of her empty cup. "I knew you had some kind of plan but I couldn't figure out what."

That was news to Wasey. "How did you know that?"

"I knew when you told him that he could kill me but you'd keep quiet."

"Listen, I'm not a very courageous guy. I could've been serious."

"No, you couldn't." She turned her face towards him. "You may not be brave, although you were very brave tonight, but you could never be anything but honorable."

Wasey hid his embarrassment behind another cup of brandy.

Miss Tatlock had something suddenly occur to her. "When did you set the fuse? How did you know when the twenty minutes was up?"

"I set it in the office when we were on the floor, then I sneaked a look at your wristwatch. All I had to do then was keep him from pulling the trigger. Why do you think I was gabbing on like a housewife?"

The table they were at hadn't been wiped down all night and bore the liquid traces of previous wine cups. Miss Tatlock doodled her cup from right to left and up and down, and considered the design uncomfortably. "Is there any chance of..." She began again. "I suppose recovery..."

"Forget it. Faraday knew what he was talking about. His body's on the way to the Yangtze."

She moved the cup again while she gathered her thoughts. "It's so horribly ironic. Faraday and his flowers. All that planning. Four weeks of scheming and masquerade to get them back, and he had them for exactly twenty minutes."

"I wouldn't worry about it," Wasey said.

"Five hundred thousand dollars? Do you know how much morphine that would have bought?"

"I still wouldn't worry about it," Wasey said.

He stuck a hand into his topcoat and put a little cloth bundle on the table.

With wide-open eyes, and zero comprehension, Miss Tatlock stared at it. "What—is—that?"

"Test your memory," Wasey invited. "Two nights back we went to Pig Alley and I bought a present for China Doll. I bought the Yellow Emperor doll for twenty-one bucks, remember? But old Feng, the dealer, hadn't finished restoring him, so he gave me the stones for the cloak and the headdress separately in a piece of cloth. I forgot to give them to China Doll. I found them tonight when I was sitting behind Faraday's desk. Right where I'd left them, in my topcoat pocket."

Miss Tatlock's eyes got a little bigger. "Then these—" She seemed to lose all power of speech, so Wasey filled in for her.

"These are the ones China Doll gave us. The real stuff that looks like glass. The ones I gave Faraday really were glass."

Miss Tatlock's mouth worked but again no sound issued.

"Don't look so startled," Wasey said. "He conned me, so what could I do? I conned the guy right back."

The stress, the tension, the punishing physical ordeal of the last hour, plus the marvelous shock Wasey had just handed her, all ganged up on Miss Tatlock. Her face puffed and stretched, her eyes filled, and she burst into tears and threw herself against him.

Wasey was surprised; he'd had half an idea she wasn't capable of tears. "Take it easy, Miss Tatlock, I'm wet enough as it is."

Miss Tatlock bawled wholeheartedly. Wasey had never heard anyone cry with a sound like "boo-hoo," but Miss Tatlock did.

"Hey, come on," he said. "You'll have me starting."

Her shoulders shook and the flood continued.

"You should be laughing, not crying. Come on, let's see a smile."

Wasey gave up and just let her wail. With her head tucked into his chest and one arm holding her to him, he reached the other arm around her, couldn't make his objective, shifted slightly, reached his other arm around, got his fingers on the object, put his chin on Miss Tatlock's shoulder, and slowly drank the remaining cup of brandy.

16

The legend on the stern of the freighter read *Estrella Verde. Valparaiso*. The captain and the first mate were from Chile, too, the rest of the crew from various other parts of the world. There was rust above the waterline, which had been painted over without first being chipped off, and the original light tan of the hull had been poorly matched with paint the color of brown paper. But the little ship still managed to look quite pretty with the late-morning sun striking it and the river lapping sunlight against it as it stood at the dock.

Wasey, at the bottom of the gangplank, put down his suitcase, turned to Miss Tatlock, and handed her an envelope.

"I wrote it all down. It's all in there, the receipt and everything. Sing Sing knows somebody who'll handle the jewels and buy the opium with the proceeds. He'll arrange to have it processed, too. He promised me he'll get you a good price, so you don't have to worry. Sing Sing's a crook but he's honest."

"Fine," Miss Tatlock said.

Wasey wrapped the ticket in his jacket pocket. "Thanks for this."

"I'm the one who owes the thanks. I can never thank you enough."

Wasey cocked his head to one side. "Do you always wear your hair in a bun?"

Miss Tatlock's mouth hinted at a smile. "Almost always."

He watched her for a moment; wearing her stark uniform, with no makeup and her hair like that, she looked exactly the way she had when he'd first seen her, except for the soft look on her face and the warm light in her eyes.

"It's been quite a week, Miss Tatlock."

"Yes, it has." Her voice was gentle, too.

"We didn't always see eye to eye, you and me, but I think we made a pretty good team."

"You weren't exactly kind to me," Miss Tatlock said.

"Me? What did I do?"

"You ordered me chicken claws."

Wasey shrugged. "They're nutritious."

"You let a man attack me with chopsticks."

"I would've intervened if he'd been eating with a knife and fork."

"You bet me in a fan-tan game."

"I won you back, didn't I?"

They stopped talking, looking at each other. Then Wasey said, "What the hell. We still made a good team." He stuck out his hand. "No hard feelings?"

Miss Tatlock took it. Wasey was expecting a firm, brisk shake but her hand was soft in his. "None whatsoever," she said.

From above their heads someone whistled a "Hey, you," whistle.

Wasey looked round. Two wharf coolies were getting ready to roll away the gangplank. Up on the ship a deck officer whistled again, pointed to Wasey, and jerked his thumb inboard.

"Gotta go." Wasey picked up his suitcase. "So long now."

He walked a few paces, stopped, turned, and came back. "Listen," he said. He seemed thoughtful. "Running round this town the last week, in the rain, do you know what I noticed?"

"No."

"A singular lack of umbrellas."

"Umbrellas?"

"I don't mean the oiled-paper kind, I'm talking about cloth umbrellas. I think Shanghai might be ready for real umbrellas."

"I see."

"I know this guy in Hawaii who runs up things like that cheap. And I was thinking, after I unload the ties in L.A., I just might give him a call and see if he wants to give me a price on fifty or sixty gross."

Silent, Miss Tatlock waited.

"So there's a chance," Wasey continued awkwardly, "just a chance, mind you, that I could be back here in, oh, I don't know, five or six weeks." Wasey shifted the suitcase to the other hand. "And if that happens, and you're still here—"

"I'll be here," Miss Tatlock said.

"Yeah, well, if you are, I could maybe swing on by your boardinghouse, if I get a moment, and we could grab a bowl of rice, or something."

"I'd like that." She kept her voice even. "I'd like that very much."

"Okay, then." Wasey leaned forward, pecked her on the cheek. "Take it easy, Miss T."

"Goodbye, Glendon."

Wasey stopped. "You never told me your first name."

"It's Gloria."

"Gloria? No kidding. I thought it'd be Doris or Edna."

He turned, walked across the dock, and climbed the gangplank to the boat deck.

The officer on duty, a ruddy-faced Englishman, said, "Blimey, that's the first time I ever saw a bloke kiss a missionary."

"You should try it sometime." Wasey waved at the figure standing on the dock below. "But get your own missionary," Wasey said. He walked by the man and pointed to himself. "That one's mine."